THE LORD OF KESTLE MOUNT

The Lord Of Kestle Mount

by
Jeanne Montague

Dales Large Print Books
Long Preston, North Yorkshire,
England.

British Library Cataloguing in Publication Data.

Montague, Jeanne
   The Lord of Kestle Mount.

   A catalogue record for this book is
   available from the British Library

   ISBN 1-85389-666-7 pbk

First published in Great Britain by Robert Hale Ltd., 1979

Copyright © 1979 by Joan Hunter

Published in Large Print November, 1996 by arrangement
with Jeanne Montague

Dales Large Print is an imprint of
Library Magna Books Ltd.
Printed and bound in Great Britain by
T.J. Press (Padstow) Ltd., Cornwall, PL28 8RW.

For my friends and companions
at Vicarage Street.

One

Grantley wanted her; of that Cassey had no doubt. She hoped that this fact was not so obvious to Tabitha or else her position in the household could become even more uncomfortable. Instinct told her that such optimism was false...the increasing chill between them was more than just a plain woman's natural antipathy towards a pretty one.

She was aware that Grantley was staring at her down the length of the candle-lit table. The damask cloth was a snowy plain stretching between them, the dishes and condiments laid out like well drilled regiments. His eyes always seemed to be following her lately, hungry, intense in his lean face. If they chanced to be alone in any corner of the house or grounds, she was filled with irrational fear and a most unreasonable revulsion for he was a handsome man. His features were regular, brown hair winged with grey at the temples, yet his forehead bore marks of severity, his mouth a touch of pride, and he carried his inches stiffly but, in all, he was personable, so why this unease? Could it be that he was her legal guardian and she resented his authority, having to ask him for every penny as he controlled the purse-strings of her inheritance?

He had concluded Grace and they were at liberty to partake of their supper. There were guests tonight, several of Grantley's fellow-soldiers, among them Edward Ruthen.

Cassey had little appetite, toying with her food, drawn by those invisible threads which seemed to link her with Edward, sneaking a glance sideways at him. He had not had time to change out of his uniform and still wore black cloth breeches, a doublet with sleeves striped in orange and a wide sash of the same colour which passed across his chest to tie in a bow at his left hip, near his scabbard. The Roundhead army were very active and he was a Captain, busy training Grantley's men with exemplary care.

'Cassandra, you have hardly touched your soup. Are you unwell, child?' It was Tabitha, always the perfect housewife, seated demurely at her husband's side. 'I'm sure 'tis no fault of Diggory's cooking which is, as usual, superb.'

Compliments to her cook rippled round the board, while she preened herself, smug in her competent management of staff. Cassey made a noncommital reply, knowing that this was all that was required. It was part of Tabitha's insistence on light conversation whilst they supped. Nothing controversial...she steadfastly refused to let unpleasant realities ruffle her serenity. Once again, Cassey marvelled at the company's ability to talk at length as people do who have little to say, covering their stilted remarks about the weather and the news with a thin shiny varnish of vivacity. No matter that there were tremendous events happening—England aflame with civil war, that most bitter of strife.

This was so different from the existence she had once known. Her father had been a scholar, their house alive with stimulating ideas, a centre for writers, artists and philosophers. Cassey, motherless from birth, was his pet, spoiled and pampered and, because of his ambition for her, educated by a succession of tutors, dancing, deportment and music masters. He had wanted her to make a titled match, but, had she really fallen in love, no obstruction would have been put in her way. He would not have insisted on an arranged marriage, the fate of most girls of her class, with wealth, property and religion of prime importance.

Life had changed drastically since his sudden death. Cassey could not yet think clearly about that terrible time, the outcome of which had been the sale of their mellow timbered house by the river, and the removal of herself to the care of his younger brother.

A surge of rebellious anger washed over her. Oh, they were immeasurably kind to her—on the surface. People said how fortunate she was, an heiress left alone in war torn London, prey to any unscrupulous adventurer, to have her uncle, Grantley Scarrier to look after her. Such a sober, law-abiding pair, he and his wife. Surely, nowhere else could she have found such a haven? Her bodily, and, more important, her spiritual welfare was assured. Little did they know, these well-wishers, with their tight pursey mouths, their trite comments, that she was turning from an enquiring, spirited girl into a withdrawn, sullen woman in such an atmosphere.

'And how long can you be spared this time, Captain Ruthen?' Mathew Ferry was their resident religious adviser. Ferret-faced, clad always in rusty broadcloth, he dabbed at his lips nervously, avoiding the direct returning stare, yet determined to converse with this young man who was actually acquainted with General Fairfax and Oliver Cromwell.

'A few hours, no more.' Edward's voice was low and pleasant, and Cassey knew that this information was for her ears. A very acceptable suitor, surely? Brave, devoted to the cause, of good family, and with a great ability to charm. Serving in Grantley's troop, he had only recently come into their lives. She knew from the first that his frequent visits were on her account.

She could feel the hot blush starting as his hazel eyes locked hers. The others were still talking, but their voices were blurred; she was fascinated by his mouth, watching his lips move as he spoke, wanting only that he should kiss her again as he had done last night. That snatched embrace in the darkness of the garden with the tang of a late frost in the air, and his urgent whisper as he leaned over her, his fine, pale hair falling forward to brush her face.

'Come, Cassandra.' Tabitha was intent

on the nightly ritual of a last visit to the nursery, to check on Megan and her charges—those six fine sprigs of the House of Scarrier.

Cassey found Tabitha's acceptance, enthusiasm and pride of achievement extraordinary. She was no more than a brood mare producing a child yearly, spending every waking moment organizing the large house and considerable staff of servants efficiently, economically and well. This was the role which they intended Cassey would later take, humbly and gratefully, thankful to have a husband. Now she was serving an apprenticeship for it, Tabitha's companion and help, until a suitable alliance could be arranged. But the war was making eligible men scarce. She was a spinster of nineteen and likely to miss her chance. A dreary prospect with her dowry in Grantley's hands to use or withhold as he saw fit. She could easily become an unpaid drudge, condemned to live in another woman's shadow, obliged to do as she was told, like Aunt Helen. That little, nervy woman seated next to Ferry, who throve on thin pleasures, her own personality subordinate to Tabitha's.

Cassey had long ago decided that this

would never do for her. She liked to exist, most emphatically, and for men to know that she did.

She rose, scraping back her chair impatiently, a slender girl, her plain mourning dress emphasising her narrow waist, the tight lacing of her bodice pushing high the full swell of her breasts. This was a Parliamentarian household and they were restrained in their attire, but Grantley did not demand the rigid standards of some. A wide white collar trimmed with Flemish lace softened the severity of the square neckline, the sleeves of her shift puffed through the slashes in the overdress. Her ash-blonde hair was arranged with as much care as any Court Lady's, the back braided into a knot high on the crown, heavy ringlets framing her oval face, while kiss-curls wisped round her forehead and nape. Beth, her tiring-woman, fancied herself as a hairdresser, spending much of her spare time gossiping with the maids of high-ranking damsels, rushing back to practice on her mistress. Cassey submitted, to keep her happy, not always too sure whether she liked the result.

The day was nearly over and a great solemn sunset came flooding across, making the tall landing windows glow, each diamond pane holding a miniature fiery disc, as Cassey came down the wide curving staircase to join the gentlemen in the withdrawing room. With a sibilant rustle of black silk skirts, she moved across the polished floor with its bright islands of Turkey rugs, and seated herself in a carved armchair by the wide, heavily embossed fireplace.

Edward was already there and he rose as she entered. Behind them a servant was going round touching a taper to the candles. Light glowed warmly on the linen-fold panelling, the room very shiny with beeswax, lacquer and brass. Tabitha joined them, satisfied that the children were safely tucked up in bed. Courteous as ever, Grantley acknowledged his wife, their formality that which was expected between couples, though routine had been upset. Grantley was no longer solely a country squire with business interests in the city. Joining the army, rising quickly through the ranks, he was now a Colonel, and his duties called him away for much of the time.

The war had shaken everyone out of their equanimity. Cassey had listened to her father and his cronies discussing the troubles long before the King left London, raised his standard at Nottingham in 1642, and then made Oxford his headquarters. In the bewildered first months, everyone took sides, either for King Charles I and his Divine Rights policy or for Pym and Parliament. In every country and village, in inn, church and market, England tore itself into hostile halves. Armour, hanging on walls time out of mind, was taken down, dusted and polished. Horses shot up in price, and every buff coat and piece of steel which could turn or deal a blow became suddenly valuable.

At first, it had seemed that the King had the advantage, although his enemies controlled London and the mint, but now;

'Our might grows daily,' Grantley was saying, while glasses were filled, and the fragrant smoke from long stemmed pipes spiralled towards the painted ceiling where well-built goddesses frolicked amongst cottony clouds.

' 'Tis no longer as it was at the onset, when their ranks were filled with men fed and equipt by their feudal lords—prepared to lead and officer them—gentlemen whose education had, naturally, included horsemanship and swordplay.' Charles Craig leaned forward to light a spill, his squarish, rough-hewn face glowed red as he puffed. With his hair straight and clubbed to the ears, his plain, no nonsense collar and serviceable uniform, he was Grantley's second-in-command.

'Whilst ours,' put in Edward, welcoming Cassey with his slow smile, 'were made up of tapsters and tradesmen and other low fellows.'

'So they mistakenly thought,' growled the portly sergeant, Amos Hawley.

'Papists—wicked Papists, led by a Jezebel Queen—,' mumbled Ferry into his wine. No one paid him much attention, he was getting deaf and feeble. Yet he was good at keeping the servants in order. No morning began without them being gathered in the hall there to receive a sermon—much of which dealt with hell-fire and damnation.

Aunt Helen set great store by him, not a day passed but they were in earnest consultation on some trivial matter blown to exaggerated proportions by her. Now she twittered, all attention, nodding her head, which seemed to wobble on her scrawny neck, the frill on her cap bobbing, little greyish streamers of hair poking untidily from beneath. Long ago, Cassey had detected a streak of romanticism in Helen which came out in a surreptitious admiration of the Royal pair. She could remember London in the old days.

'I saw her once,' she breathed, 'and the King, dining in public at his palace at Whitehall.'

'Indeed. Well, they'll not dine there again,' Grantley, as always, withered her with his scorn. 'Fairfax and Cromwell will see to that. We have a fighting force second to none.'

'And they have Rupert,' reminded Edward. Even now, when their side were beginning to take towns and cities piecemeal, the name of the King's nephew had a powerful effect.

'Rupert!' Grantley spat out the word. 'That Devil Prince—the Mad Wizard who has brought his German methods of warfare to our poor country. A plunderer! Looting and raping, leaving a swathe of ravaged land in his wake!'

'He's a professional soldier, like me,' rapped out Craig, unable to conceal the mercenaries' contempt for the amateur, no matter how competent.

'In league with Satan.' The preacher was looking at Cassey through his pink-rimmed lids as if he included her in that company. She knew that he did not approve of her, but she was accustomed to being viewed with a faintly disapproving air. Her father's unconventional ideas had offended many people. Also, try as she might to conform, she had all the traditional qualities of a beauty, and there was an indefinable aura about her which hinted at recklessness and passion and a lust for living. Her gaze was too direct for comfort, her smile alluring. It was small wonder that Tabitha and her matronly friends looked at her askance and bristled like warring cats.

Cassey ignored the old man. The feelings were reciprocal—she could not bear to be near him with his whining cant, his dirt-encrusted nails, his stale, unwashed odour. Tabitha, so fussy about her children, did not object to his dealings with them. All was forgiven because he was a Puritan preacher.

'That is not how I have heard our soldiers speak of the Prince.' Edward was getting out the inlaid chess board. 'Fairfax respects him as a General. He is noted for his fair treatment of prisoners. One knows where one is with Rupert, but never with King Charles.'

Cassey was glad that Edward held moderate opinions, very much like those once cherished by her father. Grantley and Ferry were already enmeshed in the Sectarian fervour sweeping through their party. How her father would have practised his mockery on them, very gently of course, a mild-mannered man, keeping his head amongst the heated anti-Royalist propaganda. He had sided with neither the King's men—'Cavaliers', as they were dubbed, the name having unpleasant connotations with the ruthless soldiers of Spain, nor yet with the Parliamentarians, christened 'Roundheads' by King Charles' scornful Queen, because of their short haircuts.

She recalled his irony, when in contact with persons eminent for prudence and piety, that twitch of a smile when they delivered their violent sermons, his masterful mimicry of their scriptorial way of speaking. He was equally sarcastic concerning the Cavaliers, mocking their foppish mode of dress, their earnest desire to be known as reckless, dissolute brawlers. He had admired Prince Rupert, recognizing him as an honourable, hard-headed soldier, but was equally fair about the Roundhead leader, Lord Essex. His sympathies had lain with the ordinary yeomen, loath to leave their quiet homes in exchange for privations, marching and bloody battle-fields, yet doing so in support of whichever side they favoured, with stout hearts, open coffers and armed hands.

Dreaming of a united England, ruled by King and Parliament, he had joined the Londoners in their defence of their homes, fighting those whom he considered were ill-advising the King. A Cavalier bullet had killed him at Brentford where he had taken his place among the Trained Bands.

'Still she pours her poison into his ear.' Ferry was pursuing the theme of Henrietta Maria. 'It is as though she has cast a spell over the King. He listens to her and his other wicked advisers—his priests—his Irish soldiers—heathenish idolaters!'

Cassey watched Edward from the tail of her eye, trying to stamp his appearance on her memory. When they were apart she had difficulty in recalling his features clearly. An odd fact when her thoughts were full of him—she walked through her days abstractedly, performing tasks in nursery, still-room and kitchen as in a dream. Diggory had noticed and teased her, rumbling deep in his vast belly as he stirred and sniffed, tasted and amended his concoctions. 'Ah, madam, such sighs, such starry eyes! One would think that you were in love!'

Now she could fill her mind and heart with impressions of his narrow face, his frank brow and honest eyes. The warm smile, the shyness which sometimes made his strong body seem awkward, so that he clattered his sword against the door jamb on entering, and banged into Tabitha's fussy little side tables, rattling the ornaments, but all with an infinitely endearing boyishness.

Cassey stabbed the needle into her embroidery, in and out. She was working on a table cover, the unbleached twill linen beginning to blaze with an intricate design of waterflowers, lilies and birds. When completed it would be folded into her dower chest, joining similar pieces intended to grace her bridal home one day. Would they let her marry Edward? Seeds of hope had struck a timid root when they first met, blossoming into full flower last night. But he was going tomorrow, and there he sat, wasting precious moments poring over the game, while she was dying of impatience.

Then as the clock on the mantel made a metallic whir preparatory to announcing ten, Grantley snapped a triumphant, 'Checkmate!'

Tabitha packed away her sewing with meticulous care. Aunt Helen dropped her knitting in a confusion of spiked pins and a runaway ball. Ferry closed his bible and shuffled to the door, making his goodnights in passing. Everyone took up candles. Cassey and Edward reached for theirs, bending to light them at the same steady flame. His hand touched hers, eyes intense, little sparks, jets of amber, in their depths. She slipped away, a perfume, a subtle essence of femininity wafting behind her. Gliding like a ghost up the staircase, she paused with her hand on the newel post, glancing back at the little blobs of light moving like disturbed glow-worms below.

In her room, she leaned against the door for an instant. Beth was already there, swooping about, picking things up and dropping them again, always more enthusiastic than methodical. She was Cassey's personal maid, a dependable link with the old happy life. Her nose was impertinent, her red hair and eager expression highly attractive. Now she was hovering near the bed, shaking the pillows from their decorated day-time coverings, smoothing them into virgin whiteness, lying primly side by side above the turned down edge of the sheet.

She whisked the cream lawn nightgown over her arm and came across to help Cassey undress, then she busied herself unpinning her mistress's hair so that it cascaded half way down her back and, while she brushed, they giggled about Master Ferry, and gave their tongues full rein on the other members of the household. Their characters were scrutinized, found faulty and cast aside. Cassey relaxed, Beth always managed to amuse her, a lively companion with her bubbling vitality.

Yet, all the time, inside Cassey there was a hush and a waiting, and she soon dismissed Beth who left her propped up in the big armchair by the fire, a pitcher of lemonade at her elbow and a book on her lap. Normally, she enjoyed d'Orfe's tales of chivalry and romance, but tonight they seemed impossibly far-fetched. The pages blurred and wavered before her eyes, she was not quite asleep. Still aware of the details of the room, the wall hangings embroidered with classical scenes, the high bed, like some dim cave, with its velvet curtains pulled on the window side against draughts, the firelight dancing across the ceiling.

On the table was a china bowl filled with dried herbs which gave off a warm, rich smell, strangely disturbing. The flame flickered, then burned steadily. Her eyelids began to droop; she strove to regain her senses, clinging to the thought of Edward. Would he come, and, if he did, what then? Were his intentions serious? Or would it be like her first lover, that artist friend of her father's, engaged as her drawing master, four years ago when she was fifteen? Oh, she had loved him, waiting eagerly at the top of the steps when he came to call; making excuses to slip away to his lodgings in Whitefriars, a very willing messenger of a sudden, whilst art became her favourite subject.

Twice her age, a charming, unprincipled rogue, he had seduced her without difficulty. For a brief while she knew an almost painful happiness, joy which plunged into despair when she arrived unexpectedly at his rooms one day. There was another girl in his bed, while he, looking scruffy and decidedly dissipated, tried to conceal his gross infidelity and keep Cassey outside the door. She had maintained control, her voice tight and hard with the effort to sound normal, and managed to salvage her dignity with what she fondly hoped was an air of worldly unconcern, backing off, unable to get away fast enough.

Somewhere in the bowels of the house, the long-case clock boomed eleven. On its painted face the figure of Time scythed away the crawling minutes. Cassey shifted, her neck and shoulder had gone numb from being too long in one position. An overwhelming longing for Edward welled in her. Passionately she willed him to come, spinning a strong thread of want, shivering as she remembered it said that witches could make people do their bidding by the power of thought. Both she and Beth were firm believers in the supernatural, weird stories sending pleasurable chills through them. In the Eastern Counties, hotbeds of Puritan fanaticism, there was an upsurge of witch-hunting and the authorities were hanging them.

Sometimes her own imaginings alarmed her. There was a wildness in her, an instant response to all that was dark and dangerous. Too many hours spent in the company of philosophers and those interested in alchemy had roused in her a boundless curiosity, not comfortable in one forced to live now in such a God-fearing house. Also, her confidence had been shattered by that first, miserable affair. She had needed others to assure her that she was beautiful and desirable. The men of her own class treated her with too much respect. She had found a better reception among the grooms and stable-lads who were not slow in finding the real woman concealed beneath the mask of a lady.

That was in the past. Since being with the Scarriers, she had not dared to be indiscreet—until now. Restlessly, she paced the room, her filmy nightgown and lace-trimmed over-robe trailing behind her, and paused at the arched, mullioned window, kneeling on the padded seat set back in the deep stone embrasure. A shard of moonlight severed a notch in the clouds and lit the garden. The avenues and pleached walks, sundial and statuary seemed blasted, silver-blue, as if lightning had flashed once and then been frozen.

When the tap came at her door, she did not believe it. Her heart wobbled. She held her breath, ears straining. It came again, and she flew to the latch.

'Who is it?' she whispered against the panelling.

' 'Tis I. Edward. Let me in.'

Why is it that, after dark, small noises retort like pistol shots? In the hurly-burly of daytime, no one noticed that the door hinges needed oiling.

His cool lips found and grew warm on hers, and he was kissing her as if he would suck out her very soul. Cassey trembled, feeling herself melting, wanting only to lie with him, but, 'Caution', warned a still cool corner of her brain. If she appeared too eager he would take her for a trollop and an offer of matrimony would not be forthcoming, she would never escape from the cage of the Scarriers' home.

'What is it, Cassandra?' With his fingertips, he pressed the damp curls back from her forehead most softly, a gesture which made it even harder to resist him. 'Have I misunderstood you? I thought you wanted to see me?'

'So I did. Oh, Edward, you'll never

know how much. It is just that...well, you should not be here alone with me. It is not right.' Sometimes the quick inventions which sprang to her tongue surprised even herself.

He released her, though still with his hands lightly cupping her elbows. His expression was contrite. 'Please do not be offended. I know that I should have spoken to your uncle first, but I could not till I was sure how you felt. Over the weeks I have come to love you very much, and hope that you will do me the honour of becoming my wife.'

His formality was touching, his words exactly what she wanted to hear, bringing a sense of security which was as warm as a welcome. She slid her arms up about his neck, running her lips over his shaven cheek, finding his mouth and kissing him very thoroughly.

'You'll accept?' His eyes were shining with admiration and desire, and he shook his head wonderingly as if unable to believe his incredible luck.

She nodded, smiling widely and he swung her off her feet, whirling round, laughing. 'Oh, darling, you'll not regret it. I'll make you happy, I swear it!'

Then his face changed, serious and tense, and he led her across to the bedside. Cassey was floating dizzily towards complete surrender. Now there was no need to hesitate, she had his promise and instinctively knew him to be trustworthy. He was no womanizing gallant, ready to cast her aside once he was tired of her. Her only doubt lay in Grantley's permission for them to wed; she had not failed to notice that he avoided the subject, if it came up. But these were details which could be attended to in the morning; now she responded to him warmly, while he caressed her with an eager ineptitude which betrayed his lack of experience. Cassey was confident that she could change this, but remembered that if she appeared too knowledgeable, he might start asking awkward questions.

The rushing in her blood, the sweet, melting desire, were making all thought or further talk impossible. Passion swelled and bloomed in Cassey and she relaxed, giving herself up to sheer, sensual enjoyment.

It was much later, an hour, maybe...if such hours can be measured at all...when she raised her moist cheek from the hollow of his shoulder and said sharply; 'What's that? Who's there?'

'No one...nobody...lie down,' Edward murmured sleepily. The sound came again. There was someone at the door and, unbelievably, Grantley emerged from the deeper darkness beyond.

Cassey sat bolt upright, sheet clutched to her breasts like a shield. Grantley pulled up short, as astonished to see Edward there as they were at his sudden appearance.

'What the devil's going on?' he demanded. The single rushlight he held cast harsh lines on his angry face, carving deep eye-sockets and cadaverous cheeks. His shadow loomed over them, vast and menacing.

'Why are you in my room?' Cassey countered his question with another, turning the spear of his attack against himself. Then the true reason for his visit dawned on her and she laughed, a strident, mirthless sound. 'Oh, I see...you thought to perform what Edward has already done.'

'Slut!' Grantley spat out, his expression murderous. 'I'll have you slung out in the street!'

Edward swung his legs over the side of the bed, reaching for his scattered clothing. 'This must seem a gross betrayal of your hospitality, Colonel Scarrier, but I have asked Cassandra to be my wife.'

'Get out!' Grantley seemed to have increased in stature and Cassey felt a bolt of fear shoot through her, suddenly aware of her nakedness and vulnerability. She shrugged her shoulder into her robe and got up, standing to fasten the ribbons across the front.

Grantley was staring at her, all his repressed desire etched on his features. 'Trollop! You are nothing better than a backstreet whore! You should be whipped through the streets at the cart's tail. I knew it...' there was a rising note of triumphant justification in his tone, 'you with your damned provocative walk...your inviting glances...luring a man on to expect...'

'To expect what, Uncle?' Cassey's eyes were feline and vindictive. She paced slowly nearer, till she was within inches of him, glaring up. 'What could you possibly expect? You are my guardian, and a married man too...shame on you!'

Grantley's fist jerked up as if he would strike her, then he checked himself. 'I'll see you at headquarters on the morrow, Ruthen. And you, madam, will prepare yourself for a journey.'

'What mean you?' Cassey's voice was brittle with anger.

'I think a sojourn in the country may cool your blood. It will be quiet there, and you can give yourself over to meditation, as befits a daughter still in mourning for her father. You can contemplate the error of your ways.'

'Did you not hear me, sir?' Edward was fully dressed, his hand on his swordhilt. 'I ask for your permission to marry your ward. What possible objection can you have?'

Grantley turned his back, saying over his shoulder; 'I have no intention of discussing it with you further. You have your orders, now go, Captain!'

Roundhead discipline was strong; Edward was used to obeying Grantley. He hesitated, looking helplessly towards Cassey. 'Don't despair, love. We will come to some solution, you'll see.'

He dragged her against him hard for a moment, his lips brushing hers. Then he was gone and the door closed behind him.

Cassey whirled on Grantley in a blind rage. 'Nothing you can do or say will stop me marrying him. Nothing! D'you hear?'

'Cornwall is an inconvenient distance

away, madam,' Grantley said, so smooth and cold that she wanted to hit him, to crack the veneer. 'You and your money are in my charge, remember. D'you really think I'm prepared to lose either to another man?'

The full reality of his words hit her; the fragmented suspicions and fears of months slotted in place. There had been firm foundation for her unease, then; beneath that bland exterior her uncle was an unscrupulous schemer.

'Go to hell!' she shouted, stamping her foot.

'You little bitch!' Grantley reached out a hand and grabbed her by the wrist pulling her into his arms.

Cassey was too astonished to struggle when he bent and covered her mouth with his. She felt the press of his tongue between her lips and responded by shoving against his chest as hard as she could. His strength was surprising, and then she remembered that he was a soldier and, no doubt, had helped to sack his share of towns.

'Ah, you're so warm—so beautiful.' All caution seemed to have deserted him, and he pushed her down onto the rumpled bed. 'Let me join you in sinful coupling, as you have just done with Ruthen.' He was groping under her nightgown. 'Don't scream,' he warned. 'We don't want a scandal.'

Cassey tore herself free and landed him a smacking backhander across the face. She leapt up, robe gathered in one hand for instant flight. 'You are disgusting. I shall tell Tabitha.'

Grantley got slowly to his feet, giving her a malevolent glare which should have blasted her where she stood. 'You'll tell no one, or I shall see to it that Edward is sent on the most dangerous missions. There is nothing more to be said. A few weeks of being buried in the country, away from the fripperies of city life in which you seem to delight, will do you good.'

'Nothing will make me come to you.' There was defiance in every line of her body.

'We shall see.' Grantley had his hand on the latch, an unpleasant smile lifting his lips. 'One day I'll have you crawling at my feet, begging me to take you.'

Long after he had left and the room fallen into silence, his words still seemed to ring in the air.

Two

The wind sawed the air and the sky was restless, clouds scudding across as if fleeing inland from the unseen but omnipotent sea. The heath was bleak, so exposed that it had not yet yielded to the first green spears of spring. It rolled into the distance, offering no solace to travellers, its barrenness broken only by the small cavalcade which toiled across the single track scoring its surface.

Outriders flanked the coaches, muffled to the nose, hats jammed well down about their ears, cloaks flip-flipping as the strong gusts slapped them against their horse's flanks. There were four vehicles; a hired conveyance carrying boxes and luggage; a massive hulk like a cargo ship which bore the household staff; the second-best coach housing the denizens of the nursery and their attendants, and the large box-shaped structure, slung on giant leather springs, which headed the cortege.

No comfort, then, in the view. Cassey

withdrew her head from between the leather window curtains, and settled back in her seat, pulling the hood of her woollen cloak about her head, trying to grasp the elusive edges of sleep...an escape from her mental torment. She was convinced that she was going mad. How could one suffer such unhappiness and still remain sane?

Beside her, Beth was nodding off. Opposite, Tabitha was attempting to read, or pretending to do so, her prayerbook held steadfastly before her. Aunt Helen was deeply asleep, propped in the corner, little snores wheezing from between her parted lips, soothed, no doubt, by the pious presence of Ferry who, hands clasped over his pot-belly, always professed that his closed eyelids denoted, not slumber, but profound meditation.

The journey had been a nightmare of discomfort. Any small anticipation which might have been felt at its onset, firmly squashed by the harsh reality of bad roads, rascally landlords, and the endless complaints of the servants.

Cassey began to drift, lulled by the rocking motion, though angry, bitter thoughts pursued her like a swarm of gnats. Of what good had been the fussing and attention of her childhood? She mused gloomily. It had produced nothing but a conceited goose, who thought that she should be allowed to marry for love and have control of her fortune, though knowing full well that fathers and guardians were masters of a young girl's destiny.

Oh, they had tried to find a way out, she and Edward, meeting secretly in Spring Gardens, while Beth, versed in her part, had taken herself off, settled down out of earshot and had a nap. They had sat on a stone bench and talked, and she had been unable to concentrate because he looked so handsome in his uniform with his high leather boots, and his straight fair hair falling onto his plain white collar, and the minutes were rushing away and soon she must go home. And she cried against his chest because it was all so hopeless, while he tried to cheer her with tales of other couples who had succeeded in bending guardians—but none had possessed such a rich dowry as she—nor had such a wicked uncle!

The jarring thought of Grantley and his power over her future, woke her fully to a head which was beginning to pound, a furred mouth, and the reminder that she had neither washed properly nor changed her linen for close on a week. Mundane matters to one nursing a broken heart, yet of sufficient provocation to add to the misery.

Travelling in England was bad enough at the best of times, but now there were troops crowding the towns, taking the best accommodation. In the villages they had met unaccustomed hostility. After two years of civil war, the country-folk were exceeding distrustful of any strangers...ready to fight off soldiers of either side who brought with them the threat of enforced contributions, the commandeering of food and horses. One comfort only...the Parliamentarian forces were beginning to prevail in Cornwall. Yet, Cassey could almost wish that the King's men had retained their supremacy in the Duchy—that would have prevented her hurried despatch to the Scarrier ancestral home.

Tabitha had accepted her lord's command with little comment, agreeing that, yes, sea air would be good for the children, and a visit to Troon a delightful treat after being prevented for so long by the conflict. If she guessed the real reason behind his order, she gave no indication of it. In her usual calm manner she had organized the expedition, unaware that her equilibrium was about to be effectively shattered.

'Merciful Heavens, what is Peter about? Can he be drunk again?' She dropped her book in her lap. Certainly, their coachman seemed to have lost control of the horses. The sudden burst of speed, the violence of the motion, spoke of a driver too fond of the bottle.

'He must be dismissed for this.' Cassey was about to lean from the window and give him the upbraiding of his life, when the rattle of pistol fire stopped her. For an instant she saw Tabitha's shocked alarm, Aunt Helen blinking like an owl in daylight, Ferry's face turn ashen, and suddenly knew that the responsibility for bolstering their frail courage rested with her.

She struggled to keep her feet while the coach bounced and their pace increased. One horrified glance out and upwards, showed that Peter was either dead or injured, the reins trailing as he slumped in his seat, the unchecked horses racing madly ahead.

An outrider went pounding past, firing over his shoulder at the knot of horsemen

41

who were gaining rapidly. One was pressing ahead; his carbine seemed to explode, and Scarrier's man yelled, keeled over in the saddle, dangling sideways as his mount bolted. His assailant galloped past Cassey, crouched over his beast's mane, then abruptly stood in the stirrups and vaulted on to the team-leader. The sweating animals skidded to a halt and the coach braked dangerously, hurling its occupants to the floor.

Cassey found herself in the lap of an astonished Ferry. Commands and more shots added to the confusion. The coach door was wrenched open and Cassey saw the riders who had ambushed them. The servants sat their horses, held at pistol point, hands above their heads, while the strangers curvetted, their own man unceremoniously toppling Peter's body into the dust, taking the driver's seat himself.

A man appeared, framed in the doorway. 'Fear not, dear ladies. Captain Richard Chiverton, at your service.' He bowed ironically, low over his horse's neck, sweeping off his feather-loaded hat. 'My humble apologies for this rough behaviour, but these troubled times make us sometimes forget that we are gentlemen.'

'What is the meaning of this, sir?' Cassey's indignation conquered fear, her fighting spirit roused, flashing in her angry grey eyes.

He laughed, throwing back his curling auburn hair. He wore all the exaggerated points of fashion so detested by the Puritans. His moustache was twirled up at the ends with a mocking flourish, his green velvet sleeves were slashed with white satin and frothing with lace, his great hat was cocked at a tilt, the plume dipping across it like a drunken banner, ribbons and lovelocks flaunted triumphantly.

'That's what I like!' he shouted gleefully to his grinning companions. 'A bit of fight in a wench! Especially one as pretty as this.'

'How dare you, sir!' Cassey was white to the lips, remembering all the tales she had ever heard regarding the Cavaliers and their reputation as cruel rapists.

A smile lingered about his mouth. 'Don't worry, madam. You'll be taken to a safe place until your ransoms can be arranged.' He turned to Tabitha, eyeing her wedding band. 'Never fear, lady, no harm shall befall if your husband pays up, as no doubt he will...to rescue your fair companion if nothing else!' He raised a peaked eyebrow at Cassey.

'You have killed my coachman.' Tabitha's stubborn pride roused a grudging admiration in Cassey.

'An unfortunate necessity!' he flashed, all good humour fled. 'In these parts loyal fellows still fight for their King.' He looked angry, but beneath the bravado, his eyes were haunted. His appearance and that of his men spoke of hardship. On closer inspection their finery was soiled and worn, they wore the air of lean, marauding wolves. Different indeed to the well fed, regularly paid troops of the Parliament.

The Captain slammed the door shut. 'We must be on our way. Make no trouble. I'll not hesitate to shoot again.

At his command, the whip cracked, the horses leaned into the straps, spokes creaked, wheels turned and they were moving again, with a new, sinister escort.

'Oh, do be quiet, Aunt!' Cassey rounded on her kinswoman who was snivelling into her kerchief. 'Of what use are tears? There is naught we can do for the moment.' Somehow, she had assumed the position of commander. They were looking to her for reassurance. She was blazingly angry at the audacity of the Cavaliers; in retrospect the whole episode seemed appalling now. At the time the shock had been blunted by astonishment, disbelief, a sense of incongruity, and the fear of being the butt of a practical joke. But the grim horsemen flanking the coach were no jesters.

Beth pulled herself together. There was something comforting about her spirited annoyance at the disruption of routine, a routine, moreover, to which they had only recently become adjusted. Her curls bounced, her eyes sparked, and Cassey caught a hint of something other than anger. Beth liked adventure, throve on the marvellous, the incredible.

She reached under the seat and produced a flask. 'A drink...that will do us a power of good! For a moment I feared yon ruffians would search and discover it.' Tankards were filled very carefully against the jolting and, equally carefully, sipped except by Ferry who swigged his back with smacking relish, confirming Cassey's suspicions. On more than one occasion, she had turned away from the stale taint of alcohol on his breath.

Aunt Helen's pinched cheeks became pink and her tears stopped, whilst Cassey drank slowly, letting the brandy diffuse on her tongue, its warmth spreading down to the pit of her stomach.

The coach continued its awkward, uneasy course, swinging off from the wagon-way, passing through a narrow hollow where branches clawed at the Scarrier escutcheon, spoiling the blue enamel. The hills that encompassed it on both sides were wood covered. They began to climb; the valley unfolded; rich, rural distances, a spacious landscape of green pastures and fertile fields, and, between the hills, a flash of sea accompanied by a wild, spicy smell.

Their destination was a castle looming on a crag against the dark perimeter of the sky. The ascent was through a steep wood where the view was untamed, the trees and rocks intersected by a winding river. The horses slowed, strained at their burdens, then, with a final effort, breasted the rise. Hooves drummed on planks, iron-bound wheels rumbled across a drawbridge, and the jagged shadow of a portcullis forked across the cavalcade as it lumbered into the courtyard beyond the keep.

'Come, ladies, and you, sir.' Richard Chiverton looked Cassey over with the eye of an expert as he offered her his arm. As wary as a captured tigress, she stepped down, her fingers resting lightly on his hand for a moment.

All round them men were off-saddling, the needs of their beasts of prime importance, joking and blaspheming, bawling at the grooms, before strolling off to the Court of Guard. Wide-eyed, Cassey stared at the machicolated walls, the towers which reared up, feeling dwarfed into insignificance by this massive, ancient and unfriendly pile.

Chiverton was watching her in pleased contemplation, the corners of his eyes crinkled into laughter lines. And the other men, too, kept glancing across, calling out good-natured jibes, swaggering for her benefit, similarly attired as he; with glittering breastplates and wide-brimmed hats with plumes which shivered at every movement. Cassey responded with a bold stare, discomforted, yet pleased to be the centre of so much interest. Soon they were escorted under a vaulted Norman lintel and into the Great Hall.

Men-at-arms leaned against the grey stone walls; the flagstones were grey too, and thick grey pillars rose up into the dimness. Dust motes and flies circled in the light which filtered through narrow windows high among the rafters where once there had been a walk for bow-men. Halberds, rusty shields and tattered flags bore silent witness to many a vicious skirmish fought long ago in battle overseas. Rooms led off through arches like the dark mouths of caves, while the black oak staircase looked as if it would need scaling ladders to make climbing possible.

Logs roared, lost in the vastness of a fireplace with stone supports and an enormous hood on which was carved the same device which dominated all else—two crossed swords surmounted by a snarling lion's head. This amorial bearing was repeated on a crest in the centre of the overmantel. To one side of the hearth was a chair made of ornamental wood and stamped Spanish leather, wherein lounged a man, his booted feet resting on the edge of the andiron, slim, brown hands laced round a goblet.

Chiverton went to lean over the back with easy familiarity. 'Sir, we've brought prisoners. Roundheads with money, it would seem.'

There was a moment's pause before he turned his head and Cassey stiffened, experiencing an immediate dislike for this haughty aristocrat still slouched low on his spine, giving the impression that the newcomers were beneath his notice. Then he placed his glass on the table, unfolded seemingly endless legs and stood up. Tall and lean, he possessed a lavish physical presence which had almost the force of a blow, dominating the assembly, very used to commanding and being obeyed implicity.

He was dressed in rich, dark colours, burgundy and black, trimmed with much gold braid which contrasted vividly with the white lace at his throat and wrists. His skin was swarthy, his hair black and curling, reaching halfway down his shoulder-blades. Cassey was stunned by his spectacular good looks, his wide shoulders, narrow waist and proud bearing, and thoroughly alarmed by his curved nose and fierce dark eyes which reminded her of a bird of prey.

'Sir, tell your men to release us at once...this is monstrous!' Cassey's voice sounded thin as it echoed through the hall. 'This lady is the wife of Colonel Scarrier of Troon.'

'Ah, yes, Scarrier, I know him well.' His voice was deep, resonant and cultured, its timbre sending a chill down Cassey's spine.

He paced slowly towards them, his movements as fluid and graceful as a wild animal. 'I am Leon Treviscoe, Lord of Kestle Mount.'

Tabitha seemed to shrink into herself. 'Treviscoe...' she faltered. 'My husband's enemy.'

'Your husband is a traitor!' He shouted. This riled Cassey. She might not like her guardian's wife much but would see no one treated in such a way.

'And you, I suppose, consider yourself a soldier, making war on helpless women! You dare not keep us here!'

'Dare not!... To me!' His eyes widened in astonishment at her boldness, while Richard Chiverton grinned broadly, poking him in the ribs with an elbow and murmuring:

'A spirited little piece, eh? And in our hands too...one of the Scarrier brood.'

This appeared to amuse Leon; he tossed back his head and laughed. These sneering comments aroused in Casssey an almost uncontrollable urge to slap his face. She would have given anything to have had an army at her command to see him soundly beaten, his pride ground into the dust.

Now he turned on his heel as if the proceedings bored him, giving a curt order to Chiverton. 'See that they do not escape and send word to Scarrier at once.'

'And the spitfire...?' The two men exchanged a glance as if they shared some amusing secret.

'She'll sup with us.'

Chiverton bowed, eyes twinkling at Cassey's expression, hustling her out before she had time to argue, remarking to Leon; 'You show your usual good taste, my Lord. I wouldn't mind a dip in that pool myself.'

Kestle Mount was old and very large, seeming to be filled with endless stone-paved corridors down which the dejected party of prisoners were conducted. Yet for all its imposing structure, its damp walls told of neglect, its whole appearance one of decayed magnificence, as if its present feudal lord could not afford its upkeep.

'Well...here's a fetch!' Beth blew out her cheeks in comic amazement when the heavy, iron studded door thudded behind them.

With a sob, Tabitha collapsed onto the nearest stool whilst her maid fussed, unpacking the vinaigrette and a fresh handkerchief. Cassey went at once to one of the windows set in the thickness of the wall, pressing her nose against the dimpled glass. As she had suspected by the distant sound of crashing waves, the castle was perched on the cliff edge. She looked down a sheer drop onto white spume and the ragged teeth of rocks. There could be no escape in that direction.

'Don't even think on't, ma'am.' Beth was behind her, craning over her shoulder. 'And there's the Court of Guard and the keep on the other side.'

'Oh, my children...my poor children!' Tabitha, in full spate, was rocking to and fro.

'Hush, dear...' Aunt Helen hovered helplessly over her niece. 'They are in a chamber further down the passage. Their attendants are with them; no harm shall prevail.'

This was true enough. Chiverton had seen to it that their servants had been settled, more or less comfortably, not too far away. No doubt arrangements would be made for their waiting on their mistress before long.

Cassey prowled round the chamber

which was furnished in the same faded splendour as the rest of the abode. The walls were hung with tapestries from Flanders which softened their harshness, threadbare rugs were strewn on the dark, sloping planks of the floor. There were three-cornered stools, coffers for clothing and high-backed chairs of uncompromising hardness, footstools and table covers worked by long-dead Treviscoe ladies, and a large four-poster bed, solidly made, with a ceiling supported by stout oak, a wooden panel at the head, and hung with drapes. Everything looked as if it needed a thorough clean.

'It would seem that no woman has cared for it for ages,' Cassey observed, running a finger along a dusty ledge.

'I think Lady Treviscoe died years ago...' Tabitha's sobs had quietened to an occasional sniff. 'I do not know much about them...Grantley would rarely speak of them, even before the war, although our estate borders this one. I believe there was a family feud. There are rumours that his ancestors included pirates and smugglers. Grantley forbade me to visit here.'

Cassey could well believe it; it was easy to imagine him the leader of a band of corsairs, with his strongly-cut features, his mane of hair and cruel hawk eyes.

'If his forebears were as ill-mannered as he, then 'tis not surprising that they fell out with the neighbours.' She was surprised by the strength of her own feelings towards a man whom she had only just met. 'I've never seen such arrogance. He has an almighty high opinion of himself. Someone should have put him in his place very early in life!'

'You'll be better able to judge tonight—when you sup with him.' There was an undisguised gleam in Beth's eyes. 'I'faith ma'am, I've not come across a more handsome man. I'd not say no to the chance.'

'Beth!' Cassey admonished, really shocked, looking up from transferring the contents of her valise to a large chest which smelled faintly of dust and mildew. 'He and his men are no more than blood-thirsty brigands!'

'Brigand or no...what are you going to wear tonight?' Beth refused to be silenced and Cassey suddenly realized that for the first time in weeks she had not thought about Edward. She was ashamed of the omission, feeling guilty and disloyal, but...Leon Treviscoe! 'He is a villain!' she declared adamantly, and firmly laid out her plainest gown. The sight of it annoyed her even more; she was filled with a most undutiful resentment of having still to don mourning black.

'Villain,' she persisted in calling him as the afternoon passed, and nothing Beth could say altered her opinion.

Her room led from Tabitha's, smaller, and with its own garderobe tucked away in one of the turrets where light filtered through an arrow-slit. Certainly, the accommodation was superior to any afforded on the journey. Were it not for the locked door, they might have felt themselves to be guests. But the reminder that she was a prisoner was brought home sharply when Chiverton came to escort her to supper.

Leon's apartment was the only large bedroom in the castle. It gave on to a staircase which screwed steeply up to the top of one of the four towers. It was a fine room, the Master Chamber, panelled in golden oak carved in a design of grape and vine leaves, and with a plaster frieze with a pattern of flowers and fruit, and heraldic shields, coloured in soft tints, picked out with gilding. There was a fire smouldering in the wide hearth, which was again decorated with the Treviscoe crest, and a table laid for several; some half a dozen of Leon's officers were supping with him that night.

Cassey was glad that she had had the good sense to put on her serge gown, with a high collar and no ruffles, in which she always felt old and wise, and had Beth dress her hair simply, without any lovelocks and 'heartbreakers'. She had embarked on this dangerous mission strengthened by Tabitha's and Helen's prayers, and the strong conviction that she looked a pious matron of at least thirty.

Seeing Leon again, their eyes meeting across the room, she found that she had never come across a man who annoyed her more, though she had to admit once again, that he was devastatingly handsome. Most women would be mad with desire for him...but not her! she told herself firmly. She loved Edward—the kindest man in the whole world!

This was the first of many evenings spent with Leon and his Cavaliers, who were openly delighted with her company. Yet, whilst the others complimented her effusively, teased and flirted boldly with her, each doing his utmost to become her lover, Leon paid her little attention. This piqued and provoked her; she was not used to having any man ignore her.

She began to take especial care with her appearance, rubbing her skin with rose scented lotion, unpacking her secret store of cosmetics, an addition to her wardrobe known only to herself and Beth. The Scarriers frowned on such wanton articles but now, when Beth helped her to dress, she sat long before the mirror, powdering her face with pink-tinted orris root, deftly touching a hare's foot dipped in rouge to her high cheekbones, smoothing brows and long sweep of lashes with a tiny brush blackened with kohl, and biting her lips to make them red.

Still Leon seemed preoccupied, though occasionally she would catch him watching her, his face moodily pensive, perturbing gaze sombre under the black brows.

She discovered that she had developed extreme sensitivity with regard to his presence in the castle, seeming to know instinctively if he were anywhere about... finding herself listening for his step, the sound of his voice. He was away a lot. More often than not, as the sun rose, his trumpeters would sound to horse, and he would lead his men out on foraging expeditions, with Cassey watching from the battlements, straining her eyes till he was out of sight and she could see nothing more than the distant glimmer of steel, the flash of scarlet from sash and scarf. Then would come the suspense till they galloped triumphantly back.

Sometimes, as they sat long at table when supper was over, she would listen to them planning raids on nearby villages or garrisons similar to Kestle Mount but in enemy hands. Each encounter was detailed with military thoroughness by Leon. There, amidst the smoke from pipes, the talk and laughter, it seemed that the Cavaliers often forgot that she was of Roundhead persuasion or else considered her no threat to them.

Richard Chiverton appeared to be one of Leon's cronies, so Cassey fostered his admiration, spending much time talking with him, bringing Leon into the conversation with a disinterested air which deceived no one. From him she learned how Leon had been travelling for ten years, since a lad of fifteen, fighting on the battlefields of Europe for whoever paid him most. He had spent some time along the coast of

Africa and had sailed across to America and the West Indies. Cassey was not slow to catch the inference that he had been in the slave-trade.

'There you are!' She reported back to the intrigued Beth. 'A slaver! Is that a fit occupation for a gentleman? I told you he was a ruffian!'

'That I cannot believe, ma'am.' Beth shook her head firmly. 'Look at that great pile of books in the library—his servants tell me that he's read them all! And the curios from abroad, and the beautiful paintings he brought back. You can't convince me that he's a black-hearted, uncultured rogue!'

It was true that as prisoners they were being well treated. They were on parole, having given their word not to leave the castle and its immediate surround. Tabitha and Helen kept to their rooms and tried to prevent Cassey from roaming but, whereas at one time she would have obeyed, now there was a growing rebellious restlessness forever driving her, and;

'What of women, Richard?' she asked him one day. 'Have there been many?'

He laughed and slipped an arm casually about her waist. 'Sweetheart, you are in an almighty sweat to know intimate details of my Colonel's private life.'

Cassey broke away from him, pacing the battlement which she always chose for her daily exercise, from which she could keep an eye on the road and Leon's return. 'I?... You wrong me, sir. 'Tis nothing more than idle curiosity.'

He matched his long-legged stride to hers, glancing sideways at her serious face. 'Leon has, naturally, met many ladies during the course of his wanderings. I have been with him on a great number of his adventures.'

'Has he ever been in love?' Cassey rested her hands on the parapet; the breeze lifted her hair, bringing with it the smell of cow-stalls and barns which stretched in a crooked line beyond the fortress walls which enclosed the courtyard below. This odour mingled with the acrid stench of smoke gusting from a nearby chimney stack.

Richard leaned his elbows on the stone, his shoulder pressed close to hers, joining her in admiring the view. The road by which they had entered the castle disappeared beyond the escarpment. There was a hazy distance of marshy meadows and the glint of the river, then a dense mass of trees.

'I think, mayhap, that he was hurt by some experience when he was a lad,' he offered. 'He never gives away his heart...unlike myself who is constantly being tossed in the vortex of some passion or another...and never more than now, beautiful Cassey.' He attempted a kiss which slid off her temple on to her ear.

Cassey did not protest when he held her and found her mouth. There was something reassuring about the embrace of this large, genial man with this flattering desire for her. For a moment she could forget Grantley, Edward and the enigmatic Leon. She closed her eyes as if that would shut them out, turning deliberately to him and returning his kiss.

Now he was no longer calm, she could feel the tremor of his hands against the back of her dress. His voice, against her cheek, was urgent; 'Come to my chamber—now.'

Cassey felt suddenly frightened and ashamed. 'Not yet...I don't know...'

'Please, darling...' he begged, but he was gentle with her and let her go. 'Now you'll think my manner boorish. I'm sorry, but I love you.'

'No...no...please don't be sorry.' She felt sad for rejecting such an admirable lover. He withdrew into himself, seeming absorbed in the misty distances, eyes heavy-lidded, face stoical.

She touched his hand. 'Try to understand. I am confused...give me time.'

He looked at her and smiled, then kissed both her hands and left with great dignity. The door to the tower creaked behind him and the sound of his boots clattered down the steep, winding stairs. It seemed almost impossible that she had once thought him a brawling licentious soldier. Now it was clear that he successfully covered his true feelings with showy bravado. Once she had believed villains to be dark and ugly and cruel, not handsome and gay and full of jokes. Could it be that Leon, too, was sheltering behind a facade?

Three

Cassey ordered Beth to lay out a gown of deep green satin. She had become so accustomed to the sight of herself in black, that her image, given back by the long mirror, was a revelation; she had forgotten how becoming colours were. Spring was on its way, the days growing warmer, the nights balmy, and it seemed almost sinful to continue in drab clothing amidst such an abundance of green grass, yellow catkins, the daisies and buttercups which starred the ground.

Beth fussed, straining the stay-laces an inch tighter, then adjusting the stiff, richly embroidered stomacher. This bodice was slightly high-waisted, with wide basques trimmed with gold braid. The neckline was cut very low, Cassey's breasts pushed high by the busk, that short, exceedingly tight boned corset beneath. For the sake of modesty she wore a gauze fischue, but the effect, she thought, was very worldly. Her skirt was full, with bunches of gold ribbon tying back the robe-overskirt, and matching rosettes on her shoes. The underskirt was yellow with an ornate panel down the front.

Beth stood back to admire the effect when she had dressed her mistress's hair. Then she attached a purse and hand mirror to Cassey's waist, put a handkerchief and fan into her hand, sprayed her with perfume, and set her once more before the pier-glass.

'Oh, ma'am...' Beth was overjoyed. 'You look lovely.'

'I am afraid that Mistress Scarrier will consider it a great disrespect for my father's memory, but I do not think he would wish me always to wear black for him.'

'Indeed not.' Beth was emphatic. 'He delighted in you being as fair as possible.'

Cassey had assumed that Richard and the other officers would be present as usual, but that night the table was set for only two. Alarm bells clanged a warning in her brain when Leon dismissed even his dour foreign manservant, Jan, coming across to pull out her chair, gravely bowing her into it, then leaning over to pour wine into her glass.

Whenever she had imagined being alone

with Leon, she had been full of wise and witty remarks. Now that the moment had come, she was tongue-tied and paid more than usual attention to settling her skirts.

'Where are Captain Chiverton and the others tonight?' she managed at last.

'They are engaged on a mission,' he replied—just that, nothing more. He stared at her across the table without blinking, while she tried to compose herself and eat, wondering how to prolong this meeting, establish a link between them. He offered her more wine, and she did not drop the glass as his fingers brushed hers. Instead, she laughed and he laughed too, and there was a wild glint in his eyes which said: 'Soon I shall eat you, wench. I promise.'

'In any case,' he remarked slowly, startling her by following some train of thought of his own, 'I wanted us to sup alone. Tell me about yourself.'

Excitement struck her dumb for a second, then words gushed out, her throat trembling, clinging to any topic of conversation so that she need not sit there overawed by the force of his personality. She found herself chattering inanely about her family, her knowledge of the war, listening to the foolish words tumbling over themselves. She could feel herself blushing. This made her angry and she concluded sarcastically;

'A very ordinary existence mine, my Lord. Yours must be much more eventful... filled with pillage and rape and the imprisoning of the innocent!'

His eyebrows swooped down in an alarming scowl. 'You are bold, mistress. D'you not realize that the fate of yourself and your people depends on me? I have but to lift a finger and you will all be shot.'

'Prisoners of war, sir? Even you would not do such a thing!' She was clinging desperately to her anger, a shield against this new giant emotion. She had the feeling that she was breaking into pieces, too weak to stand up and say that it was time for her to leave.

'Why should I not?' he snarled, his rage awe-inspiring, pushing his chair back sharply, pacing the room, up and down, up and down, till it seemed he might wear a hole in the rugs. He stopped dead in front of her, glowering blackly. 'The enemies of my King. 'Tis only the thought of your ransoms which stops me!'

Cassey could feel the palms of her hands beginning to sweat, fear making a dry taste

66

in her mouth, but only for a moment, then she was immediately possessed of her reason again for she saw that she had won some more time with him by making him angry.

Now he was leaning against the mantel, staring moodily down into the fire. He was wearing a claret velvet doublet, straight Spanish-style breeches with a row of small, sparkling buttons running from the hip to meet the turned-over tops of his leather boots. He kicked at one of the logs; it collapsed in a shower of sparks.

'I should be off with Maurice, Prince Rupert's brother, sieging Lyme, but that rogue Grenville bids me stay here with my garrison, bringing order to the neighbourhood, collecting contributions. God-dammit, what I would not give to be with Maurice, taking part in some real action!'

'Like your forbears...the pirates?' she said with vehemence, braving his glare. Something happened to her breathing and she coughed. She reached for her glass...being a little drunk helped, she discovered. 'What do you want of me? I have no loving parent who would pay any price to rescue me. My father was shot down at Brentford fight.'

His face set in grim lines. 'Mine was taken prisoner at Edgehill and butchered as he tried to escape. I saw it all...I managed to break free but my elder brother died in an attempt to save him. Grantley Scarrier was in command, and, though knowing their identity full well, he gave them no chance and killed them cold-bloodedly!'

'I'm sorry...' she faltered, making a gesture towards him.

'Sorry!' he roared, setting the glasses rattling. 'And you, mayhap have wondered why I hate your cause so much. You should have witnessed some of the wanton destruction perpetrated by your soldiers— churches desecrated, used as stables, great houses ransacked in the name of religion because they belonged to the Catholic families...'

'But this has naught to do with me!' she protested. 'I have suffered loss, like you. I have as much cause to feel bitter.'

'Have you?' He had restlessly moved to the window and stood with his head back, staring out at the dusk, one arm along the ledge. 'My mother's heart broke after Edgehill and, within the year, she had joined them in the crypt. They have stripped me of everything, London property, business interests. Only Kestle Mount is left, and, by God, I intend to fight to keep it!'

Suddenly, his mood changed and he turned back to her, with an ironic twist to his lips, saying, 'D'you expect me to believe that there is no one—no lover—who will want your safe return? Your looks give you the lie.'

Cassey returned his hard, unwinking stare and could find nothing to say. She was happy, just gazing at him, thinking, weakly: 'I am obviously out of my mind. I know nothing about you, Lord Treviscoe. You are handsome. Your hair is like a dark cloud falling forward when you bend over me. You are a nobleman, a Cavalier, you have a fearsome reputation and you want me.'

He was talking to her again and she had not the remotest idea what it was about. His lips moved but made no sense. She took refuge in her most madonna-like smile, with just a touch of invitation in it. And suddenly she was beginning to feel more confident. For all his hauteur, he was but a man—not a god.

He said abruptly, 'You are very beautiful,' and offered her brandy which she accepted because she needed time. They drank slowly, looking at each other across the glasses. Cassey got up and walked across to the window.

'Just look at that lovely star up there,' she said brightly, feeling ridiculous. He was behind her, his arm encircling her waist, one hand cupping her breast. He turned her slowly round and locked his mouth on hers. She returned his kiss fiercely, burying her hands in his hair, her fears in his lips.

He held her gently, her face pressed against his crisp lawn collar, and he passed a hand soothingly over her hair, pulling out the bodkins so that it uncoiled like some sensual animal across her shoulders.

'We have both suffered because of this conflict,' he said quietly. 'This makes us almost friends. Come, kiss me again, friend.'

Cassey was not prepared for that. The dryness in her throat prevented an answer but he did not want one. She was bewildered by this passion which had taken her so softly and unexpected...that wildness which heats up the blood and so closely resembles love.

They held close together and did not

stop kissing as Leon lifted her with one arm under her knees, the other supporting her shoulder-blades and laid her down on the skin rug before the fire. They did not talk at all; at such a moment words would have been impossible. Leon was an expert lover; too experienced it occurred to her later. He knew the intricacies of hooks and lacing as well as Beth. But it did not matter, neither did time or space or the fact that deep night was closing in.

Much later, they conversed, lying on the bed with drinks to hand and a pile of nutshells between them.

'This war is a damned fine excuse for the furtherance of private feuds.' Leon could not leave the subject alone for long. Cassey wished that he would forget it for a while; the last thing she wanted to be reminded of just now was the differences between them.

She raised her heavy eyelids; she had been sleepily watching him cracking nuts in the palm of his hand, listening to the cadences of his voice which thrilled her. She rolled over and lay on her back, eyes half-closed, like a cat being stroked. Leon found one of her hands, looked at it reflectively for a moment, then touched it to his lips.

'I never heard my father speak of it, but then he spent most of his life in London. He was a scholar and took little heed of what transpired beyond his study walls. He should never have volunteered and joined the Trained Bands.' She said softly, revelling in his touch, ripening, sweetening, wanting only to be taken again, 'And you...?' She slid her arms about his body beneath the quilt, resting her head against the smooth flesh of his chest. 'What have you done in the war, besides abduct ladies?'

Now, she dared to tease him a little, resentment fled, unable to believe that such a short time ago she had convinced herself that she feared and hated him.

All amusement was wiped from his face, replaced by that bitterness which lurked there at all times. 'I was in Holland when war was declared. The Palatine Princes, Rupert and Maurice, were raising men to come and assist their uncle when his Parliament rose against him. I knew Maurice well, and joined his Lifeguard.'

'What are they like, those two Princes? Such tales of cruelty and wrong-doing are reported of them.'

'Most of the stories are lies spread by

the Roundheads to discredit them. They do not wage war with kid gloves, but barbarism has never been their way, in spite of what your side would have the people believe.' There was that closed look in his eyes again, that chasm which stretched between them although they were still clasped close.

'I fought with them at Edgehill.' He broke away from her, lying on his back, with his hands locked beneath his head, staring up into the shadows of the tester. 'Oh, the excitement of that first charge...the rebels had never seen anything like it...we pounded straight through on top of them...not stopping to reload our pistols...breaking through their ranks. Our impetus bore us to their baggage wagons behind their lines.'

Cassey reached over to trace the strong lines of his features with tender fingertips. 'Were you never wounded?'

He laughed. 'Oh, yes! So was Maurice—Rupert is the only one who remains shot-free. Look, these are battle-scars from this war...' Across his shoulder was a thin, twisting line, and another on his left thigh. There were others too, from his soldier-of-fortune days.

'But now I'm out of the heavy fighting. God damn it!' A bad-tempered expression crossed his face. 'Stuck out here by the orders of Grenville, that scheming opportunist who endangers our best chances by quarrelling constantly with General Goring, his arch enemy, and a roaring, drunken bully. Two fine soldiers for poor King Charles!'

There was such bitterness in his voice that she watched him anxiously. What had he gone through? What betrayal and disillusionment had brought this about?

'The cream of the Cornishmen were lost at the siege of Bristol last year,' he went on. 'We took the city, but at great cost.'

Still the war and the prospering of the war. In his strange, harsh life as a mercenary, Leon seemed to have forgotten how to talk of much else, while Cassey's mind was reeling...where did she now stand in the conflict? Overnight, her loyalties had been divided, one fact only shining crystal clear...she would follow Leon to the ends of the earth, even if he allied himself to the devil!

She wanted to tell him this and rose on her elbow to make the point, but he was asleep, dropping off suddenly as a trained

74

soldier will do, and she could take her fill of looking at him without the returning stare of those disturbing eyes. In repose, his face was boyish, with new lines etched on his brow, high-bridged Norman nose flaring slightly as he breathed, his mouth a little parted. Cassey kissed him very softly and snuggled at his side.

She was glad that he slept, wanting to have peace in which to marshal her wits, examine in detail her seething emotions, argue with herself about her motives. Without doubt, she had betrayed Edward, completely unable to control her feelings; for 'heaven help me,' she admitted. 'Like a greensick girl, I have fallen madly in love with this brigand chief, whose garrison is nothing more than a den of thieves!'

'Beth, lay out my riding dress.' Cassey had roused her early, eager to be off. 'Today, my dear, he trusts me well enough to take me riding. I have been promised a canter along the beach.'

It no longer seemed disrespectful to the dead to be finely attired. Her sweeping habit was of amber velvet with a smart coat cut like a man's, and a hat billowing with plumes. The other Scarrier women looked sternly disapproving but their final vestige of control over her had vanished on the night when she had shared Leon's bed, a month ago.

Was it so short a time? To Cassey it seemed an eternity, though it had passed in a flash. One little month, on one side of which had been Cassandra Scarrier, spinster, who had imagined herself in love with Edward, and, on the other, a passionate, fully-awakened woman seized by the most earth-shattering experience of her life. Days of wonder and joy and fairy-tale dreams come true—dreams of Princes and knight-errants and Leon—Leon—the embodiment of it all.

Time had slid by as she walked as though in a drugged sleep, heavy with love, when nothing mattered but that she must spend every waking or sleeping moment with him, her every thought or action about or for him.

' 'Tis like you're bewitched, ma'am!' Sighed Beth more than once, staring, astonished, at her mistress's enraptured expression.

'Bewitched indeed! Besotted, more like,' snapped Tabitha, as she rustled past on her way to the nursery. 'Your behaviour is

76

disgraceful! Heaven knows what Grantley will say when he hears of it!'

Cassey's full mouth turned up at the corners. She could very well guess. Grantley would be beside himself with jealousy. At first her relatives' condemnation had hurt, but now she fronted them with lifted head and steady eyes, looking them silent, worked up into a passionate forgetfulness of duty and decorum.

She had grown away from them so much, unable to comprehend their total lack of interest in their surroundings, their only thought one of rescue. To her, the castle was an intriguing hive of activity. There was always something happening. One day it would be a bunch of privateers with the accents of Dunkirk or Ireland, come to report of their harassment of a Parliamentarian fleet in the Western approaches, on another, a party of horsemen would lie in ambush for a Roundhead troop. Sometimes, Richard would slip out wearing some disguise or other, off on a nefarious mission behind enemy lines. Often, a black-eyed gypsy lad, named Will Penrose, went with him. He knew the country like the back of his hand, making full use of by-ways, short-cuts and diversions. Cassey listened, spell-bound, to the glowing accounts of their adventures.

But, in all, confinement was proving irksome, the weather being so good. Cassey had begged Leon to let her try one of his horses. Last night, he had agreed. There was an important, pressing matter which she would soon have to discuss with him. She was anxious to get him alone, away from interruptions, so that she might voice her growing suspicions and gauge his reaction.

She was becoming increasingly bothered, having at least one symptom, doing sums in her head and counting off the days, though far too occupied with the instigator of her predicament to allow herself the soul-destroying panic which threatened to swamp her if she really stopped to dwell on it. Yet, in spite of her strenuous efforts to push it from her mind, she had begun to lie awake at night, alone in the silence with everyone else asleep, heart beginning to race, a lump in her throat when she swallowed, half hoping, yet mostly terrified by the fact she was most probably pregnant.

She knew that it could not be Edward's baby. She was thrilled at the idea of carrying Leon's child, but had few illusions as to how he would react to her news, chilled by his vehement assertions that he did not wish to marry. She toyed with the idea of declaring that she had been raped by the Cavaliers, or of pretending that it was Edward's, if she was forced to return to Grantley in that condition. But her every instinct and need cried out for her to openly declare it to be Leon's child.

Whichever way she looked at the situation, she was in a mess, clinging forlornly to the hope, slender though it was, that he might be pleased at the prospect of an heir and let her remain with him at Kestle Mount. She was determined to try, while they were out riding.

A milky-white mist was rising from the meadows as they rode out. Somewhere, high in a tree above them, a blackbird called. There was that slight dampness in the air which hints at hidden mystery, sweet with wild rose and woodbine.

Early summer lay across the land, and they followed a narrow trail which soon diverged, one to meander into the open countryside, the other to wander in a crooked, downward direction towards the sea. The going became so steep and rough that Leon dismounted, helping her down, and they walked their mounts, presently coming out through a group of rocks. The bay swept into a crescent for over a mile. The sea crashed and gulls screamed an accompaniment to the steady pound of hooves as they galloped over the wet sand.

Leon beat her, although she rode a fine bay, light and fast, but he was pleased with her, she could tell that when they pulled up to give their beasts a breather. With a smile he reached up his arms to lift her down till she stood on the firm damp sand beside him.

The morning was developing into one of warm sunshine, the air sparkling, small fluffy clouds drifting across a pale blue sky. The tide was just going out, leaving a wet, salty tang, rocks of slippery green, pools alive with little fish, and mysterious bottle-green weeds.

Cassey slipped her hand into his and they paced to the water's edge, wavelets lapping their riding boots.

'This is what I fight for.' Leon made an expansive gesture with his arms as if he would embrace the whole cove, and he proceeded to talk of his land, his eyes glittering with passionate enthusiasm, as he told her the history of Kestle Mount and how he and his family had once cared for it and its surrounding lands. Every tenant, each village and its inhabitants had been the responsibility of the Treviscoes. Cassey had never seen him so moved; this was an entirely new aspect of his character which filled her with respect.

'Now, all this is smashed by war,' he concluded gloomily, the brief fire dying, leaving his usual cynicism. 'I have neither time, money nor opportunity to carry out my responsibilities. Our world has been turned upside down, riven by conflict.'

They walked on in silence. Cassey tried out one or two conversational gambits which fell flat, that gulf of upbringing, education and divers way of life yawning between them again. She had thought it could be bridged by love, but then, Leon had never told her that he loved her. She had given herself whole-heartedly and without reserve, but quickly recognized his self-sufficiency. There were vast areas of his life of which she knew nothing.

Eager to know his heart and mind, she snatched at each crumb of information. She still feared him and over-reacted to his words, to every nuance in conversation, or even to his very silence. She was baffled and angry, alarmed at the power over herself which she had given him. Much of the time, she felt that she did not know him at all, when, by a look, he indicated that she had said or done something silly, when he was with his officers and she felt her presence to be superfluous, or at dawn when she woke first and he was cut off from her, still sleeping, almost a stranger.

They strolled back to where the horses were patiently waiting, cropping at the sparse grass of the scrub-covered rocks, tethered to the rickety rail which marked the precarious pathway winding upwards between the cliffs.

His mood changed as he took the reins and they started to climb. His manner, teasing, relaxed, totally charming, contrasted strangely with the intensity of his eyes.

'You ride well, my dear,' he said, his praise filling her with well-being, tinglingly alive; then he added, 'Almost as well as Morag.'

A sudden cold chill stabbed through Cassey, spoiling the day. 'Who is Morag?' She tried to frame the question lightly, but her voice came out unnaturally tight to her ears.

'A girl I know.' He answered casually, seeming more interested in coaxing his beast across the rocky terrain.

All the joy of this morning ride faded, turning to something sour in her mouth. It was an untimely reminder of his reputation. She hated to think of the women in his past, wanting to be the first and only one. Vainly, Richard had tried to enlighten her, attempting to soften the hurt by his mellow philosophy, warning her against becoming too deeply involved.

'Where is she now?' She pretended to be busy adjusting her stirrup, before swinging into the saddle, glad to have something to do so that she need not look at him.

As they moved off, he glanced at her and there was both amusement and impatience in his dark face. 'Off on some wild prank, I doubt not.' His mount swerved closer. His knee bumped hers.

'But she will return?' It was more a statement of fact than a question. Cassey stared straight ahead, her back very stiff, gripping the reins till her knuckles showed white. This was no time to divulge her precious news.

He laughed, showing his even teeth, and there was a callous note in the sound which struck her like a bullet. She could not wait to get back and corner Richard. He must tell her about Morag, if Leon would not.

Seeing her woebegone look, Leon leaned over to brush his lips across her cheek. 'Here, sweetheart, why so glum? Morag is miles away, and you are here with me.'

Cassey swallowed hard and said in a small, mournful voice, 'But for how long?'

For some time she had been wanting to discuss her future with him, wondering if he expected her to leave when the ransoms came, but when they were alone a strange shyness pinned her tongue and she was loath to break the spell. In those enchanted moments, her breath shortened and she seemed to melt, flowing languidly to become part of him, then such loaded topics seemed suddenly unimportant and she let the opportunity slip away.

'That is up to your noble kinsman, Colonel Scarrier!' He gave her an unmistakable answer, inclining forward to urge up his horse, whacking her bay across the rump so that he started, nearly unseating her. 'Come!' he shouted, closing the subject abruptly. 'I'll race you back!'

Cross-questioning a reluctant Richard brought little relief. It appeared that Morag was a local girl of the Penrose brood, who loved army life, wearing man's apparel, and serving with the soldiers. He was very cagey about her, refusing to be drawn in spite of all her coaxing and wheedling. So Cassey tried to comfort herself and still the gnawing doubt by contemptuously dismissing her as a mannish hoyden whom Leon could not possibly find attractive. She had heard of such females, more man than woman, and told herself firmly that this must be the case.

No matter how she tried to put it out of her mind, she knew no peace and followed Leon about, trailing forlornly after him, longing to collect and treasure any small scrap of comfort, until he rudely told her to find some occupation and leave him to his duties.

She could not shake off the sense of foreboding; it clung to the rim of her mind during the following days no matter what she was doing. Short-tempered and edgy, she upset a bewildered Beth by her fault-finding before bursting into a storm of weeping. Then Beth held and rocked her, comforted and patted her, telling her not to worry.

'La, ma'am...you're a match for any woman!'

'So I may be...' Cassey sobbed brokenly. 'But not for him, Beth. He's so difficult...I can't understand him. Just when I am beginning to believe that he loves me and looks upon me as more than just a bed-fellow, something like this happens.'

'I'm sure that you are making too much of it, ma'am,' Beth insisted, bringing to bear her considerable experience of the opposite sex on the problem. She had more than one of the Scarrier lackeys mooning after her and had collected her fair share of admirers among their captors, finding them much more to her taste than the sober-sided soldiers of Parliament. 'Now stop weeping. It'll but serve to make your eyes red. There's a troop of horsemen ridden in today, and talk in the kitchen of a welcome feast planned for tonight. It seems they've been off campaigning for the past weeks. You must look your best to greet them.'

Fires roared in the fireplaces at each end of the Great Hall. Candles flickered in circular iron holders hanging on chains from the rafters. Velvet curtains were a barrier against the night; heavy tapestries were drawn across the door end, at the two long tables which ran down each side from the shorter one at the head, Leon's followers feasted.

There was no lack of food; it had been wrung from the surrounding villages, particularly those of Roundhead persuasion. Living at free quarters, even in the most loyal areas, a troop of horse would soon outstay its welcome. It was little wonder that Leon's men bore the stamp of freebooters, while Kestle Mount became their lair.

Servants scurried up from the kitchen bearing laden platters. Wenches, recruited from the village, were busy pouring ale and avoiding eager arms and bold invitations. Cassey was on edge, proud of her position at the head of the table beside Leon, yet raking the crowd with her eyes, seeing unfamiliar faces and gathering from the buzz of the talk, that they were not yet all here; these were only the forerunners of a large troop who had been away fighting further down the coast.

Leon was so relaxed with his comrades, allowing them to treat him with an enviable familiarity, yet keeping his position as their leader. He exuded, even more, that mysterious and compelling force which made him the centre of attention. They recognized his undisputed ability to take command, won by years of hard experience in the field.

Cassey sipped her wine gloomily, brightening up a little as Richard, at her elbow, complimented her, clad in a suit of peach damask, his face flushed, his eyes already a little glazed.

'Still no word from Scarrier. That is good. It extends your stay with us.'

Leon made no comment. He tapped the side of his goblet with his finger-nail. A servant leaped forward to top it up. Then he said: 'Goring is in the vicinity.'

'Slife, no poxy rebel will try to get through with Roaring George about.' Richard stood up and raised his glass. 'A toast, gentlemen. I give you General Goring, and damnation to Essex!'

They stamped and cheered, draining their tankards in one gulp, noisy and exuberant, still believing that their side would prevail, though a few were glum, staring into their glasses as if they could read the future there and did not like what it held.

Then across the laughter and talk came a great commotion at the door. A group of soldiers appeared, newly dismounted, their finery muddied. Cries of greeting welcomed them as they clustered round the fire, spreading chilled hands to the blaze, shaking the rain from their cloaks, beating their hats against their sides to dry the bedraggled plumes.

A figure detached itself from among them. Cassey was aware of long legs, and a cloud of hair, a slim figure clad in a leather buff coat, with scarlet breeches and doublet, trimmed with silver and gold and sparking buttons, a jaunty cap of green velvet with a black heron's feather.

'God damme, if it isn't Morag!' shouted Richard with a wide grin. At the same moment Leon rose from his chair and, arms out-stretched, received her as she flung herself upon him.

A sense of sinking and apprehension shook Cassey. She was not at all as she had imagined her. Tall, strongly built, Diana of the hunt, in a man's suit. She was extremely beautiful, in an untamed way, with dark hair and eyes, an olive skin and vibrant personality. Completely confident, striding boldly among the men who treated her as a comrade. Then, across Leon's velvet covered shoulder, she stabbed a glance at Cassey. She broke from his embrace and pointed, demanding; 'Who is she?'

Cassey responded to the throbbing of the room which had suddenly become a jungle. Leon was watching them with that smile of lazy indifference which she had learned to distrust so much. He used it as a defence, a means of cutting off from her. There was an impenetrable barrier between them and she saw clearly that uncompromising strength and ruthlessness which, in spite of his breeding, marked him as an adventurer, scorning ties and bonds. Her dream of changing him, of making him love her, shattered into fragments.

Casually, he introduced the two women. Morag took a pace nearer, and stood, hands on hips, eyeing her up and down insultingly.

'A Roundhead bitch, eh!' she jeered. 'Fancies herself to be a lady, too, by the looks on't.' She rounded on Leon, suddenly furious. 'She's a prisoner. Why does she sit at the head of the table with you?'

There was a dangerous glitter in his eyes

which Cassey had learned to recognize and dread. If Morag really knew him, then she too would have had a taste of his black moods and evil temper.

'I invite whom I damned please,' he said on a sort of snarl. But Morag did not drop her eyes and tremble as Cassey did when he was angry; she returned glare for glare.

'So, whilst I am fighting my way through Roundhead troops to carry your messages to Prince Maurice, you dally with this white-faced ninny who is one of them!'

Cassey listened bleakly as they argued. It was useless to try and convince herself that there was nothing between them. They were obviously people who had been long together. Even their quarrelling on sight indicated strong emotions; they had past memories to share, common bonds, pleasurable experiences to anticipate. Cassey felt isolated; her hold on him was so tenuous. She saw this now plainly and bitterly and her jealous temper began to rise as their high words subtly changed and soon they were laughing, whilst Leon hustled an officer out of the seat next to his and Morag slipped into it. She proceeded to monopolize Leon's attention, recounting her adventures.

Cassey was seized with a violent, almost uncontrollable urge to snatch up her dinner knife and plunge it into that audacious girl who was hanging on to Leon's arm, looking up at him with wide, shining eyes. She was aware that Richard was watching her compassionately, a wry smile twisting his full lips, but even he began to join in the talk, listening closely as Morag and her companions described their escapades in short, disconnected phrases.

The company were getting rowdy. After the King's health came that of his heir Prince Charles, and every member of the Royal family, and then they fell to pledging one another, as drunk with words as with wine. Someone started to roar out a Cavalier song, ribald and witty. They were soon beating the chorus with tankards and sword hilts. Some of them still wore their soldier's garb, shabby with hard use, but others had changed into a peacock display of velvets and brocade, sending out gold and silver flashes as the light caught on rich embroidery.

Someone, probably Richard, had kept Cassey's glass replenished. The scene wavered and blurred; waves of heat laved her and she made no protest when he led her away from the table towards a little knot of his cronies. For a while she was swallowed up in their noisy exuberance. They jostled to get close to her, angling to slip an arm about her waist, bold eyes staring down into her bodice. And Cassey, swaying slightly, an empty sick feeling within her, managed a bright, returning badinage. She kept looking across, in fascinated despair, at Leon and Morag. Their dark heads were close together and her hand was resting on his with an unmistakable intimacy. Then wide shoulders and flushed, reckless faces blocked her view.

The inane chat seemed to go forever, and now her responses were automatic. The room spun dizzily, fractured across by unshed tears, and she felt Richard's hand at her elbow, firm and comforting. The company began to clear, drifting away, lured by the rattle of the dice box and the chink of coins.

Through the haze of misery, Cassey was suddenly jerked into sharp awareness. At the head of the table there was almost a glow, a ring of emptiness. Leon and Morag were no longer there.

Four

Cassey started for the stairs, skirts bunched in one hand, so that they would not trip her flying feet. She was borne on wings of murderous rage; all the pent-up frustrations, the gnawing uncertainty, the wretched insecurity of her affair with Leon pouring through her like a black torrent.

Blind and deaf to everything save her own pain, she was hardly conscious that Richard had fallen into step with her, his eyes those of a concerned friend. They passed along the draughty corridors where flares smoked, set in iron holders at regular intervals in the walls, and the wind whistled through arrow slits, coming at last to Leon's room. Without a moment's hesitation, Cassey flung the door open.

Leon spun round on his heel as she came in, his expression changing to one of annoyance. He had been leaning with one hand against the bulbous, carved bedpost, and he was wearing his breeches, boots and full-sleeved shirt. Morag was curled up on the coverlet, clad in nothing but her shift. She looked across, startled but unperturbed.

Cassey took in the scene at a glance. The years rolled back and she was once more at her drawing-master's door, while he tried to hide his whore.

'You bitch!' she ground out and then pounced. In a flash she was at the bedside, pulling at Morag, filled with the violent desire to kill her. Morag gasped and wrenched herself free. Her hand shot out and slapped across Cassey's face; at the same instant Cassey grabbed at her hair. Their feet became entangled with the bed-covers, they lost their balance and crashed to the floor, rolling over and over, Cassey hampered by her long skirts, Morag almost naked.

Biting, screaming, kicking and pounding at each other with their fists, they rocked, first one on top, then the other. Beside herself with rage, Cassey momentarily possessed an unnatural strength which succeeded in halting Morag who was well-used to fights, toughened by soldiering. Bloody scratches appeared on cheeks and arms and breasts. Cassey's skirt was ripped, her bodice half torn off, her nose was streaming, smearing them both, but at last she got astride Morag, pummelling her head and face with her fists while Morag fought her off with feet and clawing nails.

At first the men had been too astonished to move, then they each made a grab for one of the women, dragging them apart, giving them a shake, half angry, half amused. Cassey collapsed against Richard, spattering his shirt front with her blood, beside herself and screaming hysterically;

'You lousy bitch! Don't think I've finished with you yet!'

Morag crouched on the floor, her shift torn to ribbons, while Leon flung his cloak over her. Her face was contorted with rage and hatred.

'And I've not done with you, not by a long shot!'

Cassey swirled round to Leon, reckless and demanding; 'Get rid of her! The gypsy slut!'

'What!' Morag got to her feet threateningly. 'You try to order him? My God, what do you know of him? I've been his comrade for years, and you come here with your high and mighty airs and really think you can turn him from me! I'll see you smoke in hell first!'

'Both of you damned jades be quiet!' Leon's eyes flashed angrily and he stood regarding them, legs spread, thumbs hooked in his belt. 'Any more of this and I'll send you both apacking!'

Cassey could not control the trembling in her limbs, shaking with shock and fury. Morag was used to violence, giving a defiant toss of her tangled hair. And it was Richard who snapped the tension, his arm about Cassey's shoulders.

'Come away, Cassey. You can do naught here tonight. Discuss it in the morning.'

Sick with dread and humiliation, Cassey searched Leon's face imploringly, but he would not look at her and, hopelessly, Cassey allowed Richard to lead her out before she gave Morag the satisfaction of seeing her cry, drained and exhausted, very aware that her cuts and bruises were beginning to throb but managing to make her exit with as much dignity as she could muster.

She walked on blindly and Richard, matching his long-legged stride to hers, said at last; 'Where are we heading, sweetheart?'

She had been making for her room, there to seek the dark solace of her bed, to hide away and indulge her grief, to cry until there would be no more tears left in her. She stopped dead at his question, hands flying to her face. 'I can't go back yet. They might see and question me. Tabitha may still be up.'

The full realization of her plight struck her forcibly; she pictured Tabitha's and Ferry's smug self-satisfaction when the truth of Leon's treatment of her became known. 'Oh God, it's true, what they have been preaching to me for years!' she thought frantically. 'Women like me do come to a bad end!'

Then she began to cry, giving way to the horror which she had been holding in check all evening. Richard did not speak for a while. He held her firmly while she poured it all out...her adoration of Leon...the hurt because he did not love her...his blank refusal even to hint at marriage...and now, this final insult.

'Hush now, sweeting,' Richard said at length, pulling out his kerchief, mopping at both tears and blood. 'You are making a great deal of bother about nothing. Can't we go somewhere other than this icy passage? My room is not far away...' He laughed as she began to protest. 'Have no fear. I'll respect your honour.'

So she gave him her hand and followed where he led, not caring much, in that black hour, whether or no he succeeded in seducing her. They went through an archway and up a few stairs, meeting *en route* two or three revellers staggering alone, bidding them noisy 'good-nights'.

His was a strictly masculine apartment, and he knelt to stir the embers of the fire. 'That is better. Your hands are frozen, Cassey. Sit down and I'll pour you some brandy.'

It was useless to protest that she had drunk enough already. He was insistent, so, to please him, she sipped. Her throat hurt where Morag had tried a stranglehold.

'Well, my dear...' he mused, sitting back on his heels, smoothing his thin line of moustache thoughtfully. 'In truth, you have amazed me. Who could have guessed that beneath that dainty exterior lies a savage fighter? Morag is no mean adversary. I'd not risk her anger myself!'

'That woman!' The scorn in Cassey's voice should have withered her. 'I hate her!'

He was watching her with narrowed laughing eyes, then pulled a solemn face to prevent the full blast of her rage hitting him. 'She is a very old friend of Leon's.'

'Does he love her?' It was half a question, part accusation, full of tears.

His flippancy vanished. 'Love her? Whatever gave you that idea, sweetheart? Leon loves no one but himself. I should have thought you would have learned that by now.'

Cassey only heard the first part of his answer, clutching at straws. 'Then if she means nothing to him, perhaps he'll send her away again and let me stay with him. Oh, Richard, I don't want to go home with the Scarriers...I can't, anyway, not after what has happened...they will despise me. What am I to do if he doesn't want me any more?'

She looked like a lost child, dishevelled and tear-stained. He moved nearer and put an arm about her. 'D'you really believe that Morag will make any difference?' He caught a tear on a gentle forefinger as it coursed down her cheek, and with his other arm he squeezed her waist reassuringly. 'Of course he will still want you. You are a very beautiful little witch, you know, but he has not seen Morag for some time. Naturally, they will have much to discuss.'

'In the bedchamber?' There was a new hardness about her eyes, an edge to her voice.

'I can assure you, that it can as quickly be yourself who is in favour again. That is his way and has been so for years. Women come and go...sometimes he takes them...sometimes he doesn't.'

'I cannot be one of many.' She shook her head and made a small, hopeless gesture.

'You don't really mean that, Cassey.' He held her by the shoulders, looking down into her face, doing the best to ease the hurt with his kindly wisdom. It was no use denying it, impossible to deceive him; even with those tormenting images of Leon and Morag at that very moment, she knew that she would settle for any terms to have him back.

'Oh, why...why? I can give him everything. All of my love, my dowry...any way I can help him, I will. It's so unfair!' She flung herself against his chest in a storm of angry weeping.

He patted her and murmured soothingly, 'He is a strange fellow. I've known him for years; we grew up together. My own estate is not far from here, though now in Roundhead hands, curse them! We were soldiers abroad until this war began. Then nothing would satisfy him but that we came back, post-haste, to serve the King. I suppose this sad conflict has changed us all, my dear. Certainly, aspects of Leon's nature hidden before, have become apparent. He saw his father die, remember, struck down by an old enemy. His mother died, his sisters have fled to France and he has given everything to support the cause. Nothing will divert him from his purpose. He cannot take women seriously.'

'He is bound to marry, if only to produce a heir.' Cassey had, long before, deliberately put from her the cold fact that she and Leon belonged to warring factions. This in itself would prove an almost insurmountable obstacle, yet she had managed to convince herself that all could be overcome if only he was willing.

'When he does, it will be in a calculated way. He will make a union where property and money is the main consideration.' Richard's firm practicality was like a dash of cold water, reminding her of concepts which she too, had once accepted as inevitable. She had not reckoned on falling in love. And now that she had, it seemed a cruel mistake.

His arms were warm, immeasurably comforting, a balm to that desolate ache where once her heart had been. He was musing still, lips touching the top of her head where the white parting showed. 'The war has done much harm to us all. Old standards are gone, a new morality taking their place, difficult for you to understand. Oh, I know what you are thinking...that my morals are as loose as Leon's and you would be right. I fight hard and play hard...there is nothing left for the soldier with death lurking at every corner. But I tell you this truly, Cassey...I could love you, if you'd let me...' He grinned suddenly. 'That bastard, Leon! He always takes the wenches that I have a mind to lie with!'

Cassey's expression was withdrawn and sad. 'I should have known better than to trust him. I lost my virginity to a scoundrel.'

'Lucky scoundrel!' Richard murmured against her ear, making her smile. Though she had never felt more bleak, lonely and despairing, she accepted the strength of his encircling arms. Somehow, he would help her get through the night. She must stop listening for a step outside, some indication that Leon had changed his mind and sent for her. She knew now that this would never come.

The fire was dying and the room dark, save for the steady flame of a candle. The question mark hung between them on the still air. Now they were standing on opposite sides of the bed hung with faded plush curtains. He was watching her with all laughter wiped away. After a long pause, Cassey began to unlace her bodice, and he came round to help her.

'Maybe,' she thought as he reached out to snuff the light, 'Leon will get to hear of it and be hurt.'

Cassey woke with broad daylight shining in her eyes. She stretched out an arm, but the place beside her was empty. Then she remembered; all the sorrow of last night flooding back. She was in her own room, with Beth snoring on the truckle bed which was stored under the four-poster by day, and wheeled out for the use of personal servants or visiting children by night.

Her head throbbed painfully, her tongue was coated and her saliva tasked bitter. Richard had plied her with much wine during the course of the night. She wondered what he would expect of her henceforth. Less weeping, surely; that was no compliment to a man renowned for his dash and gallantry. Yet he had been roused by her angry tears, making up for her lack of enthusiasm by his own passion. She had clung to him with a savage desperation; only as dawn lightened the sky, had she let him conduct her to her own room, accepting the good sense of his discretion. Feeling bruised and broken and weary beyond all utterance, she had fallen asleep at last.

Now she groaned between gritted teeth as memory came churning up, each episode of the previous evening viewed with pitiless clarity. She flung back the bedclothes and stood up. Someone had undressed her for her clothes were in a neat pile on the chair, her gown spread over the back and she wore only her semi-transparent knee-length shift.

Her movement woke Beth who sat up sleepily. Beneath her single blanket, she was fully clothed. Cassey guessed that she had probably waited for her return most of the night and she was thankful for such patient loyalty. Beth must be dying with curiosity, constantly in a state of suspense brought about by Cassey's capricious behaviour.

Now she was yawning and rubbing her eyes and Cassey was glad to have her to talk to though it hurt her pride to have to admit, even to such a close confidante, that Leon had been unfaithful to her, and her own wretched finale to the night's activities filled her with shame. It was as if she had made a vow of fidelity to Leon, completely committed. Only yesterday it had seemed incredible that she should even think of lying with another man. Richard had attempted to explain that it did not make all that difference after all and she had tried to listen, like a child learning a lesson from a grown-up, realizing that her Puritan morals had no place now in the scheme of things. But it was more than a moral code; she had flouted that before without a qualm; it was something she felt deep inside her.

She loved Leon with great tenderness, care and deep involvement, as well as passion...it was as if she were already his wife...now she felt debased, unclean. She could do no more than push her affair with Richard to the back of her mind. It was like a useless possession without value, which cannot be discarded, sold or given away. She would have to live with it always; cover it up, hide it, maybe, but never forget.

Beth was never critical of her mistress's actions, admiring her devotedly, mothering her constantly. Now nothing would satisfy her but that she fetched warm water immediately and bathed the scars of combat. Some of Morag's scratches were deep and it would take time for them to fade; fortunately Cassey's face was not badly marked. Beth laid out a clean shift, then rifled through the clothes cupboard, pulling stockings from half-open drawers, snatching up the petticoats that puffed over a chair, vigorously selecting a suitable gown for Cassey to wear when she next faced the enemy.

'She's but a gypsy trull, from what I hear,' Beth stated firmly, 'so you'll be at your most ladylike, madam. Please, no more brawling with her. This but drags you down to her level. Take heart from the fact that Captain Chiverton cares for you. He's a good man, and will help you, I'm sure.'

By the time a junior officer arrived to summon her to the Great Hall, Cassey had got through the weepy stage and an invigorating disgust had taken its place. Very well then, Morag and Leon were welcome to each other's company! Obviously they were well matched. A pair of heartless thieves and as common as dirt!

The mystery of why the prisoners had been called was soon explained when Leon swept in. Morag strolled at his side, high bosomed and keen hipped in a rust-red doublet and breeches, thigh boots encasing her long legs, with yellow feathers adorning the hat cocked on her head. There was a smirk on her face as she looked in Cassey's direction. Cassey assumed her most aloof, haughty expression, enormously satisfied to see that she had a black eye and that her left cheek was swollen. This more than compensated for the smart of her own injuries.

There was activity in the hall; Leon's men preparing to ride out. Richard was there, talking seriously to a couple of his men, and he gave Cassey a faint smile which she did not return. The scout, Will, hovered at his elbow and Cassey noted that he stared continually at Morag with hollow, haunted eyes while she deliberately ignored him.

Tabitha had walked in with Cassey, a dignified figure in the plain grey silk. Over the days she had never swerved from her contempt and hatred of her husband's enemies, and she could hardly bring herself to exchange any words with Cassey. Now she raised her eyes as Leon addressed her:

'We have had word from your husband, madam.' Leon was holding a dispatch in one gloved hand, his manner courteous. He was dressed for riding and Cassey wanted to run to him, to smash through that cool politeness and demand that he cast Morag aside and keep her there as his mistress, but she did not move, clenching her fists so tightly that the nails cut into her palms.

'Your deliverance is at hand,' he continued, whilst Tabitha's pale face lit up with relief. 'A messenger has arrived not more than a day's ride ahead of those bearing your ransom. They will be here today.'

The morning light was streaming through the arched windows, the rays glittering on his black hair, and Cassey longed for time to stop so that she might never leave this place alive.

'Thank you, my Lord. This is indeed welcome news.' Tabitha dipped him a curtsey. She had scarcely exchanged a single word with him since that first day; always reserved, she had kept close to her room, looking after her servants, protecting her children.

'Colonel Scarrier is sending a troop to accompany you from here.' Leon was tapping his toe thoughtfully with the tip of his riding whip, leaning back against the oak table, avoiding Cassey's eyes. 'I trust that you will assure them that you have been well treated here and that they will return the courtesy to any of our people who fall into their hands.'

He obviously considered the interview at an end, tossing his long cloak across his shoulder, preparing to depart, but, as he made to pass her, Cassey put a hand on his sleeve, uncomfortably aware of Tabitha's reproving stare, and the jeering smile which lifted Morag's lips.

'My Lord, may I speak with you privately?' There was such desperate appeal in her tone that he paused; then, with a quick word, freed himself from the crowd of officers who were with him. He walked with her to the solar, closing the door behind them. Cassey felt as if her knees were dissolving, trembling so hard that she could barely stand.

There was amusement and a hint of impatience on his dark face. 'What ails you, sweeting? You are as white as a ghost.' He gestured as if to tip up her face towards him with a finger under her chin.

'What do you think is the matter?' She was suddenly furious, wrenching away from him. 'You lay with that woman last night! D'you really expect me not to care?'

He was watching her steadily, with a kind of tenderness on his face, as if he was searching for the right words which would ease the pain and humiliation, and the full force of his attraction reached out to her. She longed for him to love her again, almost prepared to crawl at his feet and beg it.

'I warned you that you were wasting your time loving me,' he said softly, 'and that it was no use to be jealous.'

'I can't help it...' she faltered. 'And I cannot understand why you did it. Do you love her?'

His dark eyes met hers unblinkingly. 'No.'

Hope flared up at that single word and the fact that he was holding her lightly with a hand on either side of her tiny, tightly-laced waist.

'Can't I remain here when the others leave?' It was difficult not to make the question sound like a persistent whine. They had been over this vexed point many times before.

His face changed, though he was smiling it was with his mouth only. 'Impossible, my dear. I need your ransom money.'

'If it were not for that...could I stay, then?' She had to have an answer, no matter how painful.

'I cannot become deeply involved with any woman just now. There is much to do in the prospering of His Majesty's armies and, when 'tis over, I must somehow find the wherewithal to repair my house and ravaged estates. I cannot be bothered with you, darling. Quite frankly, I don't want to.'

So there it was. The lovely dream was smashed. He had used her for his pleasure for a while and now it was time for her to go.

'But what is to become of me?' she whispered, grey eyes as reproachful as those of a stricken doe. 'My family will disown me, like as not. No man will want me for his wife. It will soon be noised abroad what has happened between us.'

He shrugged, then spread his hands wide in a gesture of apology. 'I'm sorry, my dear...'

'But I love you so much...' she wailed, pressing against him, hammering on his chest with small mournful blows. He did not hold her, his arms stiffly at his sides, and in his eyes there was pity, perplexity and a hint of regret. 'Let me stay, please, please, Leon. Don't send me away...I'll do anything...I won't be jealous of Morag or any other...just let me serve you...and love me sometimes!'

He gave her a little shake, holding her firmly by the shoulders. 'Tears won't move me, Cassey, they never do. Don't make it so deuced difficult. I was afraid this might happen but at first I didn't care...'

'You do now?' She perked up at this.

'D'you take me for an utter rogue?' He seemed angry, more disturbed than he wanted to be. 'You are a very lovely woman, Cassey, and I am but human.'

'Then why did you take Morag last night?' she demanded, wanting to hit him for his air of masculine superiority.

'You wouldn't understand if I tried to explain it. But I'm not going to argue with you,' he put her from him resolutely. 'You'll have to leave with the rest and there's an end on't. In any case, I shan't be here long. I have orders to join Maurice.'

'I could come with you. I have heard that women sometimes travel with the soldiers.'

'Camp-followers, d'you mean?' He looked sceptical, his eyes running down over her. 'No doubt but the men would welcome you! But it is not the life for you. You are a lady, though, at times, you behave like a strumpet.'

She was not sure if this was meant as a compliment or an insult, but she brushed it aside. There was a more important issue. 'Will she ride with you?'

Now he was becoming more angry. 'Morag? I know not what the devil she will do. Nor care much.'

He swung round on his heel and picked up his hat. 'And now...I must go.'

He spoke swiftly, giving her no chance to interrupt. He was in a hurry to get out before she started to cry again, but he had not taken three steps before she threw herself in his path.

'Leon, promise me that if you ever have need of me, or if I can help you in any way, you will send for me.'

He nodded and reached for the door handle. 'I promise. Now let me go.'

'Aren't you even going to kiss me?' It was a cry of anguish.

He hesitated for only a moment and then his arms went about her with a rough eagerness which suggested some reluctance within himself to leave her. Cassey's fingers dug into his shoulders frantically, as if she could hold him there forever by sheer force of will, her face already wet with tears.

'Oh, Leon! Don't go! Please don't send me away from you!'

He seized her wrists and forced her to free him. 'Cassey, darling...there is no other way. We'll meet again, mayhap, some day.'

There was such finality in his tone that Cassey gave up struggling, an icy numbness deadening thought, yet she could not stop herself making one last plea.

'Leon, I have told you that there is a fortune waiting me at my father's goldsmith in London. This is yours to use whenever you want.'

A shadow crossed his face, that pride which would prevent him from accepting charity, especially from a woman and she added hastily; 'Not for yourself...for your King...for the furtherance of your cause. I shall ask nothing in return.'

He looked sceptical as he always did when she made exaggerated promises or claims, and she knew that his cynical philosophy doubted human motives. But there was such sincerity shining in the eyes which stared up at him in adoration that he smiled and rested his hand gently against her cheek for a fleeting moment. Then, before she quite realized what had happened, he had gone out of the door slamming it behind him.

Cassey reached for the latch, then stopped suddenly as the full hopelessness of the situation hit her. She slumped slowly back against the table and her head dropped into her hands.

She did not know how long she sat there, lost in a wasteland of desolation, when Beth came bursting in, carrying with her an air of excitement and bustle.

'Ma'am, they are here!' she exclaimed, too preoccupied to notice Cassey's drooping shoulders and tear-blotched face. 'And guess who is leading them?' She did not pause for a reply but rushed on: ' 'Tis none other than Captain Ruthen! There, what think you of that?'

She brought this out triumphantly, like a kind aunt offering a sweet as solace to a child with a skinned knee. It was her firm opinion that Cassey should marry Edward. She was well aware of Leon's dangerous attraction, and had pandered to her mistress's desire, doing all possible to ensure that she had her way with him, and herself had a string of admirers among the soldiers, but she recognized sensibly that there was nothing so satisfying for any woman as a loving husband and a parcel of children. The harrowing times in which they lived tended to strengthen this view.

Cassey looked across at her, a wan look on her face, her eyes dull. 'Edward here?' she repeated, listlessly. She had not thought of Edward for some time; he had been eclipsed by the meteoric blaze of her passion for Leon.

In the hall, Roundhead troops and Cavalier guards eyed each other warily and an uneasy truce prevailed. Leon was exchanging stiff civilities with Edward, both of them very formal as befitted officers and gentlemen. Several heavy leather bags of coins stood on the table and orders were being given.

As Cassey came in, Edward greeted her with solemn propriety, and bowed over the hand of his Colonel's lady. Tabitha's pale, plain face lit up with relief, and she immediately became involved in the arrangements being made for the continuation of their interrupted journey. The business completed, Leon strode away without so much as a backward glance, and Cassey was caught up in the urgency of packing.

As the lids were being securely fastened on the last leather truck, Edward came to find her in her room. Somehow, he seemed to have shrunk in size from how she remembered him. Was it because she had found a god to be worshipped? A tall, dark man of an almost unearthly beauty. Edward seemed pale, faded and insignificant. She felt no more emotion for him than for a kindly friend.

Beth who considered herself the soul of tact where romance was concerned, skimmed him a curtsey as she passed him on her way out on some trivial errand, ignoring Cassey's frantic signals to remain.

Edward stepped, almost lurched, to meet Cassey, the light bright on his blond hair, glancing off the ridge of his nose. In his sober uniform and steel helmet, he looked five years older than she recalled, and travel-stained too. Dust powdered the creases at the corners of his eyes and his new, fair moustache, a shade darker than his hair. His voice speaking familiarly to her, sounded unnatural, but so did her own.

'Cassey, darling...they have not harmed you? My God, I have been so worried.'

'There was no need...they are gentlemen ...they did not seek to hurt us,' Cassey began incoherently, then stopped, doubting her own ability to explain anything at all to him. He was a stranger. It seemed that she had squeezed a lifetime of experience into the past weeks, grown so far away from him...his was like an alien world...nothing was of any significance beyond the walls of Kestle Mount.

'What ails you, sweetheart? You are as lovely as ever, but something has ruffled your serenity.' His face was troubled and Cassey turned away, laughing a little mirthlessly at this exquisite under-statement. She busied herself with folding linen, unable to meet his eyes.

'I cannot go to Troon,' she said quietly, then stopped him as he opened his mouth to reply. 'Don't ask me to give you reasons. If you still love me, Edward, then you must help me.'

A worried expression crept into his face, which had before held only relief and admiration. 'Love you? Of course I love you.'

'Do you still want to marry me?'

The hope which sprang into his eyes made her feel almost ashamed. He took the room in a couple of strides and swept her off her feet into his arms. 'How can you doubt it, Cassey?' Then he sobered, setting her gently down but keeping her in his arms, stroking her hair, running his hands over her back. 'But what of your uncle? He has forbidden the match.'

'God's Life, man...would you let that stop you?' He winced at her scorn, while from without came the noises of imminent departure; the hurried footfalls in the corridors as Tabitha's servants humped down boxes and chests while children wailed and their nurses tried to hush them, and somewhere a servant was barking orders. This discussion must be short-lived if they were to be well on the road by nightfall.

'What can I do? He is my commander.' Edward was torn between loyalties.

'Take me to your own home. Once we are married, there is nothing Grantley can do about it.' Cassey did not add the strongest factor; he would then have to relinquish his hold on her money. She had complete confidence in her ability to get her own way with Edward, intuitively recognizing that he would be putty in her hands.

Her course of action was becoming brutally clear. Marriage with Edward would offer her protection from Grantley, security, a road to her fortune, show Leon that she could get on very well without him and, most important of all, give her baby a name.

'D'you really mean it, Cassey?' His brows drew together, puzzled, wanting to believe but unable to accept this stroke of fortune. 'For if this be done out of pet or God knows what, it will quickly show itself.'

'Well, of course, if you don't want

to...' she began tartly. This discussion was getting on her nerves; she wanted to erupt into violent action.

Then Edward was contrite, swearing on bended knee that he desired only to serve her, making her feel sad and sorry and, at the same time, despise him for his weakness. Together they laid their plans.

It had been arranged that the travellers should break their journey at dusk, finding a suitable hostelry. There, they decided, when all were asleep, they would saddle-up and slip away. When their flight was discovered, it would be too late for pursuit. By the time Grantley got to hear of it, they would already be man and wife.

Their departure went smoothly, servants, children and coaches rounded up and assembled and, at last, with Edward's troopers forming a guard, they rattled over the drawbridge.

Richard had been there to help her into the coach, his eyes speaking volumes whilst he assured her earnestly; 'Remember, if I can be of service to you...' leaving much unspoken which could have been said between them.

Cassey looked back in spite of herself.

Kestle Mount clung stubbornly to its lofty pinnacle...dark and forbidding, yet she longed to be folded within its ancient walls more than anything on earth.

Five

By evening the cortege clattered into the courtyard of an inn bordering the rough road close to a moor. Ostlers ran to attend the horses, and the host appeared in the doorway, silhouetted against a glow which promised warmth and welcome. The occupants climbed stiffly from the carriages; dogs barked, horses neighed and sleepy children grizzled. Points of light sprang from smoky flares borne by the inn hands to guide the disgorging of passengers and baggage.

It was only when they reached the privacy of her bedchamber that Cassey was able to divulge her intention to Beth. Time slid by and soon, as the noises of the inn dwindled away and all became silent, Cassey stood at last in the hay-sweet stable, gazing at the deep black mystery of the heavens which hung above her, a sharp night breeze on her cheek, a cold dampness in her hair.

A figure detached itself from the gloom

and Edward was there to help her into the saddle. She hitched her knee over the pommel and took a firm hold on the reins. Behind her, Beth was hoisting herself up, groaning and complaining, no experienced horsewoman, but accepting the discomfort for the sake of her mistress. The sky cleared and a sulky sickle moon lit the way. Edward was on familiar ground and led them across heaths and moorland, following narrow animal tracks until at last he paused to point to a rise. The dim, squat shape of his home loomed against the denser blackness of trees.

Cassey was very tired and cold and her first glimpse of Mawnan Manor was dreamlike. Edward was knocking at the heavily-studded oak front door, and soon a light appeared at one of the small-paned windows, a white-haired retainer drew back the bolts and a couple of hounds appeared at his heels, tails wagging in ecstatic greeting of their master. A groom staggered from the direction of the out-buildings, knuckling sleep from his eyes, and a cock started to crow as the first pale streaks of colour heralded the dawn.

No sooner had they entered the hall

when a tall, finely-boned woman who must once have been handsome, came along the landing, and made her way down the curving staircase. She was wearing a wrapper flung hastily over her nightgown, her unbound hair streaming across her shoulders. Two younger women, round-eyed and excited, hurried behind her, obviously newly-awakened.

Cassey wished that she was a more presentable figure to meet her future mother-in-law and her daughters, now so tired, weary with travelling. Their eyes were on her, full of unspoken questions, whilst Edward, at first, attempted to explain, then gave up and burst out with:

'Mother, this is Cassandra Scarrier...we are to be married.'

Eyes were now studying her closely, the large, accusing eyes of his mother, her thoughts reaching out to bare her soul. She was weighing...judging...seeming to ask herself was this untamed creature, redolent of passion and the sweat of another man's bed, torn and broken by emotions, as savaged as a deer caught by the hounds, really suitable to be her son's bride? It was as if Cassey's most guilty secrets were being exposed and she could feel herself flushing.

Then her spine stiffened. It was ridiculous. How could this woman possibly know anything about her? It was all wild imaginings born of her exhaustion. She tossed back her snarled hair, her glance encompassing the curious girls, catching the beginnings of admiration in their shy glances. Their adoration of this eldest brother was plain. They crowded round, eager and questioning while he laughed and relaxed, thinking that his mother had accepted Cassey, unable to comprehend that anyone should not see and love her at once as he did.

His father had been Sir Mortimer Ruthen. There was an imposing portrait of him above the fireplace and Cassey found his painted features stern and uncompromising, guessing that he would have found her as unsuitable a match for his heir as Lady Amelia did. But she soon had Cassey and Beth installed in the guest room; to be anything but good-mannered was against her nature. Maids humped up water, the lavender-scented sheets were turned back on the big bed, and breakfast was brought in on a tray. There was even a bunch of sweet smelling snowdrops in a little silver vase.

Cassey had lost her appetite, a sick, hollow pain inside her which had increased with every mile which cut her off from Leon. She slumped in a chair, a picture of dejected misery.

'Lord, ma'am, have a glass of wine, do,' urged Beth, filling two glasses with splashing generosity. 'This mumpish humour will do no good. At least try to convince Captain Ruthen that you're glad to be marrying him.'

Cassey sighed and sipped, recognizing the sense of Beth's suggestion, but the more she thought about the prospect, the more wretched she became.

'Seems to be a mighty fine house. You could've done a lot worse,' commented the incorrigible Beth, casting an appreciative eye round the room.

It was furnished with the same good taste which seemed to be prevalent in the whole house. Everywhere about them were evidences of comfort and wealth. The tables and chairs had coverings of velvet or stamped leather, edged with shaggy fringe. There was the magnificent bed, and a dressing-table, fitted with drawers, on which stood a lacquered toilet-box. A pretty Venetian mirror in a gilt frame hung on the wall behind it. The floors were beautifully laid in intricate patterns of polished wood of various shades, though the one in the hall had been of black and white tiles. The furniture was mostly of carved oak, old-fashioned but imposing, and tapestries covered the walls. The atmosphere was one of sobriety...this was the home of quiet, conventional unassuming folk. Already Cassey found it so restricting that she wanted to scream.

She was in no better mood when, a little later, as she had just settled down to try and rest, Edward knocked on the door. She had already decided what to do when this happened, instructing Beth to tell him that she had fallen into an exhausted sleep and would see him at dinner. Disappointed, he went away, and, though he did his best to dissuade her, she stuck to her virtuous stand, having firmly made up her mind to keep him at arm's length until they were wedded. She told herself that it was diplomacy not repugnance of another man's embraces which made her so reluctant. She was unwittingly helped in this by Lady Amelia, ever vigilant of their morals, who saw to it that the young couple were always decently chaperoned.

Because his duties were pressing, the wedding preparations went ahead without delay. Cassey and Edward were married in the tiny church of St James in the village of Mawnan Haven. No expense was spared, and the female population of the household were reduced to a state of hysterical turmoil by the speed with which the arrangements were made. Mawnan Manor was crowded with local gentry who were complete strangers to the bride. They had put away their usual unimposing garb and, wearing gay apparel, arrived early on the wedding morning bearing sprigs of rosemary and flourishing true-lovers knots. Gifts for the happy couple were set out on trestles in the hall. Lady Amelia had driven the servants hard and the whole house had been thoroughly cleaned from attics to cellar. The pewter and silver were burnished, the waxed oak glowed warmly, hung with gilded bays, aromatic with the great sprays of spring flowers which filled every pot and vase.

There was a noticeable absence of young men in the crowd; any male who was fit and able-bodied was off fighting the war.

There was a preponderance of elderly squires, parsons, younger sons who chaffed with impatience to be old enough to join in the fray, and a large number of women and children. In spite of the wedding gaiety, black predominated. There was hardly a family present who had not lost someone, father, son or brother in this bloody war waged by fellow-countrymen on the fair English soil.

Earlier in the week, Edward had galloped off to make his peace with his commander. He did not want to be charged with desertion, so went to see Lord Essex to make his position plain and give Grantley no opportunity to malign him. He arrived home on the eve of the wedding.

The ceremony and the feast which followed passed in a haze for Cassey. She moved like an obedient doll, standing and sitting when told, pale and beautiful in a formal white satin gown, the bodice trimmed with seed pearls, the sleeves very full and slashed from shoulder to wrist to show the lace-trimmed chemise worn beneath. The overgown was slit up the front to display the fine underskirt which had a centre panel lavishly embroidered with silver thread and more pearls. It had been Lady Amelia's own bridal gown and, pushed for time, she had allowed it to be taken from the linen press where it had been reverently stored for years. The resident seamstress had made alterations, rendering it more fashionable, taking in the waist and letting out the bust so that it would fit Cassey.

Looking in the mirror when she was dressed on the wedding morning, Cassey hardly recognized herself. This brought a measure of comfort, like putting on a masquerade costume in which she could act a part. She was no longer Cassandra Scarrier, not yet Mistress Ruthen, hiding away inside a faultless, unfeeling stranger. This helped her to suppress the truth that she was not marrying the man she loved, and, if tears rose in her eyes as the ceremony progressed, these were interpreted as those of joy and considered to be good luck.

When it was over at last, and they had been bedded with as much tradition, festivity and ribaldry as their Puritan persuasions would allow, Cassey was disconcerted to find herself alone with Edward. Now it was more difficult to hide her feelings and welcome him into her bed. But she played her part as well as she was able, hoping that he was unaware of the insincerity of her embrace, his adoration and her own conscience stirring her to do her utmost to please him. She was saddened to find that he excited her no more than Richard had done. With every fibre of her being she longed for Leon, staring into the darkness after Edward slept, silently crying out for her Cavalier lover, tears streaking across her temples, running back into her hair.

They breakfasted in their room. It was early for Edward must be on the road to London. Cassey, not yet dressed, wore a green silk wrapper over her white lawn nightgown. She looked fragile, still sleepy-eyed and yawning, child-like and innocent with her unbound hair sweeping her shoulders.

Edward's face was such a picture of delight and love that she felt embarrassed. She recognized such enslavement; it was exactly what she felt for Leon who, were he to live to a hundred, would never return that intensity. She saw this bitterly and clearly while the sunshine slanted through the window drapes, winking on the silver and accoutrements of their repast, the

134

birds sang a glad carol to the spring, the old house hummed with gentle, orderly pursuits and Edward's eyes shone as if he beheld a goddess.

'My bride,' he said, enormously satisfied, stretching out a hand to enfold one of hers. 'I shall be back as soon as I am able. Mother and the two girls will look after you, beloved. Would that I might take you with me, but 'tis impossible.'

Cassey caressed his palm with her thumb. 'Edward, will you see Grantley whilst in London?'

He answered her question with a nod, busy munching cheese-cake and apple-pie. Then added ruefully. ' 'Twill take all my courage to do so. I'd rather face a battery of Royalist guns! I find it in my heart to hope that he is kept away about Parliament's business.'

With Edward gone and the preoccupation of the wedding over, the days stretched ahead into an eternity of boredom during which Cassey had far too much leisure in which to brood about Leon, recalling every incident, dwelling on each detail, torturing herself by imagining him with Morag, quite unable to accept her new life which excluded him completely. Her heart felt raw, as if she were bleeding to death inside, denied his presence. It was pure agony to be parted, not to know where he was or even if he was safe. For all she knew he might be fatally wounded somewhere, or even dead. Reason told her that this was unlikely. It seemed that he led a charmed life, never receiving more than a scratch, and common sense told her that this was due, not to any magic but to the very fact that he never dithered about on the edge of the fray but plunged right in where the fighting was thickest. His reactions were lightning swift, his aim unerring.

But Cassey would have given years of her life just to see him walk into the room, overshadowing all by his dominating personality, reaching out his arms for her. She wanted to lay her head against his chest and hear the heavy beating of his heart, to feel his hands in her hair and his mouth on hers.

They had not seen each other for almost three weeks now and she was losing hold on him...it was like a wonderful dream which, though once remembered vividly, rapidly fades to nothing. There was the colour of his eyes, dark and impenetrable, though sometimes having a reddish tinge when sunlight chanced across them, the twist to his mouth, cynical and reserved, yet sensitive too, the quietness of his voice which yet held the promise of suppressed violence. Whenever she thought of the last time he had made love to her, her blood raced and her heart began to pound. She remembered the sweetness of his mouth, the skilful caressing of his hands. Edward was an inept amateur when it came to love-making.

Yet, in spite of its strongly physical nature, her love for Leon seemed almost pure, bringing out all that was best in her. No sacrifice had been too great. With Edward it was just a question of expediency, while he did all the giving. It was a novelty to be considered and adored; she had become accustomed to so much loving attention...it made her uncomfortable.

Restlessly she wandered the abode where she would soon be in charge; Lady Amelia proposed moving to the Dower House, taking her daughters with her. Sad, dispirited thoughts were her only companions down gravel paths edged with box-yews, across the soft, velvet-smooth lawns, between troops of flowers to the herb garden where beehives sheltered their busy occupants.

Mawnan Manor was a lovely place, half timbered in black and white, with curly pedimented gables and upper storeys which jutted over the court-yard. It was a much more friendly building than Kestle Mount where the atmosphere was war-like, bristling with armed men and all the bustle of a military encampment. Here, nothing more eventful happened than shifting-day when, monthly, all the linen was gathered, laundered, and spread out on the bushes to dry, or there might be a visit to the market, or one of the men returning with tales of the war.

Her coming had been one of the most disturbing incidents for months; even now she was well aware that the maid servants were aloof, conversing in undertones which stopped dead when she entered a room. Without doubt she must have disappointed many a maiden with aspirations in Edward's direction. She took a wicked delight in being at her most cool and sophisticated when Lady Amelia had callers. Her slightly superior manner reminded them that she came from

London, whereas they were but the wives and daughters of countrified gentlemen. Playing games with them relieved the boredom, but it did not last long and she soon wandered away, a victim to her own unhappy thoughts.

Lady Amelia, struggling to be fair, showered her with kindness, though both were undeceived, knowing full well that it was only done for Edward's sake. To impress her, Cassey accompanied her to the still-room where the shelves were lined with pickles, wines and preserves, herbal remedies, ointments and potions. Most of these Cassey recognized from hours spent in the kitchens of her childhood for, though expecting a high standard of education, her father had also seen the sense of training her to be a good housekeeper. For although he had hoped she might never be called upon to practise these skills if his ambitions for her future came to fruition, at least she would know if her servants were cheating her.

Lady Amelia was surprised, impressed and mystified...and it did not make her like her daughter-in-law any the more. Her girls, however, found Cassey fascinating...they had never met anyone like her, thinking her most glamorous and worldly-wise. She was not reluctant to show-off, and wished that she had not been forced to leave most of her boxes of clothes with the coaches. But, as it was, what she had managed to bring filled them with admiration. They envied her her London modes and manners. An imp of perversity urged her to influence them; she showed them how to effect a fashionable hair style, and initiated them into the subtle use of paint. It was the same spirit which made her long to say something outrageous when Lady Amelia and her friends were present.

Then, late one afternoon, the peace of Mawnan was shattered by the sound of hooves, the snorting and trampling of horses in the courtyard, and Edward was swinging down from his sweating mount. Cassey did not go flying out to meet him as she would have done had it been Leon, but walked slowly down the wooden staircase from the gallery which connected the upper rooms, arriving just as Lady Amelia was embracing her son.

His soldiers were making their way to the mess-hall, while his sisters had fallen upon the rider who had mail-bags strapped to his saddle, dancing impatiently whilst he undid the buckles, grinning at their eagerness. They seized the bags and disappeared indoors with them; undoubtedly they contained letters, and packages bearing fripperies from the London shops. Cassey could remember a time when she too would have shared their enthusiasm; now all that she longed for was some token from Leon, and this was unlikely to be brought by a Roundhead postboy.

Edward, smiling broadly, came across to kiss her, then strode into the house with one arm about her and the other linked with his mother's. She insisted that he eat at once, and Cassey had no chance to speak with him privately until much later. Even then it was difficult for he wanted to make love to her without preamble, slipping a hand into her robe whilst Beth was engaged in smoothing the bed-sheets, glancing across to see if she had noticed. He was always a little nervous of the outspoken Beth and was glad when she had finished preparing her mistress for the night, dipped them a curtsey and departed.

Cassey was seated on a stool before the dressing-table, one leg sliding out of the opening of her robe, balancing a high-heeled mule on the tip of her toe. Beth had already brushed her hair, but she continued to work on it till it shone like satin. She knew that she was putting off the moment, unable to stop comparing this tepidity with the wild passion which used to sweep her uncontrollably when she was living with Leon. Then she wanted him at any hour of the day and night, filled with trembling eagerness whenever he was near.

Edward had taken off his doublet and was standing watching her with evident enjoyment. 'I have seen Grantley. He knows that we are married.'

Cassey paused in the regular strokes, watching his reflection in the mirror. 'What happened?'

He laughed, coming up behind her, sweeping the hair from her nape, bending to place his lips there. 'He was ablaze with fury, very put out because I had been excused duty by Essex. But what vexed him most, my dear, was his loss of control over your money.'

She swivelled round to grip him eagerly. 'You saw my goldsmith?'

'Indeed I did. But he would release nothing to me. You must needs visit him yourself, taking our marriage documents with you. There is no hurry...you have money aplenty here for your wants.' He smiled indulgently, thinking that he knew very well what feminine baubles she would want to buy. 'Your jewels can wait...you'll have little opportunity to wear them in the country. Indeed, it might be safer to leave them in the capital.'

Cassey allowed herself to relax against him, feeling his hands tremble as they examined the contours of her back, and the heat of his body pressing against her, knowing his urgency and his need. She responded almost automatically, but her brain was cool, and she was irritated...she wanted to have all her money and her assets here, in her grasp. There was no doubt of her intention once this happened...its purpose would be her escape from this stultifying marriage, and her return to Leon.

They spoke no more of her wealth and within two days he was gone again. Cassey felt nothing but relief; secure and pleasant her life with him might be, the truth was that he bored her in bed. When Leon had looked at her it had been like fire and wine in her blood; in Edward she merely saw a pleasant young man whom she would be happy to have as a friend. His rare visits over the next weeks cemented these feelings.

One sunny morning, Cassey was gathering rag-wort, privet and yarrow. Dried in the sun on muslin racks, then pounded by pestle and mortar, these would be added to hog fat to make wound lotion. She paused and straightened her aching back. From where she stood in the kitchen-garden, the hills sloped steeply down from the ruin of the old Norman keep which had once protected Mawnan Manor. On one side she could catch a glimpse of the blue ocean, flecked with a passing sail, on the other spread fertile parks, fields and purple heather moors. On the opposite side of the valley, there was an ancient earthwork, standing bleakly on a peak, relic of battles long ago.

Cassey was pondering about this, her quick imagination peopling it, wondering who they had been and if any of them had been as unhappy as she, when Beth came puffing out to find her.

'Ma'am, there's a pedlar at the back door. He's asking to see you.'

Cassey picked up her trug and followed her into the light, airy kitchen. Just outside hens were clucking and scratching unconcernedly in the dirt, protected by their master, the great russet rooster with his knee ruffles and spurs and red comb fiery in the sun. The air smelled of baking bread and fermenting fruit for the steward was making wine, the ingredients standing in deep earthenware crocks already creamed with frothing yeast.

A shabby figure leaned indolently against the jamb with his tray of goods before him supported by the leather strap round his neck. He was scruffy and ill-kempt, greasy reddish hair twisting from under a battered felt hat, a fearsome black patch over one eye. A little way off, a dark-skinned lad squatted on his hunkers, waiting.

Cassey took one look at the pedlar and stopped short in her tracks. It was Richard. She stifled the exclamation of recognition, for he had closed his one existing eyelid in a monstrous, conspiratorial wink.

'Here, mistress, look at these ribbons. This blue one will surely become you.' He had assumed a rough, Cornish accent very different from his usual cultured one.

Cassey made a pretence of being interested in what he offered, drawing nearer, out of earshot of the scullery maids, busy about their scouring. He leaned a little closer, speaking in his normal voice.

'Here's a fetch! And you married, Cassey! To a Roundhead too!' He rolled a scandalized eye. 'You disappoint me.'

'Oh, Richard, don't tease,' she whispered, hope soaring within her. 'Have you brought word from Leon?'

'Ah, so that's the way of it, eh?' He nodded sagely, holding out a spread of lace cuffing, and raising his voice. 'You'll not find better value this side of Bristol, madam.' This was for the benefit of the straining ears in the kitchen.

'The marriage is one of convenience, Richard, nothing more.' She was anxious that he should believe her. 'How is Leon? Is Morag still there? Oh, dear God, there is so much that I would know.'

'Not now,' he hissed. 'I have not the time. I have a letter for you. Can you step outside and read it without drawing too much notice?' He turned to shout over his shoulder; 'Hey there, good-for-nothing lazy-bones! Bring up the pack horse...her

Ladyship has a mind to see that bale of fustian.'

Will the gypsy rose and tugged on the rein. Leon's letter seemed to burn her fingers. Pretending to inspect the material which was unrolled before her, Cassey ran her thumb-nail beneath the blob of red sealing-wax and unfolded the stiff paper. The letter was very brief;

'My dear Cassey,

Do you recall offering your help if monies failed? Believe me, they are most desperately needed now, not for myself, but for the cause. You are often in my thoughts, more than is good for my peace of mind. Send word by this messenger,

Your friend,
Leon Treviscoe.'

Cassey read it once without taking in a word, just to see his large, sprawling writing brought him to her vividly; then she re-read it slowly clasping it against her when she had done. 'Oh, Richard, of course I'll help him!' Her voice was choked with tears. 'What must I do? Oh...' her hand flew to her mouth, dismayed, 'but my fortune is in London.'

'We thought this might be the case.' Richard was still spreading the cloth for her perusal, saying loudly: 'There's no better weave in England, madam.' He lowered his tone, speaking with quick urgency. 'Are you willing to come away with me? Good, then this is what we will do.'

He outlined the plan. She was to meet him at daybreak at an inn in the next village. He began to pack up his goods while still talking. 'It is always easier for a man to get through Roundhead pickets if he has a woman with him. We'll ride to London where our agents will help with the next stage; I'm going as a farmer with wool and hides to sell; you can pass as my wife. Once there, I can introduce you to those working within the city walls, and you can see your goldsmith. I'll tell you more tomorrow.'

The fact that she was about to act the traitor to the Parliamentarians meant nothing to Cassey; a lifetime of loyalties and upbringing swept away. Leon needed her. That was all that mattered. She asked for nothing greater than to serve him, for whatever he believed in must be right.

Bubbling with suppressed excitement she

prepared to leave. The prospect of spying made her stomach lurch with a sick thrill of anticipation. She had heard tales of women agents working for whichever side they favoured. There had been one well-born Cavalier lady who had ridden to London with secret dispatches hidden in her curls. She would show Leon that her courage was every bit as high as Morag's.

Explaining her sudden absence was not going to be easy, but she left Beth to deal with that. They concocted a plausible story of her being called away to London on urgent family business. This would allay suspicion for a few hours at least. She mulled over leaving a note for Edward, then decided against it.

She rose into an overcast morning not yet light, found her way to the stable, saddled Golden Boy, mounted and gave him his head. She wanted to shout aloud with joy at the freedom, leaving her safe home without a qualm, her head spinning with thoughts of Leon. She bent low over the horse's withers, clinging on top of the rhythmical pounding, mouth full of hair and lace collar, crashing through narrow paths in the woods where the leaves of the trees hung heavily, occasionally dripping.

It was wicked to run a horse so but she revelled in it. So did Golden Boy.

She found the right road, stopping to ask a girl who was driving her geese to the pond. She looked at her curiously but pointed an arm to direct her and she raced on. Soon the hedgerows gave way to straggling cottages which gathered into a hamlet. It contained only one inn and this was easy to find. Cassey dismounted, leading her horse round to the back, picking her way through the mud, holding her velvet skirt high.

In the yard, a scullion was busy with the pump, and its squeak and the thump of the wooden bucket against the mossy sides of the well mingled pleasantly with the cackle of poultry and the high voices of maid servants as they whisked in and out of bedrooms bearing breakfast trays of crisp bacon and newly baked bread.

As Cassey hesitated, holding her horse by the bridle, not sure what to do next, she glanced up at the gallery. Someone was coming out of one of the bedchambers, leaning on the carved rail, looking down at her. It was Leon.

Six

Cassey stood perfectly still, one arm braced against the hitching-post, staring at him. Her head began to whirl and her heart pounded and she was suddenly paralysed, unable to move or speak.

Richard came to her rescue, materializing from the stable. He walked across, kissed her casually and slipped an arm about her waist. 'You managed to find us, sweetheart. Well done. Yes, Leon is here too. This mission is of such moment that he had to come.'

Then she moved, although her legs felt as if the bone and muscle had dissolved. Leon came swiftly down the steps and she went into his arms. And Cassey closed her eyes and lay heavily against him, in a kind of disbelieving dream. She wanted that moment to last for ever, feeling his arms about her, the strong muscles of his thighs pressed against her, while she clung to him as if she would never let go. She breathed in that heart-breaking fragrance which was always Leon to her, the perfume of his long hair which trickled her nose, the masculine odour of sweat from his dark red doublet, the crisp clean smell of his lace trimmed collar. His hands were gentle on her, his voice murmuring low. She never ceased to be amazed at the way this large, immensely strong man could be so gentle when he wished. It was the same tenderness which softened his dark eyes when he spoke to children or looked at his dogs.

There, in the full view of the interested inn servants, Cassey put up an arm to coil about his neck, the fingers of her other hand moving across his face, tracing the strong jaw, the straight nose. He seized her wrist, turned his head slightly and kissed her palm, running his mouth over her fingers. Her arms were about him again and she held on tightly as if she feared he would melt away like snow in sunlight, tipping up her face so that he could kiss her lips.

Behind them, Richard cleared his throat, reminding them that there was much work ahead, so they went into the inn, ordered a meal and, over it, enlightened her as to their position.

Cassey pressed close against Leon's

side, eating little, taking in none of the conversation though afterwards it made sense. It was as if she had been dead for weeks; now her life-blood came flooding back into her, bringing with it a wild exhilaration and a blinding reality which eclipsed the sensation of trance. She really was here with Leon's hand in hers; she could actually reach out and touch him whenever she wanted. Then her life at Mawnan became no more than a nightmare from which she had just wakened. She shook her head as if to clear sleep from her eyes and asked:

'What is this important issue on which we must now work?'

They were alone in the parlour but even so Leon lowered his voice. 'The Queen is in great danger. Essex draws ever closer to Exeter where she had just been brought to bed of a baby girl. Money will be needed if we are to spring the trap and see her across the water to France and safety.'

'But Rupert, Maurice, and the King? Can they not rescue her?'

His mouth set in a grim line and even the sanguine Richard looked glum. 'Rupert has suffered a crushing defeat at Long Marston in Yorkshire. Maurice is having difficulty sieging Lyme, and the King has troubles aplenty about Oxford.'

'What can I do to help?' Even now her role was not clear.

'We'll go to London, there to glean information, deliver and collect letters. You can obtain your money, then we'll ride for Exeter, God willing.'

Richard had been employed in espionage for a long time. Leon had formed a very healthy respect for his stratagems and intelligent grasp of opportunities. There existed a complicated network of contacts behind enemy lines, and waiting for them at this inn was suitable clothing for their journey, together with a wagon and merchandise.

Richard and Leon transformed themselves into a couple of country clods, none too bright but full of native guile, and practised the correct dialect. Cassey's quick ear had already registered the singsong idiom of the Mawnan villagers and she had little difficulty in producing a passable imitation. It was not so easy to turn her into a demure, respectable farmer's wife, in spite of the sober dark woollen dress provided for the part, with its prim high neck and snowy collar, her rebellious hair covered by an unbecoming cap with a wide-brimmed plain hat set severely on top.

Richard turned her about slowly, looked her up and down. 'Hum,' he mused critically. 'You are still far too attractive, my dear. Walk more stiffly, control that provocative hip movement, you are not trying to lure Leon into bed at the moment...and the chaste wives of Puritan-minded men do not look up like that from the corners of their eyes, and their lips do not smile so invitingly. 'Twould be safer if I could cover you with a sack from head to toe.'

It was almost impossible to concentrate with Leon there watching; she was only too aware of the interest in his eyes and the tension building up between them. When evening came, Richard and Will took themselves off to the taproom and Cassey wandered out, tired with so much instruction, seeking Leon who had left to pursue some business of his own.

She found him on the footbridge which spanned the darkly flowing river. He had his elbows resting on the balustrade and his eyes were pensive. She hoped that he was not thinking of Morag for she had half expected her to arrive at any moment, but had been afraid to ask him. Now that the first fierce exultation had worn off a little, she found herself beset with worries. If he loved the gypsy it would be an agony not to be borne; she was suddenly sure that one day, if she held fast, she would be able to blot out his every thought of other women. Somehow, she must become as indispensable to him as breathing.

Now he turned towards her at her step, his face shadowed and, without a word, she went into his arms. His doublet was unbuttoned and she clasped him tightly beneath it, aware of his warm flesh beneath the thin cambric of his shirt. Her nails dug into him through the material when his kisses became more demanding, her mouth opening, ripening under his, knowing nothing but the urgent response of her body.

'Come back to the inn,' he said, his breath was warm against her cheek.

She hung on to his arm, while he slowed his pace to hers, and she was in a seventh heaven of happiness just to be at his side. He did not talk much, neither did he appear to feel the dampness in the air, bare-headed, and he had not bothered to fetch his cloak. They walked across the village green hand in hand because it was nearly dark and it was such a beautiful night and they were so wonderful together. At the inn she saw his silhouette upon the threshold, walking all golden from the light, an undeserved halo bright around his head. She shuddered as one sometimes does in sunlight.

He stood back with neutral courtesy for her to precede him up the narrow wooden staircase to the gallery. The landlord had given him a key. The flint and tinder was in its usual recess near the fireplace. Leon took it from her and skilfully coaxed a flame, lighting the wax candles and then kneeling to stir the sluggish logs.

Cassey felt that she should be performing these menial tasks, not he, and turned away to unpin her hair, the heavy locks coiling down. Sneaking a glance at him, she found him sitting on the woven wool rug, watching her, leaning back on his elbows, long legs stretched out straight before him. She came over to kneel beside him, almost shy.

'What have you been doing?' Part of her wanted to prolong this lovely morning of anticipation. She asked him about the skirmishing, the bedevilling of Roundheads, anxious to share all the thrills, the danger, to get under his skin, understand and become a part of him. Had she been born a man, he was exactly how she would have wished to be.

He shrugged, not inclined to talk. 'Oh, this and that.'

He pulled her down beside him and Cassey, no longer filled with this strange shyness, responded urgently, letting sheer animal enjoyment flow over her. In her heart she sang a song of triumph over Morag.

Afterwards, they climbed into the wide bed and slept until grey dawn began to filter through the slats. Cassey lay in an entranced half-sleep, aware of his every breath and movement. She kept touching him to convince herself that he was real, not just a figment of her longing as in her usual drowsy fantasy moments of waking. But she must have dozed at last, because the next time she opened her eyes it was to find him wide awake, lying on his back with his hands behind his head, frowning slightly up at the dim rafters of the ceiling.

'Can I get you anything?' she wanted to know, hoping that he would turn and love her again; she could never have enough of his powerful body. His eyes sharpened with recognition, although it seemed that he was so engrossed in his own problems that he had almost forgotten her existence. He smiled vaguely, sat up, leaned over to kiss her cheek and then moved into action.

'Nothing yet, darling. We'll get ready, then eat just before we leave.'

'I would that we might remain here for ever!' she said passionately, and her eyes seemed enormous in her oval face, filled with an unquestioning adoration.

'There is much to be done during the coming days.' He was moving about the room, putting on his clothes, ducking his tall head to avoid the dark beams. His energy constantly amazed and wearied those about him, a driving restlessness which never allowed him to relax. 'Money is the root cause of the problems in His Majesty's army, an unceasing demand for arms, stores, fodder and pay. I am beginning to believe that a war is won not by the gallantry of its soldiers but by the length of their purses.'

He was sitting on the side of the bed pulling on his riding boots purposefully.

Cassey sighed; it was time to be on the move again, this little oasis of peace and love must be left behind.

Will drove the wagon and Leon and Richard jogged beside it on a pair of sedate cobs. It began to drizzle as they rattled along the London road, but even so Cassey's spirits lifted with excitement as she huddled under the hooped awning which covered the bundles of wool, the strange-smelling sides of leather. The journey was uneventful, a peaceful passage through the lanes of summer, with nights passed at wayside inns, or even in the back of the wagon. Enchanted nights for Cassey, filled with the overpowering presence of her lover. She had never been happier. Then, just as she had begun to believe that they might travel on for ever, she began to recognize some of the sign-posts and knew that the capital was not far ahead.

A quake of fear shook her; till then she had not really been aware of anything but the delight of being Leon's constant companion. As the heat of the afternoon gave way to evening coolness, they passed through the outlying villages and began to wind down narrow streets where an ever-increasing population told them that they were in London.

Cassandra had never been to this part of the city before and stared up at the timbered houses which beetled over the lower storeys, the facade of each alley still further varied by the numerous signboards which swung over each doorway, a necessary appendage for every shop and lodging-house to rivet the attention of the illiterate. Whenever a wind rushed down the narrow streets, every house became a fluttering picture-gallery, all swarming with monsters, lions and swans of every colour, dragons and unicorns of every shape. Everywhere was squalor, darkness, clutter, smell and overcrowding. Different indeed to the district where Cassey had been born and brought up.

London seemed incredibly busy after the countryside; an air of anticipation galvanized everyone. Cassey had almost forgotten the sight of barricaded streets where shop-keepers jostled customers, troops and Trained Bands lorded it, showing off. The once loyal people, merchants, traders, masters and apprentices were violently Roundhead and, since she had left, it seemed that the political fire had spread more widely in the crowded thoroughfares; every man, woman and child appeared to have been caught up in the fever.

When the city had been threatened by Rupert after the battle of Edgehill, all had been thoroughly scared, portly grocer along with hot-headed youngster, the burly coal-heaver as well as the City knight, had all donned the buff and bandolier, ready to take up arms at an instant's notice to defend their town against the 'Malignants', the terrible Cavaliers, led by their mad Devil Prince. It was during an attack on Brentford, an outlying village, that Cassey's father had lost his life.

As yet, Rupert had not sieged the city, indeed it seemed that he had lost his chance and, meanwhile, though rumour ran rife and there were daily alarms, the war now appeared to be a favourable as well as an exciting event. Trade was given an impetus; the inns had never been so well patronized; wealthy men got good interest for their money; those less fortunate were bettered by its circulation. The lot of the poor was no better or no worse then when the King resided in his palace at Whitehall.

The atmosphere could not have been

more different than that of sleepy Cornwall. Cassey was very aware of it and it scared her. When she had lived in London before, she had been on the side of Parliament, now she had gone over to the enemy, though only vaguely understanding the political beliefs and religious dissensions which lay behind the war. With her new pro-Royalist feelings, she was angered by what she saw and heard, but frightened, too, when she imagined her treatment if it was discovered that she kept company with Cavalier agents.

It was very obvious that this was a Puritan city by the actual appearance and mien of its middle-class townsfolk. The men wore dark suits, their hair cropped closely about their ears, their faces unnaturally elongated by their elaborate gravity, under the shadow of their steeple-crowned hats. And the women seemed to be intent on making themselves as dowdy as possible.

Richard and Leon had noted these peculiarities on earlier visits and had adopted them as part of their disguise. Cassey contented herself with holding her tongue and taking her cue from them.

They dropped Leon off at a shop bearing

the sign of a butcher where one of their key men was in hiding, and turned into a side alley. Children scampered out of the way of the wagon, jeering and yelling, then running back to renew their gutter-games. There were several lines of dingy washing, hanging listlessly, slung across the street from top windows. An open sewer trickled sluggishly between the cobbles. Will pulled up outside a house, one of a row at the end of the alley. Cassey got out of the wagon, glad to stretch her stiff limbs after sitting in one position for so long. She peered curiously through the sooty panes and Richard banged on the dilapidated door. The house looked at if it had once been an imposing dwelling though now degenerated into a seedy lodging-house.

After a long pause during which Richard cursed impatiently, the door was opened a crack by the owner who exchanged a few hurried words with him before admitting them into a dark, musty hallway. An elderly retainer, looking even more decrepit than his master, was ordered to go with Will and take the wagon round to the back.

Richard introduced Cassey to Master Howell, and she was not very impressed.

He was elderly, wearing an old-fashioned gown with hanging sleeves which was smeared with food stains down the front, a skull-cap on his grizzled hair, and tiny frameless spectacles on his beak-like nose. But when he smiled, there was something gently benign about his face which put her in mind of an indulgent uncle. She later learned that beneath this harmless exterior he was very astute, and played a large part in organizing the Royalist spy ring. He had been a merchant for years, dealing in raw wool and woven goods, carrying out his business on the ground floor of his house, letting out rooms on the other storeys. If strangers came and went this excited no comment and he was not suspected. Many a message or illicit parcel of broadsheets had been smuggled through the city gates in bundles of fleece.

He stabbed a piercing glance at Cassey. 'And who is this young lady? Is she to be trusted?'

'More than anyone in the kingdom,' Richard asserted with a smile. 'She is mad in love with Lord Treviscoe.'

Howell chuckled and waved them into chairs, filling glasses with Rhenish. 'And is his Lordship aware of this?'

'Aware and receptive to it. She is in his trust, and shares his bed on the brief occasions when he settles long enough to occupy one.'

Howell pulled a suitably impressed face. 'Indeed, she must be a lady of rare quality to have captured the attention of that young man. Without doubt, we can use the services of such as she.'

It seemed a foregone conclusion that they would stay under Howell's roof, pretending to be merely traders, while the clandestine communications concealed in their loads were delivered to their destinations.

Richard stretched out his hands to the sullen, smoky fire. Although the weather was warm, the house was ill-lit and damp, stuffy with the necessity of keeping all the windows closed against the foul smell of the streets which was accentuated by the sunshine. Garbage lay in heaps along the pathways, and the contents of chamber-pots were flung from upper windows, often splattering their contents on to passers-by. Cassey, during her visit to Cornwall, had forgotten the putrid atmosphere of London.

'What news?' Richard asked Howell, his eyes sharp.

'A hardening of spirit in all,' the old man's mouth turned down ruefully. 'It would seem that all means of conducting an honourable peace have been tried, and abandoned as impracticable. London's temper is ugly. Their printing presses work night and day, churning out lies about the King's men...Prince Rupert in particular.'

Cassey was given a bedroom up under the eaves, with a low ceiling, and small windows set nearly at floor level. It was all muted colours of seasoned wood and old tapestry, made rosey by the glow of candles already lit against the dimness of evening. She lay on the bed, pulled the quilt up over her, weariness leadening her limbs; the journey had been more exacting than she had thought. She closed her eyes and tried to sleep, but the very air of London was oppressive with hate—misguided and misled. What chance did the Cavaliers have against such clearly managed fanaticism, their milling soldiers, the wealth of the city, its power and its munitions. The seeds of fear had been planted so skilfully by clever, unprincipled men, and had blossomed more fruitfully than even they could have dared hope.

On returning across the yard from a visit

to the communal privy, Cassey had been arrested by the sight of a young mother trying to control her naughty toddler, shaking it roundly and shouting: 'Be quiet now, and do as I bid you, or the Great Dragon Prince will come flying out of the sky to snatch you up and eat you whole!'

Cassey had shuddered, knowing that the woman referred to the rumour going round that Prince Rupert was a cannibal, and his followers equally barbarous. And Leon was still out there, lost in the confusion of the alleys and streets. All that she could do was pray that he was not discovered.

It was very late when he returned and she wakened to coil up against his back on the narrow bed. He fell asleep at once, before she could question him. In the morning she rose early to call on her goldsmith.

Samuel Reuben knew her well; she had often visited his rooms off Threadneedle Street with her father in the old days. He was a money-lender and business man, utterly trustworthy, steering a middle course in the conflict, his only thought to protect the wealth and interests of his clients. His house was comfortable, solidly built and well furnished, with an overall impression of prosperity which was encouraging to those who placed their finances in his care.

Tall, lean and middle-aged, he was always polite, obliging without being obsequious, inspiring confidence. He expressed little surprise at Cassey's unexpected arrival, making discreet enquiries as to the health of her uncle, casting a curious eye over her plain gown and at Leon who was masquerading as her man-servant.

Cassey had brought along her wedding lines, and explained as well as she could that she wished to remove her money and jewels to the country as she would not be in London often. Although he seemed a little dubious, she cut short his advice that it would be wiser to leave it, and soon he was sending down to his strong-room where the wealth of his clients was stored.

Cassey's eyes sparkled at the sight of the leather bags of coins, the packages of jewellery which he handed over for her to stuff into the valise which she had brought for the purpose. He explained that some of her money was not available as he had invested it for her in Parliamentary shipping which was trading with America. She saw the sense of his suggestion that she let him continue in the managing of this for her. Then, at least, she would have something to fall back on.

Jubilantly, Leon carried her bag into Howell's house and set it upon the table so that they might examine its contents, and Cassey was amply repaid by the expression in his eyes, his words of gratitude as he held her close while Howell and Richard pored over this horde like a couple of misers. All of her money was going to assist that dark, elegant little woman who was Henrietta Maria, King Charles' beloved Queen. And she experienced a qualm remembering that she would be almost beggared, apart from her shares in the trading company. The fact remained that she would no longer be able to return to her husband and was therefore utterly dependent on Leon. The prospect was sweet, yet, knowing him, she gave pause to wonder if the realization had yet been borne home to him, with all its implications.

Later that day, Richard suggested that she accompany him on a stroll through the streets. He had a letter to deliver to an accomplice. Meanwhile, he and Cassey must appear to be a country couple on a visit to the big city, gazing, round-eyed with wonder, at the amazing sights of war-time London.

Cassey began to enjoy the outing, once she had got over the initial nervousness. On reaching the Drum and Monkey, in Sparrow Lane, which was the appointed rendezvous, Richard found a vacant table and ordered sack and hot pies. Remembering to keep her demure pose, Cassey sneaked a glance round the room. Although the men were soberly dressed, conversing in subdued tones whilst sipping their ale, they were looking across at her. She held her cloak more closely about her and tried to shrink into the shadow of her hood, hoping that they would think her action due to modesty, not fear.

In spite of her nervousness she was hungry. The pie was delicious, crumbly pastry filled with chunks of beef and rich gravy. When Richard had finished his, he stood up, excused himself, and disappeared in the direction of the yard. Cassey was mystified, wondering if they had missed their man, though Richard always seemed so confident that she could hardly believe his plans could go awry. It was while she was anxiously waiting, twirling her empty glass, affecting an ease which she was far from feeling, that a group of uniformed officers entered, greeting the host familiarly.

Cassey, rigid with horror, met the glance of Charles Craig, Grantley's lieutenant; Amos Hawley, the sergeant, was at his elbow.

Instantly she turned away, but not before noting that his bushy eyebrows had drawn down into a puzzled frown. Her every instinct urged her to jump up and rush out, but she forced herself to sit quietly, ignoring them as if they had never met.

Richard slipped into the chair beside her and they kept up the pretence of being a devoted husband and wife, for all the world concerned about nothing more important than the quality of the food. Smiling and nodding, leaning forward fondly towards him, Cassey hissed from the side of her mouth: 'We are undone. I know those men at the bar. Where the devil is your contact?'

'Don't worry, darling.' Richard cut off a slice of cheese, balancing it on his knife before placing it on a hunk of bread. 'I saw him as soon as we came in. Our business was concluded out there, just now. We'll leave here as soon as 'tis prudently possible. No hurry now...take your time. They've not betrayed you yet, so 'tis possible that they are not quite sure. Finish your dinner and have another glass of sack.'

'I shall be sick.'

'Don't be a fool. All will be well if you keep your head.'

Afterwards, Cassey never knew how she managed to sit still, expecting at every moment that Craig or Hawley would move purposefully towards them. Nothing happened; they seemed engrossed in chat with several other soldiers, but, as Cassey passed them on her way to the door, Craig's eyes met hers once more and she knew, without the shadow of a doubt, that he was almost certain of her identity.

'I'll not venture out again!' she exploded, back in the comparative safety of Howell's house. 'We shall be shot if they catch us!'

'Hanged, more like,' remarked Leon, seemingly unmoved. 'Running into them was a piece of deuced bad luck.'

'It was a disaster!' Icy drops of sweat

were chilling Cassey's spine. She could almost feel the noose about her neck.

'We shall leave at once.' Leon began to gather up his things. 'Our work here is done.' He turned to Cassey. 'Up to our room now, post haste, and don the man's clothing which you will find there. It will be a hard ride ahead, and you must not be hampered by petticoats. We will abandon the wagon and take horse.'

Swift as the wind, Cassey reached the attic and changed, all fingers and thumbs, pausing momentarily to swagger before the mirror, pleased at the dashing appearance of her doublet, breeches and riding boots, cloak swirling about her, hat at a jaunty angle on her bright hair. She still looked very feminine but, with any luck, the Roundhead sentries at the city gates would not be too eager to dally long over their passes.

She was halfway down the staircase when there came a hammering on the front door. Howell had already opened it by the time she reached the hall. She heard male voices raised in argument, and one rising above the others, urgent and commanding, instantly recognizable as Edward's.

'I have been told that my wife is here,'

she heard him saying. 'Don't waste time in lying, old man. She was followed. We have but a short time...Colonel Scarrier will be arriving at any moment to make an arrest.'

'You are a Roundhead officer.' Howell's voice was crisp and cutting. 'Why come to seek her out and give warning?'

'She is my wife. I thought her safe in Cornwall, now I discover her in a nest of Royalist spies. I must speak with her.'

'I am here, Edward.' Cassey stepped from the gloom of the stairs and he spun round, bewilderment in his eyes.

'Cassey! Oh, my darling...' He made a step towards her, his one instinct to take her in his arms, protect and shelter her. 'So it was you that Craig saw; I had hoped he was mistaken.'

'It will take too long to explain.' Cassey stared at him without emotion. He was like a stranger, wearing the uniform of the King's enemies. 'I should never have married you. It was unjust, for all the time I have been in love with Leon Treviscoe.'

'So that is it,' he said softly and the light went from his face, leaving it grey and old. 'I had half suspected there was something between you when I saw you again at

Kestle Mount. It was the way you spoke to him, and then, back home, there was a curious reluctance on your part to talk of your experience there. And sometimes, at night, you would call his name in your sleep with such a depth of longing in your voice...'

'I am truly sorry.' Cassey spread her hands helplessly. 'I hoped that, in time, I might forget him, but...'

For a moment he paused, as if still wondering whether to take her in his arms and plead his case; then he said: 'I understand, sweetheart. I shall always be there, if you need me. Now go quickly. Get out of London and do not return. If they catch you, there is nothing I can do to help, and Grantley will be hell-bent on revenge. I can only pray that this night will see you safe among friends.'

Simultaneously, their hands reached out and his was warm and firm on hers. There was a stricken look in his eyes and she knew how much she had hurt him, but there was no time to think about that now. Cassey made for the parlour door where Richard was already waiting, sword in hand. He picked up a road map and a bundle of papers and thrust them at her.

'If Leon and I are stopped, you must get through with these. We'll meet you at the Cock Inn at Chelsea.'

A rumpus at the front door behind them denoted that Grantley had already arrived with his men. He did not wait for it to be opened; someone fired at the lock and they came bursting in; the candlelight flickered dully over gleaming weapons and lobster-shaped helmets.

Leon hastily stubbed out the rush light, plunging the kitchen into darkness. Cassey was at his heels as he flung open the door and made towards the stable. The night air struck chill and, just before he helped her to mount, Edward held her against him, a dark figure in the gloom with only his face glowing palely above her.

'Cassey,' he whispered. 'Go to Mawnan. You will be safe there and I want to look after you.'

Scared, sorry for him, Cassey could only shake her head and regret the tangled circumstances of their lives, seeing again that gallant Captain of happier days.

'Dear Edward.' She touched his cheek with her gloved hand. 'It is impossible. Come what may, I am bound to Leon. Try to understand. He is a very great gentleman and loves England as much as you. You could so easily have fought on the same side. Thank you for the honour you have done me. There is no one that I would rather have wed, saving Leon.'

'Oh, Cassey...' There was pain, regret and real despair in his tone, and his mouth suddenly closed over hers, and in that little space, suspended in darkness, she knew that this man would have been good to her all her life long. Then the uproar from inside intensified and she broke from him to scramble into the saddle.

For a moment the scene was etched sharply by lantern light, glimpsed through the window. A shot rang out and Howell's hands clawed at his chest as he began to buckle slowly, the blood running from between his fingers.

Leon and Richard shouted to her, reminding her of the rendezvous and then they were gone, setting spur to their horses. Cassey urged her beast to follow but was too late, galloping full tilt into a troop of riders who swept round the corner from the alley. In the confusion of shouts, shots and oaths, she met a barrage of blows from a mounted man. A hand closed on her rein, slewing her to a standstill. Her hat was knocked off and her hair streamed across her shoulders. Some came running with flares, pushing them into her face, dazzling her eyes with their glare.

' 'Tis the woman, by the Lord!' her assailant thundered, while she tugged furiously at the reins.

'Leave her to me, my man.' It was Grantley, coming from the direction of the kitchen.

In that sad hour of capture, small, vivid vignettes imprinted themselves on Cassey's mind; being roughly man-handled as she was pulled from her horse and marched into the house; the sight of Howell lying dead on the floor; the questions fired at her and Grantley's face swimming through the haze, filled with savage satisfaction. There was only one thought uppermost in her mind—Leon must get away—for his own sake, and that of the money in his saddle-bags.

Angered by her stubborn refusal to talk, Grantley had her bound and bundled into a waiting carriage. They drove through the darkness to his house, where Tabitha and the rest of the family had returned after their experience in Cornwall. Now he refused to let anyone speak to Cassey, stern and uncompromising, ordering that she be locked in her room, ignoring Tabitha's alarm and Aunt Helen's stuttered protests.

She was conducted to the bedchamber which had once been hers, her bonds were loosened, candles were lit in the branched flambeau and her guards went out, carefully locking the door.

In a fury of indignation, Cassey hurled herself at it, hammering and pounding with her fists, calling Grantley every filthy name she could think of, and these were many; her vocabulary of curse words had increased since living with Leon. Desperately she looked round that familiar chamber for a heavy object, snatching up the brass coal shovel from the fireplace, but though she battered the lock with all her strength it was strong and solid and she did nothing more than scar the polished mahogany of the door. When she finally realized that her shouts and violence could gain her nothing, she started to smash every breakable object in the room. When the place was a shambles she suddenly gave up, trembling with exhaustion.

Morning dawned to find her pale and wan after a sleepless night, yet still with enough spirit to be defiant when, with the scrape of a bolt and a brisk order to the sentry on guard, Grantley came in to see her.

He made no comment although he glanced at the ruin of one of his best bedchambers, his voice smooth as he said; 'Come, my dear, you must eat,' and he nodded towards the untouched breakfast tray. 'It would be foolish to starve. There may not be such opportunity where you are destined to go.'

'Prison, d'you mean?' Cassey's voice shook in spite of herself and she did not stir from the leaded window where she had been staring out at the garden, measuring her chances of breaking out that way. It was going to be a fine day, a light mist rising in the early warmth of the sun. Cornwall would be beautiful just now. With a little luck, Leon might soon be crossing its border.

'Yes, this will mean prison. You will be tried as a spy and a traitor.' Grantley came across to stand close, looking down at her.

'What proof have you of my guilt?' she countered warily, her skin crawling at his close proximity.

'Proof aplenty.' His mouth tightened and

there was a warning spark of impatience in the blackly dilated pupils of his eyes. 'There was gossip about your behaviour at Kestle Mount. It is said that you are Leon Treviscoe's mistress.'

'And what if I am?' Her lip curled insultingly and she ran a scornful eye over him, leaving him in no doubt that, whatever happened, she would never be in that position with him.

He reached out and gripped her wrist in a way which jarred right through her. 'You seem to forget, fool, that I hold an important position in the army and am not to be trifled with! You have displeased me much. Running off and marrying Ruthen against my wishes!'

His face was near to hers; she could smell the faint odour of ale as he breathed. More angry than frightened she struggled to get free, raking at him with the nails of her free hand, but he was strong, his hold vice-like and she could do nothing but glare at him, her eyes fierce and slanting as a cat's. 'You have no right to stop me,' she shouted. 'You are my guardian—not my father!'

'Right?' he ground out, the muscles in his cheek working in the effort to suppress the violence which she had always instinctively known to be there under his chill exterior. 'How dare you talk to me of "right"? D'you really think that I will ever relinquish either you or your wealth? How little you know of me.'

'What of Tabitha?' Her eyes were ablaze with hatred and disgust.

'Tabitha is of no consequence,' he said brutally and she felt instant pity for his meek, loyal wife. He stood back a little, letting her go, the light playing on his harsh features and the fire which burned in his eyes. He was a man who would never forget or forgive an injury, fashioned as he was of repression and ungovernable pride. He would use any means, religion, politics and country to gain power for his own ruthless ends. She had the sudden thought that it would be terrible indeed for England if men such as he gained control.

'I made up my mind, long ago, that one day we should wed.' Sure of his power, he no longer felt the need for caution. 'Then all the Scarrier property will be mine. It was unfair that my elder brother, your father, should have so much and I but a paltry portion...Troon and a few miserable acres.' For the first time ever he was voicing his grievances which had been boiling beneath the surface for so long, envy and spite surging up. 'It was fortuitous indeed that he died and left you in my care. What a fool I should have been not to seize the chance...a young, lovely and, more important, wealthy bride.'

Cassey crouched, chaffing her bruised wrist, naked murder in her eyes. 'You forget one thing...you already have a wife, whilst I, dear Uncle, have a husband.'

He shrugged both of them off as of no importance, minor inconveniences easily disposed of. 'Tabitha can very easily be taken ill and die; no one will suspect me. It is not known that I have made a study of poisons.'

'And Edward?'

'Edward is a soldier. He lives dangerously. Who is to know if it was my bullet or that of an enemy which killed him? Agree to my wishes and I will see to it that your part in the affair is minimized. You will be pardoned...the charges annulled.'

'And if I refuse?' Like an animal in a trap, Cassey pressed back against the panelling, wildly seeking some means of escape, yet knowing that there was none.

'Then I can promise you that you will

suffer under their interrogation.'

'You'll not get my money,' she flashed. 'Leon has it and it is already on its way to Kestle Mount.'

For a moment she thought that he was going to strike her, his face contorted into a mask of fury. Then he lowered his clenched fist. 'He shall not get away with it. I shall pursue him myself. I have an old score to settle with him. When the war is over and the Cavaliers beaten I shall appropriate his lands.'

'How can you be so sure that they will be beaten?' Cassey held her head high, outfacing him, her loyalty to Leon and his cause strengthening. 'If the King prevails, you will be the one to pay the penalty.'

'Charles Stuart...that traitor,' his eyes narrowed, mouth brooding. 'He will never be King again. Cromwell won't allow it. He is the man to watch now...his will be the power in the end, and his friends will be well provided for.' His mood changed as he looked at her and his voice became a seductive purr.

'Come, Cassey... beautiful Cassey...are you going to be sensible?'

Cassey had never felt more alone. She clenched her fists into tight balls and sent out a prayer for Leon's safety. 'What do you want of me?'

His lips curved in a faint smile which never reached his eyes. 'You will tell me all that you know of Leon and his accomplices and, in return, you will remain here under house arrest, until they are captured. Then we will wait until everything dies down. You will give me your promise to wed me as soon as we are both free, and in the meanwhile, you will be nice to me.'

His arms came about her quickly, crushing her against his chest. One hand was in her hair, forcing her head back, and his lips came down painfully upon hers, jarring her lips on her teeth. Cassey wrenched her head aside, pushing hard against muscles that scarcely felt it. Then he released her so forcibly that she stumbled back against the wall.

'Now I shall leave you to think it over.' He turned towards the door. 'Tonight I will return for your answer. I am sure that you will be sensible and save yourself needless pain for, make no mistake, they will extract information from you using any means at their disposal.'

The door closed behind him and she heard the key turn in the lock.

Seven

Time could only be judged by the pattern of sunshine moving across the dark boards and the bright woollen table carpet on the bench below the window-sill. Noises drifted through from outside, that real world of which Cassey no longer felt a part—strident cries of street-traders, the clatter and rumble of horses and carriages, the bustle of the house servants going about their duties, and the voices of the gardeners under her window.

She got up and glanced out, aware of children's shouts. Aunt Helen was exercising her charges on the verdant lawn. One of the boys was playing with a ball, whilst a little girl trailed behind, clutching a wooden doll to her chest. She tripped and fell, hampered by her long stiff skirts, letting out a wail which made Aunt Helen pause. At that moment Cassey tapped on the glass and Aunt Helen glanced across hesitantly, taking a quick peek to see if either of the guards was watching, but they were too hot to be vigilant, leaning on their muskets, grumbling and wiping the sweat from beneath their helmets.

Cassey signalled to her urgently, throwing caution to the wind. Aunt Helen was a friendly soul and, though dutiful, there could not be much love lost between her and Grantley. Cassey recalled the numerous occasions when he had snubbed and humiliated her.

Like a fussy hen rounding up her chicks, Aunt Helen collected the children and marched them indoors. It must be time for their nap. It grew so quiet and still that it was as if the whole of London slept in the heat of the midsummer afternoon. Cassey sat schooling her impatience, willing her Aunt to come, convinced that if she could only talk with her she would be able to bend her and enlist her aid. Soon there came a timid rattle at the latch and the door opened a crack to admit that rather flustered lady.

'Oh, my dear, such dreadful happenings.' She fluttered across, half lifting her hands to embrace her, then withdrawing, filled with reticence. 'And you, child, so pale and so brave. What has Grantley been doing?'

'You must help me, Aunt. Oh, God, I've got to get away...' Cassey began to cry and beat her hands together and walk up and down the room, careless of how it might alarm her. She hopped along beside her, patting her sleeve, watery-eyed.

'Now, now, hush, Cassey, my little one,' she murmured comfortingly. 'Tell me about it.'

So Cassey poured out the whole story, whilst amazement, horror and alarm chased across Aunt Helen's face and she interrupted with little indignant cries.

'That Grantley!... How wicked! Poor Tabitha...so unsuspecting! I always felt him to be a severe man, but my dear...he is a monster!'

'More important, Aunt, is the poor Queen who has just had a baby and is now being hounded by Lord Essex.' Cassey was glad to be able to tell Aunt Helen the truth about Grantley, to confirm that the unhappiness which she had endured for years had been through no fault of her own.

Aunt Helen sighed and shook her head. 'Such a lovely lady...she and the King are both tiny people, you know, like something from fairyland. I saw them once, shining like stars in that resplendent Court. They were at dinner.' Cassey nodded, trying to be patient, she had heard the tale so many times before. ' 'Tis said that he is a patron of the arts, his collection of paintings is without price. I heard him speak on that occasion, from my place in the crowd of onlookers, his manner was so slow and stately—with a very slight stammer in his speech. What can have happened to make his subjects turn from him?'

'No doubt there are many filled with ambition...like Grantley,' Cassey snapped contemptuously, then gripped Aunt Helen's hands. 'Will you help me to escape?'

'My dear child...how?' Aunt Helen asked nervously, glancing apprehensively around as if expecting Grantley to appear out of nowhere.

'Let me have the key. Where did you get it? 'Tis surely not Grantley's.'

'He forgot that I have its twin on my chatelaine.' Aunt Helen jingled the ornamental bunch of short chains bearing keys, scissors and looking glass which hung from her waist. 'Oh, dear...but I'm not sure. I don't think I dare.'

Cassey brushed aside her qualms, sweeping her along with her own enthusiasm. 'No one will blame you. It will be unthinkable that you would disobey his orders...you, who have always been so compliant. When all is over and this dreadful war behind us, you can come and live with me. I will look after you.'

To leave at once seemed the solution, whilst the household was deep in the somnolence of the July afternoon. Aunt Helen showing admirable, and unexpected, aplomb, managed to coerce the sentry on duty at Cassey's door, telling him that there was a refreshing jar of ale on the kitchen table. Cassey slipped out like a wraith in her aunt's wake, and they sped silently along corridors, down flights of twisting back stairs till they came to a neglected door which led into a secluded, overgrown part of the garden.

There, amidst a jungle of wood vetch, nettles and burdock, they said their whispered goodbyes, and Cassey had never seen her Aunt so animated. Her cheeks were pink with excitement, her hair wisping untidily about her small face. Cassey made a silent vow to do all in her power to improve her lot as soon as it was humanly possible. Her last view was the astounding spectacle of her scrambling through a gap in the hedge, determined to circumnavigate the drive and enter the house by a completely different route. Then Cassey turned and ran, filled only with the desperate need to escape.

She traversed a lane which was little used and where she was spattered with the light and shade of the leafy trees overhanging its rutted surface. The Roundheads had taken her maps, so she had no hope of finding the rendezvous without aid. She knew that Will would wait there for her as directed. There seemed to be nothing for it but to find a busy highway and there conceal herself until such time as a suitable vehicle rumbled by.

She skirted the edge of the road, ducking behind the hedges and for a while there was nothing in sight but this shivering veil of green punctuated only by bird calls or the frightened scurrying of an animal. Then, all at once, the banging clatter of a heavy conveyance resounded through the countryside, lumbering heavily towards her. Recognizing it as a public coach travelling from London to the outlying villages, she stood up and shouted. The driver hauled on his reins, came to a stop some yards further on and turned in his seat.

Cassey had already reached the door and pulled it open. 'Take me to the Cock Inn in Chelsea Village!' she cried. 'And be quick about it!'

He took her at her word and it was as much as she could do to stay on the hard wooden seat as the coach careered and jolted over the sun-baked ruts. Almost before the wheels had stopped turning, Cassey was reaching up to slap the shilling fare into his outspread palm and off at a run towards the inn, ignoring his curious stare.

The building was old and pleasantly weather-beaten; the host and his wife a genial pair in the pay of the Cavaliers. They helped her as much as they could. In the low-beamed bedroom, she changed from her man's suit, putting on the tight-laced bodice, white blouse and dark green fustian skirt of a peasant woman, stuffing the discarded things into a valise.

Will had been waiting her arrival anxiously, and his swarthy face lit up when she appeared. He told her that Leon had escaped and that they were to join him near Exeter, if they could break through enemy lines. Will had many contacts, including bands of gypsies, tinkers, traders and strolling players. These still managed to traverse the country by simply attaching themselves to the armies of the Cavaliers. The Royalists were lenient towards such people, looking to them for entertainment and help, whereas the Roundheads called them vagrants and beat them if they were caught.

Will and Cassey left at once, she riding pillion behind him and they journeyed for three days before meeting up with a regiment marching to assist the King in his struggles to reach the Queen before it was too late. These soldiers were camped overnight and Will rode boldly up to their pickets who greeted him as if they knew him and let them pass into the circle of wagons which formed the camp for their followers.

There was the sound of cheerful voices and singing, children scampering about, enjoying the freedom and Will led Cassey through the crowd, where men called greeting with easy familiarity and he accepted a pull at a proffered blackjack, and tossed off some retort to the women who called out to him. Back among his own kind, he suddenly seemed to grow in stature; Cassey hardly recognized him as the lowly stable-hand and scout.

There was a thicker press of people over in one corner where a wagon had been turned into an improvised stage. A girl was dancing, saucy and inviting, whilst someone scraped out a jig on a fiddle. Will and Cassey watched her till, her performance completed, she dipped into a deep curtsey amidst the applause. Will, who had pushed to the front, reached up for her and she leaped down into his arms, hanging on as he set her on the ground. She had pert features and a mane of mahogany hair which fell to her waist, a sensual, pliant body displayed rather than covered by the very tight, low-cut bodice of brown velvet and the full emerald silk skirt which swirled above her slim ankles and bare feet.

Will introduced the two women and a smile tugged at his lips as he noted their instant suspicion of one another. 'Mistress Ruthen...meet Loveday.'

Loveday stared at her, wary and hostile. 'Who is this high and mighty madam? Her clothes don't fool me. She has the hands and bearing of a lady. Why have you brought her along to sneer at us poor players?'

Will shook his head, thrust an arm through each of theirs and drew them along to a trestle where the sutlers sold ale. There he explained the situation and Loveday's eyes grew more friendly when she realized that she was not facing a rival, though she became guarded again when Morag's name was mentioned. It appeared that they all belonged to the same family, and Cassey was astonished to learn that Morag had been betrothed to Will from the cradle.

'Though it would seem that she has chosen to ignore that childhood pledge,' Will muttered darkly. 'She plays the whore and disgraces us.'

Cassey did not sleep much that night, her mind rocking with this new information. She shared a blanket in the back of the wagon with Loveday, who chattered almost ceaselessly, a talkative, outgoing, inquisitive creature, who was soon in possession of all the relevant facts of Cassey's life and history. In the morning they rose early, stiff and yawning, shivering in the chilly dampness of dawn, taking their cooking pots to the communal camp fire.

Cassey washed her face in the stream and dragged a comb through the snarls in her hair while Loveday stared, nonplussed by such fastidiousness when she scrubbed at her teeth with the bone-handled toothbrush which she carried among her personal possessions. Loveday was obviously a stranger to soap and water. Her smock was grey with dirt, there were rusty sweat stains in the armpits of her bodice, a long rip in her skirt had been cobbled together with cotton of another colour and there was a rank, unwashed odour about her which made Cassey's nose wrinkle.

But, withal, though fierce and quick in her dislikes, she was friendly and warm-hearted to her selected comrades and she had taken Cassey under her wing. She introduced her to those who could help her and was of invaluable assistance in accustoming her to the way of life in the leaguer.

Will had already been in touch with the commander of this army which consisted of a miscellany of foot soldiers and a small troop of horse. They had been mostly recruited from his village by their seigneur, Sir Harry Marchmont, but had gathered others on the march, and it was a patchwork enough company. Will took Cassey across to meet Sir Harry; apparently he already knew him through association with Leon. The commander came yawning from his tent, disengaging himself from two half-naked women who hung about behind him.

Cassey looked up into a gay, dissipated face and a pair of bold eyes, which twinkled with obvious pleasure at the sight of her. He wore all the trappings of a Cavalier carried to the extreme. Yet these absurdities of fashion were flaunted by him so superbly that it seemed the natural wear for a soldier and a gentleman.

'Ah, my dear.' He made a sweeping bow to Cassey, his eyes mocking, admiring, a dashing challenge of a man, infinitely dangerous, but intriguing too. 'I welcome you to our camp. Consider yourself under my protection. No doubt but that we shall be able to bring you to Lord Treviscoe with all speed. Meanwhile, believe me to be your humble and devoted servant.'

Obviously Will had told him all about her, and once again she was conscious of the respect accorded to her among the Royalists because she was Leon Treviscoe's woman.

Sergeants were bawling orders and the camp was preparing to move on. Cassey returned to the wagon to help Loveday. Soon the straggly cortège was on the march, and they plodded on all the morning, halting at noon. Cassey had packed some bread, cheese and portions of chicken, together with a flask of wine. Now she brought out these provisions and took them to where Loveday was sitting, back braced against a cart-wheel, legs out straight before her, neatly crossed at the ankles, gnawing at morsels from the red and white spotted kerchief spread over her lap. With a gesture, she casually presented Cassey to other members of her party. These numbered a juggler, a couple of acrobats, a fortune teller and an old fellow who played the fiddle.

The leader of the troop was a lively, middle-aged man with a short greying beard, hair thinning on his high forehead, intelligent eyes which sparkled under bushy eyebrows and a figure more comfortable than spritely. His name was Ralph Killigarth, and he assured Cassey that he had been well known in London before the trouble started when the Parliamentarian authorities closed all the theatres.

He had taken to the road, convinced that there was a living to be scraped together by amusing the soldiers. Some half a dozen actors had gone with him. They lived in the wagons along with props and thick bundles of scripts, mostly the plays of Shakespeare and Ben Johnson. They erected their improvised stage, doubled up on roles; somehow got through the performance without too many disastrous hitches, and shared out what was collected when the hat was passed round.

Young men still acted the parts of women, and Loveday was called upon to sing and dance, but not allowed to speak. Killigarth assured Cassey that this would not always be the case.

'My dear, in France and in Italy, civilized countries which recognize the worth of true artistes, females already tread the boards.' He managed to retain his poise, though making his points with a flourish of his dagger on which he had speared a sausage. 'Ah, those theatres! The scenic effects...the magnificence of the lighting...the costumes! One day, England too must see such productions. But now these damned Puritan kill-joys have condemned us as vagabonds...they with their particular brand of Christianity that's worse than bad breath!'

'Aye, that is true, my dear fellow,' asserted Sir Harry who had strolled over to join them, a leathern flagon of wine in his hand. Cassey had the distinct impression that he was pursuing her in a somewhat bored, desultory fashion. 'We Cavaliers have the vices of men...the love of wine and women; but the Roundheads have the vices of devils...hypocrisy and spiritual pride!'

'God damn me, sir!' agreed Killigarth, in high indignation. 'They say we out-swear the French, out-drink the Dutch and out-paramour the Turk!'

Sir Harry meandered away again, weaving unsteadily on his feet. In passing he slipped an arm round Loveday, giving her a squeeze and pinching her cheek.

A sergeant came clumping round, thick-set and aggressive, intent on getting the camp on the march again. 'Come on, there. This ain't a bloody picnic party! Don't you know we're at war?'

Loveday rose slowly to her feet, a mocking smile lighting up her brown eyes. As he half turned away she made an insulting gesture with her right hand.

He saw her from the tail of his eye.

' 'Ere, you saucy trull!' He glanced down over her and a grin lifted his bushy moustache. 'I'll be back to deal with you later!'

'You, and who else?' she retorted, hands on hips. 'Fancy your chances, don't you? I'll report you to Sir Harry.'

'Oh, Gawd, you another of his whores? Stow it, love...I don't want to fight no duels with the gentry over their fancy pieces. Plenty more fish in the sea.'

Cassey was kept fully occupied in adjusting to her new life; at best it was downright uncomfortable, and at its worst, squalid. At first she was interested in everything going on around her, beginning to lose her shyness at the admiring whistles and boldness of the soldiers, riding her pony proudly, cloak draping her shapely body, the hood pulled up over her head to protect her from the sun. Then the days began to drag monotonously, and still they had not met up with Leon. There was nothing to relieve the boredom but the flurry of an occasional skirmish in the van if they chanced across a Roundhead ambush.

Cassey became convinced that she would

never have survived without the good-natured Loveday. She had given the actual mechanics of the march little thought, assuming that it would be no harder than the hunting-parties which she had attended at home, forgetting that there had been a gaggle of servants always on hand to perform the chores. Now there was kindling to collect, water to scoop from the streams, while the great iron cauldron was a demanding despot and had to be kept stocked with snared rabbits, or a hen grabbed when it strayed from its backyard, and vegetables purloined from gardens when they passed through villages.

Will helped her as much as possible but, after two days, her hands were rough and blistered; she felt thoroughly scruffy and ill-kempt, and very much in need of a bath.

At last they arrived at their meeting-place on the outskirts of a small walled town which they were under orders to attack, both to replenish their supplies and to draw Roundhead troops away from the Exeter area, making it easier to reach the Queen.

Cassey, breasting a rise, reined in her horse and looked down over the town. She listened to the bells pealing out frantically; warning bells from the church spire, shattering the peace. She was astonished at the apparent size of the Royalist army; even allowing for the fact that they were marching wide to increase the effect, they were still a formidable spectacle as they drew up in battaglia before the beleagured walls.

Back in the camp she found Loveday on her hands and knees blowing on the tinder to stir the sluggish flames beneath the tripod. She glanced up as Cassey joined her, cheeks pink with effort. 'Any sign of Leon?' she enquired.

Cassey shook her head sadly. She had no doubt that he was out there somewhere where the fighting was thickest, in the forefront of a charge, impervious to danger. Then she resented her position among the women and children, longing to ride again at his side as she had done on the journey to London. Disgruntled, she watched a company of horse gallop off to reconnoitre, then, as the sun cast long shadows of evening in the valley, she settled down to chat with Emma Waring, wife of one of the foot soldiers who had been as determined as Cassey to follow her man.

The army approved of wives coming along too, agreeing that the soldiers were then better fed and looked after.

An odd friendship had sprung up between this quiet, timid country girl and a rather blowzey but kind-hearted trollop from one of the brothels of Oxford. Emma had recently given birth to her first child and her milk was proving inadequate. The hungry child wailed incessantly.

'Here, missus,' Polly had offered one day, having just wrapped her own fat, satiated baby in a fold of her shawl. 'The poor little devil is starving! I'll give 'im suck for you. I've enough for a dozen!' And after that it was a common sight to see Polly with her round, opulent breasts bare and a baby glued to each nipple.

They were setting up camp, gossiping about births, deaths, men and other women with the avidity of females the world over, while the children played about, got under the feet of the men, fell out of trees and into ponds, and came crying back to mother with grazed knees. Apart from the gleam of weapons, the heavy guns being lugged into position, and the tents springing up like mushrooms, it was an idyllic enough scene. The cavalry came pounding back, exuberant and cocky.

The attack was to be at dawn next day, the town having refused the command to surrender. Cassey had half hoped that Leon would come seeking her, but no message arrived. Will reported to her that he was there, among Prince Maurice's troops and she lay awake long after it was dark, listening to the small sounds of night; the murmured exchange of the sentries, the continual hum of the leaguer and occasional bursts of shot as both sides exchanged fire. She prayed for Leon, tense and worried. Soon she could bear it no longer, rooting through her valise, kitting herself out in boy's clothing again, borrowing a back and breast-plate and a helmet from Killigarth's property box and sneaking his sword while he slept.

It was just beginning to get light and Loveday was furious when she awoke to find out what Cassey intended. She grumbled continuously as she helped her into her armour. 'Where the devil d'you think you are going in that lot? Here, take this pistol. D'you know how to use it? You do? Good. Though much good may it do you. You realize that you'll probably get killed, I suppose?'

Cassey did not answer, clapping on her helmet, swinging on to her horse and spurring behind a little cavalcade who were moving off under orders. She could think of nothing but that Leon would be out there where the fighting was hottest, and that if he were to fall then she no longer wanted to go on living.

The Cavaliers had brought their guns into play and blasted a breach in the city wall on the north side. Squashed between grim-faced riders, Cassey was borne along on the impetus of their charge over the litter of fallen masonry and down into the town, a hell of noise and confusion. They were fired at from the houses so they took possession of other buildings from which they could retaliate. The firing from each side never ceased; Roundhead marksmen picking off the invaders with deadly aim. Most of the combatants were inexperienced, and few understood the principles of war, but the fighting was bitter in spite of that. Down the narrow, twisting streets poured the attackers, while the sky seemed to hail bullets and everyone was hacking and slashing determinedly.

Cassey was deafened by the terrified shrieks of the women inside the barricaded houses, the screams of the wounded, a tangle of men tumbling from their horses to be trampled underfoot, the overall boom of cannon fire.

This proved too much for her staid little pony used to a quiet country existence. A shot, whistling by his ear, caused him to rear and plunge, unseating Cassey who crashed to the cobblestones, her helmet flying off to be pounded by those murderous hooves before he bolted, whinnying shrilly, his eyes rolling with fear. For a moment she was knocked senseless, then instinct made her roll into a doorway to save herself from being pulped. Her mouth was full of blood, a raw, bitter taste where her teeth had snapped on her tongue as her head struck the ground. She moved her limbs cautiously, but, though thoroughly bruised, there appeared to be nothing broken. Her ribs hurt where the heavy breastplate had hammered them.

Her one thought was to crawl into some safe corner and hide. She edged along the wall until she was on her feet and able to draw her sword. At the same instant an armed man dashed round the corner and fell full tilt against her. He gave a savage bellow and lunged with his rapier. Cassey parried, more by luck than judgement; she had only done a little fencing with friends and that for fun, but this was in deadly earnest for he was intent on killing her.

Her feet nimble with terror, Cassey dodged and feinted, a scream rising in her throat, yet knowing that a call for help would be useless; everyone was too occupied with their own part in the mêlée to rescue her.

'By the Lord, 'tis a woman!' snarled her assailant. 'A Royalist bitch. Damned whore of Babylon!' His eyes shone with another emotion besides fanaticism. She guessed, correctly, that he was assessing his chances of dragging her into one of the empty buildings and raping her. Her sword arm was numb, breathing laboured, with one ugly fact foremost in her brain...she was about to die, impaled on her opponent's rapier.

With a crafty twist of his blade, he sent hers spinning off across the roadway, leaving her at his mercy. The piercing yell of a soldier just hit by a bullet seared across her hearing. She tried to turn and run but she was paralysed, watching, with a kind of sick horror, as her enemy closed in, the smirk of the taunting bully on his face. At that instant a huge rider forced his way through the litter of struggling men and horses. It was Leon, laying about him like a fury, gouts of blood running down his flashing blade.

Cassey found her voice and yelled, her high woman's scream rising above the grunts and moans of the warriors.

Leon swung round in his saddle, saw what was happening and bore down on them. In a flash he had leaned over and run the Roundhead through the throat. The warm blood from the punctured jugular fountained out, spraying Cassey who recoiled in revulsion. A glance up at Leon did nothing to reassure her; she could well understand now why he was feared by both the enemy and those of his own side. His eyes glittered in his smoke-blackened face which was streaked with sweat, and he was blood-spattered. His right gauntlet was dark where it had run down his sword and dripped off the guard. He seemed so indomitable that she could almost believe him capable of winning the town single-handed.

He glared at her, furious and worried. 'What the devil brings you here?' Without waiting for a reply, he bellowed over his shoulder to a couple of musketeers who had just finished clubbing a Roundhead with their butts: 'You there! Take this lady back to camp!'

At that moment a galloper came to find him. There was to be a cease-fire; the town had surrendered and a parley was taking place.

Cassey was escorted ignominiously up the hill by grinning soldiers who did not stop teasing her all the way. She was so tired and battered that she could hardly put one foot before the other, dreading meeting Leon again. He had looked so angry. So much for her attempt to be a she-soldier, like Morag. Tears stung her eyes; she had wanted to impress him so much.

Back in the leaguer, seeking out Lovejoy, wanting her kindness and sympathy, she was jolted out of her self-pity by the appalling suffering of the wounded. These were being brought back on stretchers or supported by friends. They were taken to the tents where the surgeons had set up hospital quarters. Those not badly injured were waiting in patient queues for minor dressings, some green-faced and stunned, others cracking jokes with the false gaiety of men who have looked into death's face and been reprieved. A small huddle of women were attempting to comfort Emma who was sobbing distractedly, clutching her baby, her tears dripping on to his shawl.

Cassey pushed through the throng. 'What has happened?'

Emma shook her head and moaned, incapable of answering and it was Loveday who said: 'Tom's leg was smashed by a cannon ball. They are about to take it off.'

What was there to say? Except... 'Can I help? I know about nursing the sick.'

Loveday was tying back her heavy hair with a ribbon and rolling up her sleeves purposefully. 'Not this time, love, tho' they'll be glad of your assistance later. The surgeon works fast. He has to...'tis the patient's only chance. Take Emma away from here. There is nothing she can do.'

She disappeared through the tent opening where figures, red to the elbows, their aprons as dark and sinister as any butcher's, worked over the injured men. Even as Cassey led Emma away, she saw the flash of the surgeon's saw and heard the moaning cries of Tom turn to the gurgling screams of an animal tortured beyond endurance.

Emma stopped dead in her tracks, nearly dropping the baby. It took all of Cassey's strength to prevent her from running back. 'Stop them!' she was screaming. 'Please don't let them do it! Oh, Tom...Tom...'

Between them, Polly and Cassey managed to conduct Emma to a quiet corner of the field out of earshot of the tents. She collapsed suddenly, sobbing in a hopeless monotonous way, rocking to and fro, her arms clasped about her body as if she was chilled to the bone. Polly was nursing the baby.

'This damned war...' Emma said brokenly. 'Why can't they leave us alone, them up there in their great palaces? We were happy working on the farm, Tom and me...we didn't want no part in it. But 'twas the squire, Sir Harry...he talked the lads into going with him to fight for the King. His words sounded so grand...and he promised us good pay, more'n Tom could earn in years, but 'twas all lies...we never saw any money. Tom just got carried away with his words...he didn't understand what it was all about, but the others were going, and he didn't want to be left behind and called coward!'

'That Prince Rupert now, he didn't want to involve the people,' Polly put in reflectively. 'I've heard the lads say that, in the beginning, he sent a formal challenge to Lord Essex offering to fight him in a duel and so settle the trouble with just the two of them at risk.'

The sun was a crimson ball slung low on the horizon; the evening bland and warm. Cassey unbuckled her armour, tossing it on to the grass and stripped off her buff-coat, leaving only shirt, breeches and high boots. Polly cast an experienced eye over her trim figure. 'Well, now, if you don't make a pretty lad. Why don't you join forces with me...we'd clean up a fortune together. You with your looks and gentility and me with my knowledge...we'd fleece 'em very nicely, between us.'

Cassey's shocked, reproving glance made her laugh, so she shrugged and added: 'All right, lovey, I won't press you, but just remember what I've said. You know where to find me if you change your mind. What were you doing in the fighting?'

So Cassey told her all about it, boasting a little, feeling rather pleased with herself now that it was over, although her bruises were aching and her mouth was sore.

Emma had grown very still, then she suddenly struggled to her feet, her face ashen.

'I must go back. Surely 'tis over by now.'

Cassey walked along with her, a curious sinking sensation in the region of her stomach. They were met at the tent flap by Loveday and a weary, sweating surgeon.

'Is this the wife?' he asked, then sighed and turned to Emma. 'We did our best, my girl, but your husband died a few moments ago.'

Loveday was just in time to catch Emma as she keeled over. The surgeon ran a hand over his hair. 'Poor soul...how will she shift now?'

'I'll keep her with me.' Loveday was essentially practical. 'She can travel with us players; we can always use an extra pair of hands.'

'Is that her child? Another fatherless brat.' Cassey had never seen a man look so disillusioned.

'There's plenty of them around' put in Polly, jogging the infant against her shoulder. 'At least he has a legal name.'

Leaving Emma in Polly's care, Cassey went inside with Loveday. There they assisted the harassed surgeons who amputated, sutured and bandaged without pause. Relatives came in, anxiously seeking their men and, if they were fit to be moved, took them off to nearby billets. Those who died were taken outside and laid in neat rows covered with sheets, to be identified and later buried in the tiny churchyard. The Cavaliers had taken the town, but the cost had been high.

After the first shock, Cassey became numb, doing what was necessary without thinking about it, accepting the surgeon's orders, fetching water to hold to dry lips, swabbing wounds, dressing ugly rents in human flesh. It was gone midnight when she straightened her aching back, battered by fatigue, and crawled into the rear of the wagon, pulled a blanket over her, and was at once plunged into a deep, exhausted sleep. Although he was always there at the back of her mind, even Leon no longer seemed as important as rest. Nothing could hold her back and she sank into oblivion as if it were a soft black cloud.

Eight

'He is in the town,' Will asserted, coming back from a search through the stricken streets to greet Cassey with the news. 'Lodging at the Red Lion inn. He says I'm to take you to him.'

Cassey's heart gave a leap and she paused in ladling soup into basins for the players, looking at him quickly. 'Thank God! He's not been hurt?'

'Hurt? Lord Treviscoe?' Will snapped, his face darkening. 'Not he, ma'am; the devil looks after his own, so 'tis said!'

He sounded so bitter that a pang of alarm shot through Cassey. If his resentment and jealousy still rankled he might well intend him harm. She said nothing but handed her duties over to Polly who shrugged good-naturedly, rolled her eyes heavenwards to indicate her despair at her besotted friend, and continued to serve the food.

The town was beginning to recover; barricades had been taken down, citizens were repairing smashed windows and sweeping up debris. Will and Cassey jogged past innumerable narrow-fronted houses which darkened the cobblestones but, unlike London, the air here was clear. This was a country town, enlivened almost daily by the sight of cattle and sheep herded along to the market, women balancing baskets on their heads, farmers rumbling by with their carts laden with produce, and milkmaids walking sedately under the burden of the wooden yoke. Their peaceful existence had been unceremoniously shattered by suddenly finding the war at their own doorstep.

Cassey felt wretchedly uneasy for the part she had taken in this disruption for they were, after all, her fellow countrymen. The Cavaliers apparently shared no such compunction; the inn yard swarmed with their victorious soldiers. Loveday was greeted enthusiastically by them as she swept up to the door.

'Here we go again,' she announced jovially to Cassey, slipping an arm through hers. 'Whenever we storm a town, we always take over the best taverns, though, I must say, this one leaves much to be desired.'

She was enjoying herself, impressing the

few rustics who had dared venture in. One of the young actors trailed admiringly behind her. She treated him as a great lady might use a lapdog or a footman. As usual, he carried his guitar slung across his back.

'Why don't you leave it in the coach, Lucien?' Harry Marchmont was baiting him in an indolent way. 'No one is going to run off with the damned thing.'

He had brought them in his large, ornate vehicle. It was interesting to note the way in which Loveday was beginning to inveigle her way into his life and affections, snapping her fingers at the jealous glares of his other ladies.

'He's hoping they will ask him to play,' another voice suggested. Lucien blushed furiously, lower lip rolled out in a pout.

Cassey patted the space beside her on the settle near the bar and he slipped gratefully into it. She was glad to have friends around her, tired of being left alone while Leon racketed around the countryside or dealt with yet another administrative crisis. Some of Leon's best men from Kestle Mount had tramped into the inn; their excitement and triumph crackled in the air around them. They were like men reborn to be on the march again instead of being cooped up on garrison duty, spirits raised after a stiff fight and the joy of beating up rebel quarters.

Soon a gaming-table was flourishing in one corner of the taproom. Lucien was coaxed into strumming the tune of one of their favourite bawdy songs and the chorus was being roared beneath the smoke-darkened ceiling. They beat time on the knife-scarred boards of the trestles.

Some tried to sleep, heads down among the beer mugs and plates of cold beef and rye bread, but the veterans scorned to do this, claiming that they could rest by merely cutting off and staring into space for hours. They tried hard to imitate Leon's stamina and his apparent ability to go without sleep. He was dedicated to the army, fighting was in his very bones, and he often drove himself beyond the limit, denying fatigue.

Loveday, tired of waiting for service, hammered imperiously on the table. The landlord's shabby appearance, like that of his hostelry, was not very impressive.

'I hope the beds are cleaner here than in that last pigstye of an inn at Tonbury,' Loveday drawled, smoothing the skirts of the gown which Sir Harry had given her that morning, no doubt looted from the house of some leading citizen.

'I thought I saw a couple of rats in the stable.' Sir Harry winked at Cassey.

'Rats!' shrieked Loveday, making much of pretended alarm.

'Don't worry, sweetheart, they looked quite friendly.'

'To you, I expect they did! You probably have a lot in common!' Loveday whisked out the fan that she was carrying in her new game of masquerading as a lady of quality, and began to wave it violently, turning to give the host another slating.

Whenever the Royalists either entered or took a town by attack, their coming caused instant upheaval. Not only did the troops have to be accommodated, but also the officers' wives, and other females who were neither ladies or wives. Servants, grooms, pages and attendants, all had to be fed and found billets not too far from their masters. In times of peace, small towns would have welcomed such trade, but now there was no knowing when, if ever, they might expect to be paid. If they were the vanquished, their hopes of recompense were slender indeed.

Cassey looked up expectantly every time

there was a commotion at the door and men ducking their heads under the lintel, but she always experienced an acute pang of disappointment—Leon had not yet arrived. So she continued to converse brightly without taking in a word, a brittle smile on her face, while she wanted to scream aloud at the pain of the intensity of her desire to see Leon.

Consequently, when he did walk in, she could hardly believe her eyes, almost taking him to be some creature born of her longing and despair.

His eyes met hers above the crowd and he smiled and she was filled with that same irrational excitement which she had felt the very first time she saw him. Loveday gave her a nudge.

'My dear, is that him?' she murmured, looking him over boldly. 'What a magnificent man! You are quite right to be so enamoured, but Lord! Control yourself! You shine like a star. All may read what you feel by your face. Men enjoy the chase...don't make it so easy for him...'

Cassey did not care, she could not help that bedazzled expression, gazing at him with her heart in her eyes. He strolled over and took the vacant space at her side and she had to fight hard to restrain the impulse to fling her arms about him. Instead she stared at her lap, pleating the folds of her skirt, watery green silk over a deeper shade in the crease.

Richard was with him and he grinned at her and raised his glass in salute before his roving eye lighted on Loveday, but Lucien was dominating her attention, full of awkward, puppy-jumping admiration, like an infatuated schoolboy.

Richard, quickly seizing up the situation which afforded him a great deal of amusement, clapped Sir Harry on the back and dropped into a winged armchair at his side. 'Seems like we are out of luck tonight, old friend,' he said. 'I intend to get as drunk as a fiddler's bitch. Will you join me? A little celebration. My Lord Treviscoe, here, has seen fit to recommend me for promotion to his Illustrious Highness, Prince Maurice.'

'Dear child, you should see that Maurice, he's nearly as handsome as your bold hero,' Loveday remarked to Cassey from the side of her mouth.

Cassey was much more interested in listening to the talk of the men than the gossip of the flippant Loveday. She wanted to know what their plans were and if they included herself. Now she heard Leon telling Sir Harry that the Commanders had met in a house not far from where they had made the first breach, articles had been drawn up and quickly signed. It had been agreed that the Governor and his soldiers should march out next morning, with the honours of war, and the town would be garrisoned by Royalist troops.

'Is the King still confident?' Cassey asked; much of her future hinged on this answer; she was still too shy of Leon to ask him outright what his next movements might be.

'From the scanty news which reaches us, it would appear that he is, as usual, building up his hopes and listening to such dangerous advisors as Lord Digby and George Goring.' Leon's mouth twisted sardonically. 'Maurice is furious at the foolhardly plans put forward, instead of heeding the soldiers. Even now, they still waste time while there is danger on every side. Rupert has lost the North through his defeat at Marston Moor, and the West is falling rapidly...'

'Oh, I wouldn't say that, sir...' interrupted Sir Harry.

Leon ignored him; his intelligence service was better and more informed. 'And Lord Essex' army rushes towards us, trying to trap the Queen.'

'Fortunately, we have such leaders as Prince Maurice in the vicinity,' Sir Harry stated soothingly, before being distracted again by the disarming smile and candid brown eyes of the flirtatious Loveday.

Cassey, while joining in this serious discussion, could not help wishing that Richard would not keep looking at her in that way, silently reminding her of that night at Kestle Mount. That unfortunate secret hung between them every time they met, and she fancied an echo of it reached both men. Certainly there was a new alertness in Leon's dark eyes whenever Richard engaged her in conversation. Could it be that he was jealous?

Cassey sat quietly, elbows on the table, watching Leon raptly while the afternoon deepened into dusk, the golden light mellowing, making little crimson shadows beneath their wineglasses. All about them the revelry became wilder. She feasted her eyes on the profile turned stubbornly away from her; Leon needed to talk with his officers; she must wait till later for his

225

attention. And, for a while, she was happy to gloat on every familiar, attractive feature; the straight nose, sardonic brows, sensitive tormented, self-willed mouth. His hair had grown longer during the time she had known him, well below his shoulders, curling over at the ends into great rings, and he was wearing a leather doublet, with the neck of his shirt open, well-cut breeches and black riding boots.

It was only a few days since she had last seen him, but it seemed an eternity since she had lain in his arms. The strong fumes of wine were driving away the remnants of her self-control, his body drawing her like a magnet. She was envious of his comrades, angry because he insisted in ignoring her. With all the force of her being she willed him to look at her, her hand pressing against the long sweep of his thigh, feeling the soft texture of velvet, the supple softness of leather, the strength of the muscles beneath. Slowly, he turned his head and they exchanged a glance. His eyes were dark and unfathomable, and he opened his lips to speak, but:

'We are in desperate need of more men.' Sir Harry's remark sliced across the moment.

Leon turned back to him, but not before leaning over and brushing his lips across Cassey's cheek. She was wildly happy; now she could be generous and lose him to his fellows again for a little. He was not angry with her.

'If I could but have a month, I'd double them.' Leon sounded so confident in his own recruiting abilities.

'Talking of man-power, sir,' Richard leaned forward. 'We are having trouble with deserters. Young Farriday is missing again.'

The black brows of his Commander drew down in an alarming curve. 'I've given him fair warning. Get after him!'

Richard got up, motioning Sergeant Cole to go with him. He heaved to his feet grumbling, wiping his fingers down his showy coat, none too pleased at being disturbed, muttering: 'I didn't sign on to go chasing after homesick soldier-boys.'

Still another delay...another call on his sense of duty, when all that Cassey longed for was the privacy of a bedchamber with him, but, as time passed, it seemed that Richard was dealing with the emergency. Flares were burning in the courtyard when they decided to leave the confusion in the taproom. A fight had broken out between two musketeers over one of the women; their comrades were hurling themselves into the fray and Leon's party did not wish to become involved.

She had Sir Harry, too, to thank for their relatively early retirement. He was eager for Loveday who had been mercilessly teasing him all the evening, flirting outrageously with everyone else. Now she paused on the staircase leading up to the gallery, turning to smile down at him, her face full of witchery and provocation, one hand holding up a bunch of satin skirt.

' 'Tis such a fine night,' she announced, appearing to hesitate. 'I swear, I have a mind to go down to the woods and listen for the nightingale.'

Sir Harry's expression of exasperation and disappointment was almost comical, but Loveday only laughed and stretched out her hand, encouraging him to follow her. He was too good a catch to provoke too far.

In a clatter of hooves and clink of harness, Richard and Sergeant Cole rode under the arch with their prisoner. They halted and the boy sat, drooping on his mount, his hands tied behind him. This attracted the attention of passers by and soon a circle of interested spectators had gathered. Cassey, stepping out into the lantern light beside Leon, recognized him as one of the men who had taken her prisoner in what seemed a lifetime ago.

'Sergeant, I don't want to have to look up at him!' Leon's voice was clipped, his face grim.

Cole raised a booted foot from where he sat in the saddle and kicked the young man from his horse. He fell awkwardly, and crouched trembling, the blood welling from a gash where his head had struck the paving. Wide-eyed with apprehension he stared up at his Commander who towered above him.

'Trooper, you are going to be shot,' Leon said sternly.

Richard swung down from his horse and stepped forward. The boy's eyes swivelled to him, the sweat breaking out on the greenish hue of his face.

'You going to let them shoot me, Captain?'

Richard had been in charge of him; it reflected on his reputation if one of his men was a deserter. Farriday had been warned often enough already; like many another, despite his eagerness to enlist and his brave dreams of glory, the actuality of war terrified him and he wanted to get back to the fields of home.

'I'm obliged to, son.' Richard was poker-faced.

Like a desperate animal in a snare, Farriday raked their faces. He spotted Cassey and hope flared. 'Madam...you remember me, surely...I did you no harm when you were captured. Don't let them kill me...I am needed back on the farm...there is only my mother there...she cannot manage alone.'

Emma's face, pale, anguished, flashed across her inner vision...if he died it would be yet another woman left to grieve. Leon had troubles enough without adding a mother's curse. She shivered and tugged at Leon's sleeve, whispering urgently: 'He is but a lad. Have mercy, darling.'

He shook off her hand angrily. 'An example must be made.'

'Richard will keep close watch on him. Don't have his blood on your hands. Be merciful, Leon.'

'Christ, I am merciful!' he exploded and she flinched beneath the blast but stood her ground. 'Has not this town been treated honourably? You know well that by the rules of war a garrison which is taken after refusing the summons to surrender can expect every man, woman and child to be slaughtered. Did we do that here? I wish that you would keep out of matters of which you understand nothing!'

Sir Harry had been watching silently, looking from one to the other. 'Sir, we are desperately short of men,' he reminded. 'Can we afford to lose another unnecessarily?'

For a long moment Leon paused, then abruptly turned on his heel and mounted the steps, two at a time, shouting over his shoulder to Richard:

'Captain, he is your responsibility. Don't forget it!'

Richard nodded with the world-weary eye of a man who knows all that life can do and no longer fears it, his grin as cynical as when he had first met Leon and thrown in his lot with him. He pumped Sergeant Cole on the shoulder, snapping the tension. 'Come on there, you old ruffian. Get that young fellow to quarters and then let us find ourselves a couple of whores for the night!'

'Would you really have had him shot?'

Cassey asked Leon later.

'Of course,' he grunted as if he found her question superfluous.

She propped herself up on one elbow in the wide four-poster bed, wanting to gaze and gaze at that beautiful face, the awe which she sometimes felt for him melting in admiration and love. He was truly magnificently built with broad shoulders, a narrow waist, slim hips and those legs which seemed to go on for ever. His body was tanned, and she knew that he liked bathing naked and lying in the sun to dry.

He sensed her concern and smiled gently. 'In war one must often perform duties that are odious. Prince Rupert will hang enemy prisoners if his own men have been similarly treated, and he is noted for his scrupulous justice. I did warn you that there would be situations which would distress you.'

Alarmed that he might send her away, she rose to her knees, leaning over him, her long hair falling forward to shade them both. 'Believe me, I am not complaining, Leon...' Even now the name still seemed a shocking informality; she had to check herself at times from calling him "my

Lord". 'Yet it seems so wrong to be shooting one of the same race.'

His face grew sombre, that melancholy which always lurked there beneath the surface. 'That is the terrible thing about civil war, and it hurts the older generations even more. I believe that my father allowed himself to be killed on the field rather than continue in a conflict in which he was forced to fire on old friends.'

'I have heard it said that the King was very troubled.' Cassey wondered if she might soon see him, this ruler who inspired such loyalty in his followers.

'Indeed he still is, my dear.' Leon reached for the brandy glass on the bedside table. 'Forced to make war on those whom he firmly believes God has placed under his protection.'

'Do you believe that he is right?'

He shrugged, reaching for one of her hands, turning it and kissing the palm. 'Why are you worrying about such matters? He is my Sovereign...I follow him without question...besides,' he added with a wry twist to his lips, 'I'm a mercenary and we live quite well by it.'

Cassey felt again that annoyance which stung her when he, or one of his comrades persisted in treating her as if she were just a pretty toy and not too bright at that! Their attitude was insufferable! She was quite prepared to be indignant, and, maybe, even quarrel with him a little, but his arms were going round her again.

She could never have enough of his kisses, hungering for them when he was away. That finely moulded mouth, which rarely smiled, now closed on hers firmly at first, then relaxing, seeking, as if he would absorb her into himself. She sometimes thought of this, while thought was at all possible, and wondered at the complexity of love, wanting to be lost entirely, engulfed, made one with Leon. She wanted to tell him that she was with child, but a strange shyness pinned her tongue.

Next day, Cassey and Loveday were amusing themselves, walking in the garden at the back of the inn. It was still early but already hot; the leaves on the bushes, the grass underfoot and the moist, steaming earth began to smell sweetly. They stopped by a rose bush. Loveday drew out the scissors from her embroidery basket and snipped off two fat, pink buds, giving one to Cassey and tucking the other down into her bodice.

She was dressed in all the splendour of a countess; Sir Harry was more than generous to her and had arrived early with a stolen box of finery through which she had rummaged with little shrieks of joy. He had sat astride a chair with his arms folded across the back and watched her, grinning, as she stripped off her nightgown and danced around the bedchamber snatching up this lace petticoat or that gossamer-thin shift, holding it against her as she came to rest in front of the pier-glass.

Now she seated herself demurely on a stone bench and carefully spread out her blue taffeta skirt so that it would not crease, then opened her basket and took out a pillow case which she was embroidering. Cassey sprawled on the grass at her feet, glad that her own gown was not so fine that she had to bother about it, and amusing herself by stringing a daisy chain. A little quake of anticipation began to run through her because Leon would be coming home soon, to dine with her and while away the afternoon in an almost domesticated peace.

'Has Harry told you where we are going from here?'

Loveday tugged at a knot in the yellow

silk. 'He has hinted, my dear...but you know how self-important men become if they imagine that they are engaged on some serious enterprise. I think we but delay awaiting orders.'

'I would that we might remain here for ever!' Cassey burst out passionately. 'No more wandering and separation.'

'You love that man more than is good for you,' Loveday said sagely, poking her needle in and out of a moon-daisy very nearly as realistic as those bordering the path. 'You should be like me...enjoy 'em all, but give your heart to no one. It is not worth it and you'll only end up being hurt.'

Loveday had given this advice before, and Cassey respected her experience. At the moment she was intent on squeezing a settlement from Sir Harry, pressing him to place her in the position of his acknowledged mistress. Not that she had any intention of being faithful to him. On the contrary; her eye was at the moment irresistibly drawn towards the tall figure coming towards them with long, athletic strides.

'My dear,' she could not conceal her interest, patting her curls into place. 'Who is that dashing person, I wonder?'

Cassey looked across idly, screwing up her eyes a little against the glare. She froze in recognition. A phrase of Homer's describing Helen of Troy rang in her head... 'She moves a goddess, and she looks a queen'. How else to think of Morag for all her vagabond blood and man's clothing? There was no time to give answer for in a few lengthy paces her rival was upon them. A bad-tempered expression spoiled the classical beauty of her face.

'So the soldiers spoke the truth when they told me that you had returned,' she ground out. 'Tired of your Roundhead husband, were you?'

In back of her, Cassey could feel Loveday bristling like a warring cat when she guessed who it was addressing them; Cassey had told her about Morag.

Now she stiffened and replied with as much cold dignity as she could muster: 'I have come to help Leon in any way I can.'

'How very noble!' Morag jeered, eyes hard as agates, flecked with gold. Then her face changed, contorted with hatred. 'I know your real intent, madam. You try to oust me from my place with him.'

Morag was standing before her with her fingers clenched in white-knuckled fists and Cassey stood up to cheat her of the satisfaction of being able to look down on her; as it was she topped her by four inches, a most intimidating female, but Cassey stood her ground, trembling with rage, not fear.

'And who has been sharing his bed since you last saw him, think you?' She spat out with blistering scorn. 'D'you believe for a moment that he can resist me?'

'Slut!' Morag thrust her face close to Cassey's. 'What man will refuse if it's handed to him on a plate! But don't deceive yourself. It means nothing to him and neither do you. I know him. I've been with him for years. We've often laughed together at women like you who imagine that because he swives 'em, he loves 'em! You won't win. I shall yet be mistress of Kestle Mount.'

'You!' Cassey's tone could not have been more insulting, and she stood her ground, feeling strength of certainty flowing into her, remembering Leon as he had been to her last night. Surely, he could not have been so insincere? If he was, then there was no goodness left anywhere in the world. Her lip curled as if there was a bad smell under her nose as she considered Morag coldly. 'You haven't the breeding to be Leon's wife. Leave that position to your superior, gypsy!'

Loveday, who had been rendered momentarily speechless by their violent outburst, now rose to take Cassey's arm and say: 'Come, sweetheart, waste no more time bandying words with this trash,' and as Morag swung round on her with a stream of highly coloured invective, she added: 'Out of the way, mistress, or you'll find that I haven't been a leaguer-bitch for nothing. There is no female alive who can best me in a fight. Get you back to your horse, tho' the poor nag deserves better company.'

Morag shot her a look which should have blasted her where she stood. 'God damn you!' she shouted, swinging round on the high scarlet heel of her riding boot, and to Cassey: 'I'll see you dead before he ever weds you!' She stormed off in the direction of the stable.

'Have you ever promised Morag marriage?' Cassey wanted to know when Leon sought her out later.

A scowl darkened his brow. 'Has she been making trouble again? Damned jade! I've ordered her to leave you alone.'

'Then you have been seeing her...' she quavered accusingly, though telling herself sternly that she must keep this rush of jealousy under control. A show of possessiveness was the sure way to lose him.

'She has been riding with my soldiers. She's a useful member of any troop.' There was a twitch of a smile on his lips.

He was sitting on the low stone balustrade which encircled the lawn, one foot braced on the rim of a lily pond, watching her in a way which made her blood rush. With a sob she lost control, throwing herself against him, pounding on his chest in frustration. 'Leon!... Oh, Leon...you won't marry her, will you? Say that you don't love her!'

The familiar feel of his hard muscles, the scent of his skin, the way in which the single gold earring flashed against the dark fall of his hair, made it all harder to bear, making her doubly conscious of all she had to lose. For an instant he remained still, his arms slack at his sides; then he spat out an oath and pulled her close to him roughly, holding her between his thighs.

'My God, Cassey!' He gave her an impatient shake. 'Women! All you think of is love! I have a war to fight! I've a mind to send you both apacking to Kestle Mount!'

Cassey could have bitten out her tongue for making him angry, blaming Morag as the cause of the strife between them, but she could not stop herself, her voice thinly persistent as she asked, unhappily: 'Why do you lie with her still if she means nothing to you?'

He was looking across to where a group of officers were waiting for him, wanting to be off if she insisted in prolonging this troublesome scene. 'Oh, grow up, darling. You must know that there are many reasons why one shares a bed...expediency, apathy, weariness, loneliness...or plain, straightforward lust. I have told you before, Morag is someone I have known for a long time. She thinks that she is in love with me, and I don't like hurting her.'

'What about hurting me?' she said on a rising pitch of indignation. 'Or is that of no matter?'

There was a wary, withdrawn look in his eyes. He was smiling down at her still but with his eyes only. Cassey's heart sank. Because he was angry with her the beautiful summer day seemed to darken. She knew that it was foolish to argue yet, as always when the first intense joy of being with him again began to wear off, all the old resentments and frustrations reared up. The sudden appearance of Morag had thoroughly disturbed her, shaking her frail hold on certainty.

'She has been fighting elsewhere over the past weeks. She has not been with me.' There was a puzzled look in his eyes as if he could not understand his own reason for bothering to give her an explanation. 'We are but friends now, not lovers. She has always known that marriage is out of the question.'

The sudden rush of relief was almost bearable; she wanted to laugh and cry at once, but Leon was straining to leave and she knew, with a pang of guilt at delaying him even this far, that there were a myriad things requiring his immediate attention.

She could feel him weakening and had to push home her advantage. 'Then there is now only myself?' she tried to say through the strangling in her throat.

There was exasperation and tenderness

in the glance he turned on her. 'Don't try to tie me down with promises,' he warned. 'Stop worrying. Wait and see.'

More than that she could not wheedle from him and was sensible enough not to bring up the subject again. If she wanted to complain about it, she did so to Loveday who was always willing to lend a sympathetic ear. Morag did not confront her again whilst they remained in the town, but Cassey was certain that Leon must have rebuked her for whenever they happened to meet, in corridor, tap room or garden, Morag strode coldly by her. No words were exchanged but, had they been cats, they would have passed on with tails doubled in size.

Two strong-willed women in love with the same dominating man. Cassey felt sure that England was not big enough to hold them both.

Nine

'No one will suspect the players,' Leon lay back in the great carved chair at the head of the table, touching the tips of his fingers together, waiting comments. He had summoned his friends for a Council of War.

They had left some of the troops to garrison the town, while the rest had despatched towards Oxford hoping to link up with the King and add to his reinforcements. Leon's men had removed to the manor house of Sir Harry; that likeable rogue had flung open his doors and put all his facilities at their disposal, his only condition that he should be allowed to assist in the Queen's rescue. Leon readily agreed. A handful of men, picked for their courage and resolution, were essential for success.

'Is it your suggestion that we travel with them, with enough money to oil the way?' Sir Harry asked, his shrewd eyes encompassing Cassey seated next to

Leon, resting her cheek against his sleeve while he took no more heed than if she had been a dog fawning on him. Morag slouched low in her chair, sulking, for Leon had taken even less notice of her than he had of Cassey. He was busy; there was no time for dalliance.

Sir Harry gave his sensual smile. 'And the women, sir? Do they have a part in this charade?'

'It will be necessary to have a lady assist the Queen don her disguise and slip out of the town. I have selected Cassey for this task.'

'Cassey!' Morag shot up in her seat, a flashing eyed termagant. 'Why not me? D'you think I lack the courage?'

'You have the courage but not the finesse.' Leon did not bother to look up. 'The Queen is a very haughty lady. Cassey will understand how to respect her.'

'Damn you!' Morag sent her chair crashing back and knocked over a wine goblet; puddles of claret spread across papers and maps while Leon froze into icy hauteur, but she refused to be intimidated, raging at him, 'That mincing bitch! It was different before she came. Then you cared for me. Now you say I'm unfit to serve the Queen!'

Leon's men exchanged grins, but there was an undercurrent of impatience; they were here to get down to serious planning, not to listen to squabbles between their Commander's wenches.

'Sit down at once, Morag!' Leon ordered, his voice as cutting as a lash. Morag's face reddened with anger; she opened her mouth to make a retort, then caught his eye and thought better of it. Cassey sat through the argument with smug satisfaction, giving Morag a little fleeting smile which flicked at the girl's already raw temper. Her naked hatred of Cassey was almost tangible; anyone must be the butt of it and now she directed her fury on Will, finding an outlet for her ill-natured jibes, while he took on the thankless task of humouring her. Cassey had long hoped for some miracle which would make Morag return his love, thus easing his suffering and putting an end to her dangerous passion for Leon.

The meeting concluded swiftly, but not before their plans had been laid with the military precision and thoroughness which was always Leon's method. There was no time to be lost if Queen Henrietta was to slip through the net being spread wide for her by Lord Essex.

'But I don't want us to be separated,' protested Cassey, frantically following Leon about their bedchamber, getting in his way while he was preparing to leave. He was attired in a plain dark suit with an edging of white linen at cuffs and throat. A leather baldrick crossed his chest to his left hip, carrying his serviceable swept-hilt rapier. His riding cloak swirled from his shoulders as he moved about, methodically assembling essentials for the journey. He intended to ride ahead and scout the country, assuring that the way was clear for the Queen, every rendezvous noted, allies alerted.

'I'm sorry, darling,' he grunted, pre-occupied, standing before the mirror, passing a comb through his long dark locks, one eye on her reflection as she stood at his shoulder, watching him anxiously. 'We cannot be together. Your part is to be with the Queen. Richard knows where we plan to meet.'

'And when it is all over and the Queen safe?'

He frowned slightly, though slowly

turning and taking her hands in both of his. 'Let tomorrow take care of itself,' he began, but Cassey brushed aside this well-worn phrase which merely indicated that he did not want a serious discussion.

'What of us, Leon?' she insisted. God only knew when she might see him again. The uncertainty was driving her mad.

A shutter came down over his eyes, though he still smiled. She knew this withdrawal well enough, a barrier which constantly baffled her. 'What is it that you want, Cassey? I have nothing to offer you. When the war is over I shall be penniless, whichever way it goes. The Continent and the life of a soldier of fortune are all that is open to me.'

'I know this and am prepared to accept it. Hardship will mean nothing to me if I can be at your side...don't you understand? If you love me, nothing else matters.'

He seemed moved by the pleading in her voice, and gently stroked her hair. 'You have my love,' he averred.

Cassey wished with all her heart that she could believe the softness in his eyes, those easy words, but had grown increasingly wary of having her hopes dashed. She moved away from his caressing hand; this time she must keep a grip on her emotions and the desire to melt into his arms and think no more.

'Your love?' she queried, trying, unsuccessfully, to keep her tone light and bantering. 'D'you not always say that you love us all?'

Now he gave an impatient shrug, contemptuous of the things which bother women. Cassey knew that she should have learned from bitter experience not to probe, keeping a tight rein on her feminine desire to peel away layers in an urgent quest for sincerity. She had recognized, long ago, that there could be no placid areas of tranquillity as there had been with Edward or even, very briefly, with Richard. She had forced herself to appear calm, to subjugate her own personality and will to suit Leon, telling herself that she was glad to pay the price to be at his side and in his bed.

It was only of late that she had begun seriously to question her motives; now her vehement assertions, during the long silent discussions which went on in her own mind, had a hollow ring.

He picked up his hat, half turning towards the door, his mind streaking away to the difficulties ahead. 'I must go. You know your part. Richard will tell you what to do.' He swooped her up against his chest and kissed her.

With this she had to be content, but was in an angry mood when she stepped out into the warm morning sunshine. In the stable-yard there was confusion as the players assembled their wagons and prepared to leave. Horses were being backed between the shafts, Ralph Killigarth stamping about, giving orders. There were six men already mounted who were to act as escort, led by Sir Harry, clad in the clothing of peasants, their weapons concealed in their packs.

Richard was once again adopting the guise of a pedlar, one of his favourite roles. He liked the grotesque, and over-acted outrageously, sometimes crouching with one shoulder higher than the other, or developing a spectacular limp, a patch over one eye, his face screwed up in a fearsome grimace. His nimble tongue was conversant with a variety of accents, and it was small wonder that he managed to hoodwink the Roundheads, exasperating them when they realized that, once again, he had slipped through their fingers. There was a price on his head and he was proud of it, one of the Cavaliers' best agents.

His eyes lit up when he saw Cassey and he came across, at once sensitive to her moping, seeing the droop of her shoulders as she bent to stroke the stable-cat, a large striped tabby who was arching her back with thrumming purr.

'*Mon dieu!* You make a pretty farm-wench, sweeting,' he exclaimed, turning her about with one hand so that he might admire her...neat white blouse, tightly-laced black bodice, woollen skirt which fell to her ankles, looped back over a red and white striped petticoat, feet encased in sturdy high-laced boots with stout wooden soles.

Her heart warmed to him; he was never too busy to soothe her with attention; his flattery lifting her flagging spirits. He put an arm round her and gossiped about Morag.

'She's stormed off in a tearing rage because Leon refuses to let her accompany him. At any rate, dearest, you'll have no more trouble from her for a while.'

This Cassey doubted, vividly recalling the gypsy's murderous expression at the War Council, very aware that she sought a suitable opportunity to slip a knife between her ribs.

Loveday and Polly were loading their bundles into the back of one of the wagons, together with a wan, sick-looking Emma who was trying to cope with her baby as well. Cassey was very worried about her. Much under the influence of Polly, she was drinking too much and often seen hanging around with the foot soldiers. No longer the neat, reserved countrywife, now her appearance was as sluttish as that amiable prostitute's. There was a new hardness in her face, despair in her eyes, and Cassey felt helpless, unable to aid her.

It had occurred to her to try and send her to Mawnan Manor where she was sure Beth still resided, cared for by the kindness of Edward. But this was almost impossible to arrange...there were too many other issues on her mind. First and foremost her own fears about Leon. How could she concentrate on the well-being and future of others, no matter how much they tugged at her heart-strings, when so sadly unsure of her own position?

It was a pleasant enough ride through rich dark oak woods, all softness and peace, a far cry from the conflict.

Cassey and Loveday sat on the tail-board, legs dangling, revelling in the sunshine which spattered through the dense green branches. Between the deer-parks of the gentry and the neighbouring country towns stretched great tracks of wasteland...moors, heaths, fens and marshes. The best areas were used by adjacent villages as common pasture. Cassey dozed and dreamed, lulled by the heat and the jolting, thinking about this fair country ravaged by war...England, with its orchards and cherry gardens, its gravel walks by the riversides in provincial towns, its sleeping village greens, ancient churches and gabled manor-houses...now all disrupted.

She woke with a start, aware of her clammy skin and dry mouth, rising into the headachy heat of afternoon, knowing that there was something wrong. They were passing through a village and had stopped to ask the way. A group of yokels watched them suspiciously and, in minutes, a hostile crowd gathered as word spread that they were strangers. Quickly their mood became more ugly, like many another small community, the war had begun to affect them adversely. Everywhere the countryfolk had suffered;

their young men had been taken, they had starved and died, their cattle had been stolen, their homes burned, their women ravished, their hard-ploughed fields laid waste.

The soldiers of both sides had bled them white, they wanted no more of strangers in their midst. The voices rose angrily as Richard tried to speak with them. They flourished their clubs and hurled stones at riders and wagons. Sir Harry had difficulty in preventing his men from retaliating.

'There's naught we can do but ride through 'em, lads,' shouted Richard, setting spur to his horse. Whips cracked, wheels turned, beasts strained against the cart straps as they bore down on the mob which broke to let them pass, a final barrage of stones rattling in their wake.

Cassey was thoroughly unnerved by such relentless hostility; there was little doubt that they would have been torn in pieces if the revengeful yeomen had managed to get their hands on them. She did not begin to recover until there were miles between them and the hamlet. Even so, Sir Harry and Richard would not risk another, similar encounter and took instead unfrequented paths which, though slower, were judged to be much safer.

By next morning, they had nearly reached Exeter and, just ahead on the hedgeless road which encircled the old town, sleek white oxen approached dragging carts on their way towards fields heavy with harvest and cheerful with bright-coloured wild flowers.

Exeter was yet another ancient town originally protected by a wall which had, over the years of smug, secure peace, been allowed to fall into disrepair. During the last hectic wartorn months hurried attempts had been made to patch it up. As the Queen's would-be rescue party rumbled beneath the imposing arch of its main gate, they found it bustling, active, rife with alarmist rumours of the advance of Essex. This would be a ripe plum for the Roundheads to snatch, for it was famous for its manufacture of baize and other light cloth, with a flourishing lace-making industry.

They had been informed that the Queen was staying at Bedford House, home of the Russell family. First of all they made their way to a tavern where the landlord was one of their trusted men. Although Exeter was loyal, secrecy was essential. They learned that Leon had already made a flying visit and that the Queen was expecting them.

With fluttering stomach and a dry throat, Cassey walked into the great, imposing Russell mansion, still hardly believing that she was about to meet this famous Frenchwoman who, so rumour had it, King Charles loved to distraction. One of her personal attendants came to greet them as they waited in the steward's room. Cassey registered a delicate woman with a profusion of flaxen ringlets and eyes which appeared very large in a small, heart-shaped face. She exuded a confident air of aristocracy, beautifully, expensively gowned, in an elegant, restrained manner as befitted a Queen's lady-in-waiting.

Cassey felt her cheeks burn under her scrutiny, immediately conscious of her own low neck-line and her shabby, unclean clothing. Richard, however, swept her a bow, undismayed by his ragged garb, as she rustled forward, saying:

'Her Majesty expects you. I am Lady Dalkeith, and I must warn you that she has been, nay, is still, very ill indeed. We have despaired of her life both before the birth of the Princess and since...and that

257

scoundrel, Lord Essex...' She faltered and Richard put in:

'He will not give her a pass to go to Bath?'

Lady Dalkeith wrung her long slender hands together, very worried. 'He has refused, saying that her safety was no concern of his, and giving us no indication as to whether he intends to bombard Exeter or no.'

'And the King?'

'She still writes him many letters, or rather she dictates them to Lord Jermyn; she is too weak herself to hold a pen for long, but what can he do, poor man? He is greatly distressed by her condition, and will reach Exeter as soon as he is able, but meanwhile it is not safe for her to linger.'

'Take us to her,' urged Richard and, within minutes, they were following her up a back staircase and into an anteroom. There she bade them wait and disappeared through a doorway, returning shortly to conduct them into the Queen's bed-chamber. The room was over-heated and filled with a stuffy, medicinal odour. Undoubtedly the best that Bedford House could offer, it was large and splendidly furnished, oak panelled and tapestry hung with deep, recessed windows giving a fine, sweeping view of the garden.

Cassey was so acutely nervous that she was hardly aware that she was being led across a carpeted floor. The tiny, shrunken figure seemed lost in the massive bed and Cassey was on her knees, bending to kiss the slender white hand extended to her. She looked up into a pale oval face, with deep hollows under the eyes, which were large and black and of a shining, mournful beauty. Wisps of dark hair which still curled lankly, softened her forehead from under the lace nightcap. Her thin fingers quietened the miniature spaniel on her lap, who barked in shrill defiance at the strangers.

'Hush, Mitte,' said the Queen, her voice sweet and lilting, heavily accented. 'These are friends, come to help us. Jermyn...' she called to the large, florid young man with the air of ineffable condescension who hovered close by. 'Come, let me present you. These are my rescuers.'

Polite, murmured introductions followed which appeared so ludicrous to Cassey, under the desperate circumstances, but she had been warned that at the Court of

King Charles, dignity and decorum was the order of the day. Even though she would soon be a fugitive, the Queen still expected this. The incongruity of the situation was deepened by the presence of her dwarf, introduced as Jeffrey Hudson; he was under three feet tall, perfectly proportioned with fair hair and an amiable expression. He bowed solemnly, then picked up Mitte who was still barking with indignation. It was odd to hear a man's voice issuing from this being of child-like stature.

'You must rise, madame,' Lady Dalkeith came forward with a hiss of taffeta skirts. 'They have brought clothing in which to disguise you.'

The men were shooed out, but Cassey was invited to remain. It took herself, Lady Dalkeith and another waiting woman named Mary Clare, to get the Queen to her feet and into the garb of a peasant. All the while she was voluble in a tongue which she spoke most imperfectly and displayed abundant un-English gestures. The operation obviously exhausted her and Cassey was appalled to see her in such a sorry state. Was this really the vivacious elegant Sovereign of whom she had heard so much? The proud daughter of that great warrior Henri de Navarre? This sick, bent woman, partially paralysed down one side, not yet recovered from her lying-in, suffering acute pain from a breast abscess and weeping tears of weakness and distress.

The sight of her reflection in the mirror brought a fresh storm of tears. *'Mon Dieu! How awful I look. What would they think of me now, my brave Cavaliers?'* She turned to Cassey, eyes feverish and bright, taking her hand, pathetically eager to impress her. 'I used to ride on horseback at their head. I was their She-Majesty and Generalissima. They called me "Mary", so much easier for their English tongues, and "God and Queen Mary" was their rallying cry.'

Well might she gaze at herself in bewilderment and despair, this woman whose winning manner and brittle beauty had thrown a fatal fascination over all who succumbed to it. Effervescent and, in the opinion of the professional soldiers, with an incorrigible desire to meddle in affairs which she did not understand, she had imparted to her withdrawing-rooms and salons, the deep, agitating importance of the Council Chamber. There every political or social intrigue had been gossiped about, places canvassed and schemed for. Behind the suave, well-bred masks, a great deal of mischief had been concocted which had eventually helped to rock her husband's throne.

Her ladies, beautiful and persuasive, had belonged to the same circle, but it was her charms, talents and rank which had secured her the adoration of the gay soldier-poets scribbling their verses, dashing off to fight, returning pale and romantic and, perhaps, slightly wounded, to rattle off a few more sonnets praising her.

She had been the bright star of that courtly world, but now the Royalist power was waning. There were to be no more sunny days of masques, balls and fetes in which her gay soul delighted. She was reduced to the status of a refugee, parted from her home, her children and the husband she adored, and now forced to abandon this last, precious baby.

This thought was more agony than her physical discomforts. '*Mon enfant, ma petite* Henrietta...I must leave her threatened by those tigers.'

'You know that I will protect her with

my life.' Lady Dalkeith's eyes were filled with sympathetic tears. 'Mayhap, the King will come soon.'

'Not soon enough to save me, *ma chérie*.' The Queen shook her head dolefully. Mary endeavoured to tuck an escaping curl under the unbecoming white cap; a tattered cloak placed round the Queen's bowed shoulders completed the outfit. Her doctor, Sir John Wintour, was at the door, anxious to observe the effect of the sudden rising from bed of his famous, and sometimes trying, patient. He felt the responsibility keenly and was mopping over his face with a kerchief, her confessor at his heels, both of them in disguise as they were to accompany her. Mary Clare was going along too.

At last the moment of departure could no longer be delayed and Lady Dalkeith brought in the little Princess so that her mother might give her one last kiss. Henrietta cried and hugged her then, through her tears, proudly showed her to Cassey and Richard. It was indeed a child of exceptional beauty, tiny, flower-like and delicate, and Cassey could feel her own throat constricting with compassion for the Queen. At last, with the greatest reluctance,

Henrietta placed her in the arms of Lady Dalkeith, and the fugitive party slipped out the back way.

Horses awaited them, and they made their discreet way down side streets through the gates and out into the hazardous open country. About three miles beyond Exeter, Richard, who had ridden ahead, came pounding back with the warning that there was a Roundhead picket not far away. A barn lay close to the bridle-path and Richard hustled them quickly within. The women, Doctor Wintour and the priest, who had abandoned his soutane for a farmer's smock, mounted the rickety ladder to the loft, pulling straw over them until they were well concealed.

The Queen's woman did what she could to make her mistress comfortable, but it was a poor enough lodging for a Royal lady. Doctor Wintour clucked and fussed and bemoaned their fate when out of his Sovereign's hearing, his long, lugubrious countenance pulled into an almost comic expression of concern.

The evening passed in apprehension; they were afraid to talk above a whisper. Henrietta Maria fell into a troubled sleep, but Cassey was too strung up to rest, wandering out to find Richard who kept watch with a couple of his men, under the stars. She could see the outline of his head against the blackness of the trees.

'Hush, sweetheart,' he warned, pulling her into the shadow of a broken wall where he had taken up his post. Moonlight winked on a pair of primed pistols on a tree stump at his feet. 'Will has hidden the horses. I do not think the enemy are near at present, with any luck they may not come this way at all, but it is too dangerous to risk falling into them.' His arm tightened round her waist and he laughed softly. 'There is some relief in bad fortune, then, if it brings you to seek me under the romantic light of the moon.'

Cassey relaxed against him. It was comforting to have his strength during this time of fear. She knew that he was more than half in love with her and this fact sometimes made her sad, for she could give no more than she gave Edward; Leon had her heart. Yet she recognized that both of them were probably more worthy, unselfish contenders for true affection than he.

Richard's hand caressed her hair, and his mouth found hers under a pale searching finger of moonlight, and she wished, as often before, that she had never set eyes on Leon, yet she knew that an hour of his love-making was worth a life-time with any other man. If they had not met, she would always have been waiting for something, mysterious and tantalizing, expecting to find it round every bend.

'Why won't you let me love you again?' Richard was insisting, one experienced hand exploring her breasts. Cassey liked it, and was immediately ashamed of herself. Where was her loyalty if she began to stray like an arrant bitch when Leon was busy elsewhere? Her feelings confused her. Richard was very good, very facile at kissing.

In a desperate attempt to bring them both back into line, she said: 'But you are Leon's friend! Is there no goodness and honour left anywhere in this Goddamn world?'

She could feel Richard laughing and guessed at the expression of amusement on his face. 'Sweetheart, d'you really believe that Leon would care if I borrowed his whore for the night?'

This made her angry and she struggled free, giving him a resounding slap across the face.

'Marry, come up, Richard Chiverton!' she exclaimed, pulling the front of her bodice together. 'Leon would call you out if he could hear you!'

But Richard only threw back his head and laughed, and she could still hear him chuckling into the darkness as she flounced back to the barn with burning cheeks and a hot, uncomfortable feeling within in. She was not very proud of herself.

It was strange to be cooped up with the Queen of England, who proved to be no more than a sick, saddened woman, hounded by her enemies, her only comfort in the presence of her priest with whom she spent much time in prayer.

They had brought some food with them and a couple of wineskins, but this was soon used up and Cassey began to experience the pangs of hunger as well as the thrill of danger. Both of these sensations were new to the Queen and her party who chaffed at the close confinement.

'Surely, 'tis safe for us to move on.' Doctor Wintour insisted every time Richard showed his face in the loft. 'Her Majesty grows ever weaker. I cannot vouch for her life if this continues longer.'

'Sir John, I am sure that Captain

Chiverton knows his business.' Henrietta would rebuke him gently, the most patient among them although suffering the most discomfort.

It was while discussion of this sort was taking place during the morning that Richard's trained ear caught a sound in the distance. A troop of men were advancing, close to the barn, sunlight winking on steel breastplates and those odd helmets with the long, plated piece covering the neck, much in favour with the Roundheads. The noises grew nearer, marching feet, the drum of horses' hooves, the clink of harness and arms, voices raised in talk, and occasional laughter.

'Roundhead soldiers, no less,' muttered Richard, squinting through a crack in the daub and wattle wall.

The loft occupants froze in momentary terror, then erupted into action, hiding their belongings and themselves under the straw. The enemy party obviously intended to halt by the barn. They paused in its shade to drink from their canteens and rest their horses. A couple of foot soldiers, with an eye to the cooking pot, chased a roaming hen into the barn where its astonished squawk was brutally cut short.

'Here, Ben,' one shouted to his companion, tossing over the bloodied bundle of feathers. 'We'll not go hungry tonight.'

'Gawd, but I'm sick of army fare,' the other man grumbled.

'We'll do better than this when we take Exeter.' His friend was crashing about in the straw, searching to see if the farmer had any vegetables in store. 'And if we are lucky enough to take the Queen, my lad, you know what the reward will be.'

'Aye, fifty thousand crowns for the first man to carry her head to London!'

Cassey, listening to them, was in a cold sweat of fear, letting the breath slide slowly through her nostrils lest even this would startle them so that they started to mount the ladder. Behind closed eyelids she pictured the scene vividly; the straw whisked back as they poked about with their swords; their startled surprise changing to triumph; one of them daring to lay hold of the Queen; their shouts which would bring the rest running...the terror and violence which would follow.

But nothing happened. Pleased with their loot, the men stamped out to join their comrades. Soon all were mounted again, or in their lines, a sergeant shouted an order and the cavalcade moved off through the trees taking the road to Exeter.

Richard gave a long, silent whistle. 'Phew! That was close. Now will you believe me right in keeping Her Majesty well hidden?'

It was not until dusk on the third night that Richard deemed it safe to press on. Will fetched the horses from the gully where he had concealed them and, somehow, they got the Queen up behind Doctor Wintour. They turned aside, following a rough track with Will leading them through terrain he knew well.

On and on, seeming to pass through a wall of damp darkness with the horses stumbling on the uneven ground, mud sucking at their fetlocks, and the trees solid on either side like ranks of sinister foemen. Cassey, riding pillion with her arms round Richard's waist, aching with weariness, nodded off, her head falling against his broad back. Dear, dependable Richard...she dozed and dreamed, waking fully just as a blackbird was stirring and a pale, coppery sheen smearing the eastern horizon. There was the gentle, sweet sigh of leaves borne on the breeze.

Cassey glanced across at her companions.

In the grey light their faces were haggard, dark lines carved beneath their eyes. The Queen looked like a dead thing, clinging to Doctor Wintour; crippled by rheumatism as she was, the journey must have been a nightmare, but now Will was leading them off the path and deeper into the woods. They passed into a clearing, waist-deep in weeds, with a small wooden hut in the middle. In the dawn light, a single rush still burned in the tiny window.

Ten

It was a squalid enough place, with the
door hanging off its hinges, and nothing
inside but a rough bench made of logs, a
pile of ashes under the smoke hole in the
roof, some straw and bird droppings on the
floor. A strong odour of mouldy feathers
assailed the nostrils. But the poverty of the
surroundings was eclipsed by the warmth
of welcome from the group awaiting them.

Supported by Doctor Wintour and
her priest, Henrietta Maria crossed the
threshold to be greeted by her large,
stately chamberlain, Jermyn, the squat
figure of Hudson and, yapping excitedly,
her favourite spaniel, Mitte. It was a strange
encounter in the early light made eerie
by a ground mist. The sun was growing
stronger, fingers of gold penetrating the
dark recesses of the hut. The Queen's
faithful retainers were grouped around her
like figures from some fantastic fairytale,
yet, for Cassey, the most marvellous thing
was the presence of Leon.

'My men wait to escort you the rest of the way, Your Majesty.' He swept off his beaver and made her a low bow. 'There is no time to be lost.'

'Madame can travel no further on horseback,' put in her medical adviser firmly.

'I had thought of that.' Leon, ever practical, seemed always to find himself in charge. 'We have had a wagon prepared. I must urge you to make haste.'

But they had to let her rest for a while, huddled on the bench, shivering with fever in spite of the warm cloak, holding her little dog close, finding comfort and solace in the warm furry body. Then they dared delay no longer, the Queen, Mary Clare, Mitte and Jeffrey Hudson travelling in the wagon, the rest on horseback.

At noon the party split up. Leon wanted to do his own scouting, so he left the Queen in the charge of Richard and Sir Harry with a group of experienced soldiers, while he made off through the woods, taking Cassey and Will with him. She was overjoyed at being allowed to go along, though knowing perfectly well that this was but a strategic move; a woman among riders was much less likely to cause suspicion.

They rode for miles, guided by Will, and the shadows were lengthening as they clopped over short, springy turf between avenues of oak trees, coming out on a winding road leading towards an inn on the edge of a village. The ride had made them hungry and they dismounted, leaving their beasts tethered to the rail. This tavern was one of several along the route, meeting places where messages could be left and agents contacted. In this instance the host was not in their confidence, he and his wife were ignorant of the fact that Cavaliers met there. The vicinity was militantly Puritan and they followed the general trend.

There was nothing to arouse his suspicions; they appeared a very sober party, and the landlord served them supper just as if they were the husband, wife and serving-man which they acted so well. Cassey began to enjoy the adventure, delighted because Leon had not trusted Morag enough to include her in any way with the Queen's rescue. Hope had struck a timid root in her heart. Leon's attitude towards her had undergone a subtle change. For a fleeting moment she thought that she caught an expression very akin to respect in his eyes. Every time she was party to some successful operation, her behaviour seemed to impress him more. It was as if he was taking her measure against some impossible yard-stick of his own.

Now, it was very sweet pretending to be his wife, the simple action of sharing a meal heightened. Just for a moment she could dream that this was but one of many. Perhaps, at some lovely future date, they could always be together like this, and she would really be Lady Treviscoe. She quite forgot that she was already married...to another man. She was suddenly snapped out of her delicious reverie by a noisy commotion from outside.

Dogs began to bark, horses' hooves clattered on the cobblestones, and there was a babble of voices...men shouting, a woman's scream. Will, who had been in the yard, suddenly appeared waving frantically at her. And Cassey, terrified, leaped to her feet, while Leon grabbed for the sword which was no longer at his hip. In his disguise as a farmer he could not wear one.

' 'Swounds!' he ground out. 'What the devil is amiss?'

' 'Tis Roundheads!' Cassey cried wildly, glimpsing steel morions and the hated black and orange striped sleeves. 'Quick! Let us get to the horses!'

'Too late!' he snapped grimly. 'They are coming in the front door.'

The voices were nearer now and Cassey —able to think of nothing but escape— started towards the door at the rear. Then she heard the unmistakable sound of Morag's voice screaming:

'It's the woman you want...she is the spy...none of the others!'

Cassey ran blindly into the landlord. He reached for her and caught hold of her skirt. She jerked it free, hearing it tear, and rushed on into the hallway just in time to see half a dozen soldiers burst in. There was no escape. They seized her and dragged her back into the taproom, where Leon was already struggling with his captors.

Morag was there, white-faced and shaken for it seemed that her plan had mis-fired. She was shouting: 'Not him, you fools! He has naught to do with it. Only the woman is to be taken!'

A quick glance round assured Cassey that Will was nowhere in sight. Unless he had been apprehended outside, the chances were that he had run off. At that moment a shadow appeared in the wide open doorway and Cassey, standing defiantly between two soldiers, looked up into Grantley's mocking black eyes. He recognized Leon instantly.

'Lord Treviscoe, is it not? You are now my prisoner, sir. There are questions I shall want you to answer.'

Morag rounded on him; she had not been prepared for this eventuality. 'You told me that he would be unharmed!'

Grantley stared at her coldly; she was exactly the kind of female to arouse his detestation. 'D'you really expect word given to such as you would be binding?' He tossed across a purse which she caught expertly. 'Here. This is the price we agreed for information. Take it and get out before I change my mind and arrest you too!'

Morag hesitated, unable to meet Leon's scornful gaze. Cassey had never seen such misery on anyone's face; her eyes were those of a damned soul. Although filled with hatred and disgust at her treachery, she also experienced a flash of pity, but this was lost as Morag turned to curse her:

'This was your doing, damn you!' And she rushed from the room, colliding with a couple of surprised troopers who gazed, open-mouthed, as she slashed them with a virulent tongue before slamming out.

A grim smile played about Grantley's mouth. He jerked his head in Leon's direction and barked an order. 'Tie him up, and the woman too.'

Without the slightest compunction he commandeered the inn, the quivering host and his menials, too scared to argue, hurriedly obeying his demand for food, while his men quartered all over the building, using his hay for their horses, his ale for themselves.

'Wine, my dear?' Grantley was at his most suave, as pleased as a cat who has been at the cream, when the guards brought Cassey to him in the tavern's best parlour. He had obviously been engaged in writing, probably a report to his superiors. There were papers strewn on the table where a meal had been set, together with a quill and ink, and he was just sanding a letter before carefully folding it. A very precise man, her uncle. Cassey remembered this from former days and how his meticulous attention to detail had always grated on her nerves.

Even now, there was deliberation in the way he filled a wineglass and offered it to her. Cassey shook her head. He raised an eyebrow questioningly, then ordered her bonds to be removed and dismissed his men.

'What is it that you want?' Cassey spoke through gritted teeth, rubbing her wrists where the cords had been drawn cruelly tight.

Grantley smiled, tapping his glass with a thoughtful finger. 'Why do you assume that I want anything?'

'Don't play cat-and-mouse with me, Uncle.' Her voice rang with loathing, more angry than frightened.

His chill deepened. 'It was the most incredible stroke of good fortune that Treviscoe has fallen out with his other doxy,' he goaded her. 'She lost no time in finding me with the story of a plot to aid the Papist Queen. Although she lied, saying that only you were implicated, I was not surprised to find him at the bottom of it. Now I want further information. You will tell me the Queen's destination.'

'I'll tell you nothing!' Cassey retorted, facing him with chin uplifted. The candles had been lit, the soft glow reflecting on her white face and wide, almond-shaped eyes. 'Do what you will. Torture me, if you must. I shall not speak.'

'All very noble, my child,' his sarcasm coiled out smoothly. He seated himself on a corner of the table, fixing her with his eyes. 'I don't doubt that you would be stubborn, but, tell me, d'you think you will be able to hold your tongue if it is Treviscoe who suffers?'

Cold sweat broke out along Cassey's back. 'You would not dare!' she gasped.

He gave a light laugh, filled with an intoxicating sense of his own power, driven by revenge and greed, determined to capture the Queen and claim the reward, ears already ringing with the praise which would be heaped on him for such an action. The war had brought to full flower ambitions once frustrated in his position as a country gentleman. He had grasped every opportunity and never more so than now.

'Would I not?' By his tone she could not doubt it, but:

'As your prisoner, he must be given the honours of war.'

'He is a spy!' His expression changed, dark and malevolent. 'Plotting so that the evil woman shall escape with her priests!'

An image of the pathetic fugitive flashed across the mirror of Cassey's mind. A proud woman no doubt, maybe unwisely intentioned at times, but never wicked. Who but madmen would believe the vile lies circulated about her?

'I know nothing,' she said sullenly.

Grantley strode to the door, flinging it wide and shouting for Leon to be brought. He entered, jostled by heavily-armed guards, and he was dishevelled, his eyes wild with fury, his face bruised and bloody, his knuckles raw where he had fought them before being overpowered.

Grantley motioned his men to step back a pace, then stood to begin the interrogation.

'Sir, you will tell me where you are to meet the Queen.'

'Go to the devil!' Leon stared arrogantly down his aquiline nose at this strutting jumped-up civilian turned Colonel. As a soldier of long standing, he recognized the type and did not bother to conceal his contempt.

'Be sensible, my Lord.' Grantley's glance shifted to Cassey's face, noting her reaction. 'Why suffer needless pain for something which we shall get out of you in the end?'

'I am an officer,' reminded Leon,

stiff-backed and haughty. 'I demand the courtesy of arms.'

'You are in no position to demand anything.' Grantley was uncomfortably aware of Leon's ancestry which made him feel inferior no matter how much he might bluster. 'No one will report what happens here today. Come, tell me...where is the Queen?'

'I don't know.'

Grantley drew himself up to his full height, attempting to command the situation. 'Lord Treviscoe. I order you to be taken outside and flogged. Mayhap this will loosen your tongue.'

'No!' Cassey shouted, feeling hysteria rising, her eyes imploring Leon to tell all that he knew. No cause, no matter how momentous, could be worth his pain.

'Cassey, be silent!' Leon ordered grimly. 'I forbid you to speak!'

Trembling, Cassey stood with her hands clenched at her sides as they marched Leon away.

'And you, my dear, shall watch.' Grantley grabbed her and propelled her to the window. The yard was illuminated by flaring torches in the light of which she could see the group, with Leon in their midst, coming out of the back door. The parlour was on the first floor and from the window there was an uninterrupted view. In disbelieving horror, Cassey looked down on the scene. The soldiers were tying Leon to a stout post, his bound wrists stretched above his head, his face to the wood.

They had already stripped off his doublet and shirt and his broad back glistened, tanned and smooth, under the flickering light. His ankles were lashed so that he could not move, and the sergeant in charge was running the thongs of the nine-tailed whip through his fingers, checking on the iron tip of each. He made a few practice strokes, glancing up for Grantley's signal to begin.

Grantley let her take it in fully, a tight smile on his lips, then he gave her a shake. 'Well?'

'Oh, Leon...' she leaned from the window, 'let me speak!'

'No.' His voice came back on the breeze. 'Say nothing.'

'Proceed,' barked Grantley. The sergeant raised the whip, its thongs swishing through the air, then snaking down to cut across Leon's back.

His body bucked against the ropes and

a gasp of pain rushed out on the breath knocked from him. Cassey crammed her fist against her mouth. It was as if the blow had gone right through her.

Again the hiss of leather, the impact on flesh now criss-crossed with bloody stripes, again, and yet again while the soldiers, lined up on each side, watched, mouths set sternly under the peaks of their iron helmets. A breeze gusted across the yard and the flares wavered, making patterns of light and shadow, and, among the group of officers nearest the prisoner, Cassey saw a familiar face. It was Edward and she wondered, in that terrible moment, what emotion he was experiencing seeing the torture of his rival. Was it satisfied revenge? The justification of a wronged husband? Or did he feel compassion, for herself if not Leon?

It was as if God had deserted them; there was no answer to her prayer that merciful oblivion would sweep herself and Leon, transporting them from this realm of pain and humiliation. Nothing happened...no band of rescuing Cavaliers came hacking into view, yelling their war-cries, no host of avenging angels flew down from on high. The only reality was the whipping-post and

Leon's instrument of agony.

The nightmare stretched out, protracted and wracking. She could see and hear nothing but the hypnotic lash, now dripping with blood. She struggled in Grantley's hold, demoniac in her fury, half demented so that she possessed an unnatural strength against which he had to use all his own, her energies centered on the instinct to fight her way to Leon and attack the man wielding the whip with such deadly effect.

'Leon!' she screamed. 'Tell them! Please ...please...'

Grantley swore and caught her in a vice-like grip, clapping one hand over her mouth, shouting to the sergeant to continue.

'He has fainted, sir,' came the reply.

Cassey tore her face aside from Grantley's restraint. 'You murderer!' she yelled, and sank her teeth into his hand.

Grantley started back, loosening his hold and, amidst his anger and hatred, there was something glowing in his eyes which sickened her. 'We'll revive him—and continue!'

'No!' She gripped his sleeve in frantic fingers. 'No more. You'll find the Queen on the road to Pendennis Castle.'

His eyes glistened. 'You speak the truth?'

'Yes! Yes! Untie him!'

Leon was lowered to the cobbles where he lay inert while someone threw the contents of a bucket over him, the water running in bloody channels on to the stones.

Fierce as a tigress, Cassey rounded on Grantley. 'I want to see him.'

Having got his way, Grantley was preparing to play games again. 'Later, later, my dear. You are as pale as death. Here, take a sip of brandy; we cannot have white cheeks, eh? Nothing must mar such perfection.'

He came close, handling her with gross familiarity, seeming to be in no hurry to carry out his search for the Queen, lust roused by Cassey's revulsion. 'Come, Cassey. Do not be stubborn. I can do a great deal for you, you know. Nothing need be known of your part in this affair nor the escapade in London.'

'And Leon?' Her head ached, and she felt so tired that it was as if every bone and muscle in her body was crumbling, yet she still had to bargain.

'I am afraid he will have to be shot.'

He was eyeing her in a cold, considering way, playing with the feathers of the quill, touching the tip to his chin thoughtfully.

Cassey's heart gave a lurch and seemed to settle, sickeningly, in the pit of her stomach. Here it was then...that situation which she had always known she must face some day. Clearly she could foresee, step by step, every move of the game Grantley played. She remembered a scene in her bedroom; was it only months ago? It seemed another lifetime. And Grantley promising her that one day he would have her crawling to him, imploring him to take her. She had thought then that it might be for the sake of Edward...now she knew otherwise. It was Leon's life for which she must bargain.

With a gesture of uttermost weariness, she passed a hand across her forehead. 'You could save him.'

'Of course...with your co-operation.' He had grown very quiet, waiting, a predator ready to strike. 'You already know my terms.'

Cassey could feel all her defences crumbling, one by one. He was implacable. Useless to appeal to any feeling of decency or chivalry...he was quite bereft. And what would Leon think of her now? She longed to run out to him, yet shrank from the condemnation she would read in his eyes.

She bowed her head and Grantley, satisfied, watched the fight draining out of her. 'Please let him go,' she whispered.

It was as if he throve on her despair, a bloated spider gorging on the unhappiness of others, his voice loud and harsh. 'You'll do anything I ask in return?'

She nodded, all emotion numb, wanting only that they would let her creep away, find some dark corner and sleep, waking later perhaps, to find this bad dream over. But there were still practical considerations to work out.

'How can I be sure that you will not cheat me?' she demanded in an icy voice, wondering how a man could face such hatred and still desire her.

He raised his lean shoulders in a shrug. 'You have no alternative but to trust me. Of course he will have to be kept under restraint until the Queen is captured. He is far too dangerous. I think the Keep at Troon will prove a stout enough prison. Then, later, I'll see that he escapes to Kestle Mount. You must keep your side of the bargain now. I've waited too long for this. You've tormented me enough.'

Cassey was gripped with an almost overwhelming awareness that he was lying. Never had she felt so inadequate. 'And if I don't do as you ask?'

'He dies at dawn tomorrow.'

So this was it then. All her hopes crashed in ruins. For an instant the thought flashed that she might remind him of the old days, before her father died, before the war which had changed men so much. One glance into his face convinced her that it was useless. And outside it grew ever darker and Leon was still prone in the yard, needing attention.

'I want to see it in writing,' she demanded. 'A pass for him to be conducted to Troon.'

Grantley gave his cynical smile. 'Nothing easier, my dear. I'll do it now. Please be seated, and try a sip of wine. There is no need for uncivilized behaviour.'

He turned to the table, dipped the quill in the silver inkpot and began to scribble. Cassey watched him, eyes narrow and cat-like. Her hatred had reached obsessive proportions. This man had made Leon suffer. He could not be allowed to live.

Official business finished, he pushed

back his chair, and stood, turning to face her. He was looking at her, hands hanging at his sides, legs apart to balance his weight and Cassey was more sharply aware of his body across the space between them than she had been in his forced embrace. She glanced at the door, measuring the distance. His mouth curved into a chill smile. He let her wait, nerves strung out to breaking point, then suddenly moved, flinging off his sword, reaching out for her. One hand thrust into her hair, the pale locks streaming over them both. He grabbed a fistful of it and jerked back her head.

Cassey fought like an animal, astonishing herself with her own violence; sick with dread and humiliation she could not believe that this was really happening to her. The blood was beating in her throat, making her a wild, frantic creature filled with helpless hatred. He had her down on the daybed near the window, getting his knee between hers, pushing her skirts back over her thighs. She raked at him with her nails until a backhanded blow made the room reel.

Desperation urged her to one final effort before his weight crushed her into submission. Before they had started to struggle she had half-consciously registered the heavy brass candlestick on the side table close by. Now she grabbed for it; it bit into her palm, its chill hardness giving her strength. The lighted candle fell out, spattering them both with hot wax and, before he realized her intention, she had brought it crashing down on the back of his skull.

He grunted in pain and astonishment, rolling to one side in an attempt to avoid her next blow. Cassey sprang up, summoning her resolve, gripping it in both hands, raising it high before clubbing him again. He lay perfectly still, blood oozing darkly from his hair.

Eleven

For a moment Cassey crouched, staring down at Grantley, then at the blood on the base of the candlestick, dropping it suddenly as if it had stung her. Instinct was urging instant flight, but there was a cold, factual functioning of one part of her brain which told her to snatch up the pass, rifle Grantley's money purse and arm herself with his dagger before leaving.

Grantley was not dead, as she had at first thought; she could hear his laboured breathing as she conquered her revulsion and bent over him, going through his pockets, weapon at the ready for any sign that he might be regaining consciousness. Then she stiffened, hardly daring to breathe, when she heard footsteps in the passage. Someone was trying the door which was bolted inside.

'Colonel Scarrier,' a man's voice was saying. 'I have a message for you, sir.'

'Who is it?' Cassey quavered, dagger gripped firmly, a comforting hardness in her hand, resolved to kill herself rather than be taken again.

'It is Ruthen,' he replied, then his voice changed, holding a note of anxiety. 'Cassey! Is that you? What has happened?'

On a rush of relief she staggered to the door, throwing the bolt and Edward, puzzled, paused on the threshold, but one glance round the room made the situation clear. He shut the door hastily. 'My God! Have you killed him?'

'No. He is stunned, but I wish that I had!' There was such loathing in her tone that he reached out for her, swept with pity and protective concern.

She was trembling, shaken by sobs, threatening to break down completely at his touch. He shook her gently. 'No time for that, Cassey. You've had courage enough to go this far. Hold fast a little longer, whilst I think what we should do.'

Cassey clung to him, Edward, who always seemed to be there when she needed him most, a bulwark against despair, and now he would help her again in this desperate hour. Yet there was still that other who obsessed her thoughts.

'Leon...' her fingers dug into his sleeve as she gripped him feverishly. 'We must save him. Help me, Edward. Grantley has written a pass, 'tis here.'

The thought crossed her mind that why should Edward make any move to save the man who was his wife's lover? What right had she to demand it? Yet he hesitated for only a fraction of a moment, his hand pausing in its comforting stroking. In her eyes he read her dilemma. It did not occur to him to condemn her, much as he might hate Treviscoe, her happiness was of prime importance, and his answer was in the coolness and calm of his voice.

'Give me the pass. It is very necessary if we are to succeed. We must act at once. There is not a moment to lose.'

The curtain cords proved strong bonds with which to truss the unconscious man, a table napkin a convenient gag. No doubt Grantley had given orders not to be disturbed, with Cassey's seduction in mind. With any luck, he would not be found till morning, by which time they would be miles away.

A stealthy glance outside proved the passage-ways to be deserted. Noise came from the taproom where Grantley's troopers were whiling away the evening. It was only a matter of minutes before they were facing the first hazard; the stable where Leon was under guard. Cassey left the talking to Edward, hearing him giving orders in a brusque, soldiery manner, brooking no argument, his demands given authority by the paper in his hands. For her part, her attention was focused entirely on Leon, almost overwhelmed with horror at his plight.

He was slumped in a corner on a heap of dirty straw, his wrists still securely tied, a rope passing round the bonds tethering him to an iron ring in the wall. He was semi-conscious, his head hanging forward on his chest, his tangled hair wet with sweat. Cassey, on her knees at his side, mopped over his face with a corner of her kirtle, murmuring to him soothingly, hardly aware of what she was saying, only knowing that he must hear a familiar voice. She ran out to the well in the yard, bullying one of the ostlers to pull up a bucket of water, filling the pannikin and carrying it carefully back to Leon.

He drank greedily, the water spilling over the shirt which someone, maybe more merciful than the others, had pulled on over his raw back. Cassey, arm braced against the wall, taking his weight, whispered that help was at hand, not certain if he understood her, afraid to say too much lest she be overheard. Meanwhile, Edward had selected three of his own men to accompany them, stout fellows with sworn loyalty to him, their liege lord, than to any party. Horses were saddled and between them, they managed to get Leon to his feet which he spread wide to keep his balance, his shoulders weaving slowly from side to side, a look of worried anger on his face.

When he reached his horse, he acted by instinct and the habits which years of hard riding had made second nature to him. With teeth gritted against pain and this new, unaccustomed weakness, he swung up into the saddle. Cassey was filled with concern, raking his face anxiously, seeing how he swayed, almost falling forward over his beast's neck, while the sweat ran from his hairline, drops sliding along his jaw. His eyes were screwed up with the effort of marshalling his wits, and he moved like a man half drunk.

She was so worried about his ability to stay mounted without falling sideways through sheer exhaustion, that she guided her own mount automatically, following

Edward's big bay as he made his way past the guards and out under the arch of the inn courtyard into the darkness beyond. They kept close together for fear of getting lost, their horses' hooves skidding and slipping on the rutted road in the gloom. Then, as they drew rein at the cross-roads, the clouds cleared and the moon hung, a great pale orb, remote and pitiless, washing the scene in blue-silver and betraying the presence of a lone rider who had been waiting for them in a copse.

It was Will, who had used the hours profitably, hanging around the inn, finding out what was happening, now appearing, to offer his services and guide them off the main road, down a little used side track. Edward dropped back, swerving close to Cassey in order to say:

'Will suggests that we go with him. His people have their camp well hidden in the forest. There Treviscoe's injuries can be attended, and he will need to rest before we journey further.'

'But the Queen...?' Cassey whispered back, that terrible feeling of guilt tearing at her.

'Do not forget that it will be morning, most like, before Grantley is discovered and he alone knows where she is to be found. This will give us a few hours' start, and messengers can be sent to find and warn the Queen.'

More travelling through darkness that was almost tangible, with branches brushing across her face, showering her with dew, while leather creaked, scabbards thumped against saddles, bridles jingled, hoofbeats thudded dully on sodden turf and Cassey kept her eyes fixed on the dim outline of Edward's broad shoulders just in front of her. Leon was riding beside him, bowed over the reins, head hanging forward, so that every so often, Edward would reach across and ensure that the beast was keeping up with the others.

Will disappeared into the density of trees ahead, returning very soon accompanied by two horsemen who said little, exchanging but a few words with Edward and subjecting them to scrutiny before nodding, and wheeling their steeds around with orders that they were to follow them.

Edward had no alternative but to trust them, leading his party on through what appeared to be impenetrable trees, but the thicket parted on a path which followed the course of a stream which meandered, slowly descending, across the forest floor, its cool splash adding to the other sounds of the night; the cry of a screech owl, the small, mysterious rustling all about them. Cassey shivered and was glad that she was not alone.

The stream widened and they forded it where it glittered in the moonlight, gaining the path on the other side, passing through an avenue of trees which suddenly cleared so that they came out in a natural circle surrounded by the densely massed woods.

Leaping flames from the cooking fires flecked the scene with crimson. There were wagons drawn into a ring, reminding Cassey of the leaguer, as did the smoke drifting across the clearing, the mouth-watering smell rising with the steam from the iron pots slung from tripods over the embers. But here any similarity ceased; as they rode into the glade they were met by silence and the unwinking stares of these dark-eyed, swarthy people. The air was thick with suspicion, wariness, and an over-riding hostility.

The men squatted on their heels by the fires, their women well in the background, dressed in smocks and rough cloaks, scarves covering their braided hair, the firelight sparking off the rings in their ears. Some of them had small children hiding behind their skirts, peering out at the strangers with those luminous, unwinking eyes, others had a baby swaddled in a shawl or straddling their hip. Lean, starved-looking hounds tethered to the wagons or lying at the feet of their masters, raised their heads to growl ominously until cuffed into submission. At the rear of the wagons were the shadowy outlines of a number of horses, cropping the short, springy turf.

Edward's grim-faced soldiers dismounted, ready for trouble, eyeing Will apprehensively as he went to converse with a man seated a little apart from the others. The respect accorded to him signalled him out as a being of some importance. Edward, controlling his men with a word, stood quietly waiting until Will had finished explaining to his leader in a strange, incomprehensible tongue. Cassey was far too concerned about Leon's condition to pay much heed, watching him like one hypnotized as he slid awkwardly from his saddle to stand at his horse's side with the look of a men so drunk that he was about to pitch forward onto his face.

A wild surge of rage against Grantley

swept her uncontrollably. She bitterly regretted that she had not succeeded in killing him.

Will's conversation with his chief seemed to have the desired effect. Welcome was extended and they were presented to this man who called himself a Duke of Little Egypt. Cassey was impressed with Edward's behaviour for he treated him as an equal without the slightest trace of condescension, sensitive to the fierce pride of these nomads.

This Duke, whose name was Anthony Lalow, was older than he appeared at first. He was very dark with a brown skin, hair which fell across his shoulders, and a long, black moustache. His eyes were the strangest Cassey had ever seen, with queer orange pupils and a light in them which seemed to come from within. They bored into her as if they would unravel all her secrets. He was grandly dressed in black velvet with a beautiful silver belt, finger-rings and jewels in his ears, a contrast to his followers, many of whom were clad in rags.

Cassey viewed him with misgivings. Will she had learned to trust, and Loveday too had been a friend. She had met tinkers, horse-dealers, musicians on her travels with the army, but gypsies were a race apart, with an unsavoury reputation for thieving and cheating. Then her fears gave way to astonishment at the extraordinary sight of Lalow embracing Leon, greeting him as an old friend, instantly concerned about his injuries, sweeping all out of the way so that he might conduct him to the largest, most ornate wagon.

'Now there will be no doubt that he will give you every assistance,' Will informed her. 'He has no time for Colonel Scarrier, who has ever hounded our people from his land, but Lord Treviscoe was always fair in his dealings with us. See, he has taken him to Nona Lalow. She will heal him quickly. Go with him, madam, she may need your aid.'

A strange time indeed for Cassey, the sequence of events taking on a dream-like quality in her high-strung, weary state. Nona Lalow was a stately lady, high in the tribal hierarchy, the Duke's mother and a Princess in her own right. The interior of the wagon was surprisingly neat and comfortable with a bed-place at the far end to which Leon was helped. Further rush-lights were brought and Nona leaned over him, examining his back with little comment, then she dismissed the men, her shrewd eyes noting Cassey's white, anxious face and bidding her stay.

She worked quickly, with skilful movements of her gnarled brown hands, preparing herbs taken from a carved coffer, spreading the mixture across Leon's back and fixing a dressing of clean white linen.

'What is this you use?' Cassey had studied plants and their usage as part of her training as a prospective housewife. Doctors were scarce and expensive, especially in country districts. The Lady of the house was expected to have a sound knowledge of nursing. The still-room was used not only for the storage of food; its shelves also contained home-made cordials, medicines and ointments.

'Adder's tongue, mixed with oil, excellent for wounds such as these,' Nona answered and the eyes which regarded Cassey were shrewd and intelligent still, though set in a face as wrinkled as old parchment. They made Cassey uneasy; this woman was alien to her, reared in a life-style utterly different from her own, and Nona too seemed unwilling to talk much. But, at the sight of Leon's back, striped with blood, she forgot everything in her anger and indignation, pouring out the whole story while Nona listened.

'That accursed Scarrier! A mean, vicious man. You will be safe here for a while, child. Your man will mend quickly...he is healthy and strong. I know him well, and his family before him.'

Leon had been prone on his stomach, suffering their ministrations without complaint. Now his eyelids flickered and lifted; for the first time he seemed fully conscious of his surroundings.

Nona inclined her head with grave dignity. 'Greetings, my Lord.'

He struggled to sit, a puzzled frown rucking his forehead. 'What has happened? Cassey, tell me. Did I betray the Queen?'

Cassey's heart plummeted; this was the moment she had been dreading. The urgent appeal in his drawn dark eyes was more than she could bear. She drew her tongue over lips gone suddenly dry, fists clenched into white-knuckled balls. Question and answer flashed between them, that white heat of silence which built up intolerably.

'You told them!' Even as he said it, he shook his head as if unable to believe it, and the accusation in his voice was almost the hardest thing of all.

She was unable to meet his gaze, and nodded, dumbly. Nona was watching them closely, picking up the vibrations in the taut air around them.

'I'm sorry, Leon,' Cassey found herself trying to explain, hammering desperately at the barrier which had sprung up between them, made of misunderstanding and pride, ending lamely: 'They were hurting you. It had to stop.'

'Lay aside your anger, my Lord,' Nona put in quickly. 'Can you not see 'twas but her love for you which made her act so? She is true to you and to your King. I read it in her.'

'I should never have trusted you!' Leon ground out furiously, frustrated by the weakness which made him sweat and prevented him from going on the hot spur to the rescue of the Queen. 'You are a Roundhead!'

'My Lord, be calm,' urged the older woman, lifting a cup to his lips. 'Drink this. It will make you sleep, and you can do nothing yet to help. Messengers have already been despatched to find and warn the Queen.'

Cassey shrank from the condemnation

in the eyes which continued to glare at her, though he obeyed Nona. Then he eased down again under the patch-work coverlet, rolling on his side, his face to the canvas wall and black despair in the set of his wide shoulders stubbornly turned away from her. Soon Nona's potion began to take effect. His breathing became regular and he was deeply asleep.

'Thank you, Mistress Lalow.' Cassey touched her hand in gratitude. 'You are right. I do love him. He is my whole world.'

'I know.' Nona nodded sagely, adding with heart-warming conviction: 'And he is the man for you.'

'How can you be so sure?' Hope sprang full-blossomed within her but she had become so afraid of disappointment.

'There is little that escapes me.' The understanding smile which lifted Nona's narrow features made her seem much younger than her seventy years. 'Come, let us see what the cards have to say.'

Cassey was deeply disturbed; she had been brought up to be wary of fortune-tellers and their like, yet she desperately needed advice and encouragement. She hesitated only a moment when Nona brought out a box carved with most curious designs, lifted the lid and carefully removed a bundle wrapped in black silk. She whisked this off with a flourish, revealing the pack. Cassey looked at them curiously; they resembled playing cards and yet were strangely different. Nona told her that they were the Tarot, wherein lay the destiny of those who enquired. She fanned them out on the floor...pentacles, wands, swords...and the Court cards, Kings, Queens, Knights and Pages...most mysterious of all the strange Trump cards...the Hanged Man, The Tower, Death and the Universe.

Nona handled them in fingers which were like claws, with a half moon of dirt beneath each nail, gathering them up, passing them to Cassey with instructions to shuffle and cut into three packs. The smoky rush-light planed shadows on Nona's face, her eyes burning with concentration as she formed a spread with the selected cards, pondering deeply.

'You have come through great danger, and there is more to come,' she mused. 'There is one who intends you harm.'

'This I know,' Cassey broke in. 'It is Grantley Scarrier.'

Nona nodded. 'Aye, he who should have been like a father to you, but has allowed his avarice and desires to dominate him. There are trials and sorrow—your road will never be easy, not for some time at least. And there is death, too.'

Casssey felt the cold sweat break out on her body. 'Not Leon?' she gasped.

Nona shook her head with that closed, withdrawn look. Her lips moved wordlessly, while her intent, listening expression gave Cassey the eerie feeling that she was conversing with invisible beings. She sat in this waiting silence for a long time, so still that Cassey began to wonder if she was asleep. Then she suddenly said; 'I see you both across the sea. There will be no returning to England for a long time.'

'But we shall be together?' Cassey ventured, only half believing. This must be laughable nonsense, games for children, yet she could not resist asking questions.

Nona continued to stare at the real or imagined drama which the cards unfolded. 'You will be together, I promise you. There is soon to be a child—an heir for Kestle Mount.'

Cassey's heart leaped and then she trembled with fear. How could this woman know what she herself had kept such a closely guarded secret? She was still slim, her waist as slender as a boy's, only her breasts betrayed her, larger and more full, the nipples darker than before, but Nona could not possibly be aware of this.

Her chief emotion was one of joy. Nona's words rang sweetly in her ears. She was to give Leon a son. This would surely make him love her, for she knew full well just how much Kestle Mount meant to him, and the continuation of the Treviscoe line must be of equal importance. As she listened to Nona, she wanted his baby with passionate intensity, and not only for its own sake. There was a greater issue.

'Kestle Mount!' she demanded, old ambition flaring up.

'You will be mistress there.' Nona spoke with such certainty that Cassey would not but believe her. The eyes of the two women met and locked and Cassey knew that if everyone else failed her, Nona never would. She had made a life-long friend. But there was one more vital question.

'And the cause? Who will win the war?'

Nona's face darkened; it was as if the sorrow of this bitter, fratricidal conflict was reflected there. 'Many have asked me this. There is but one reply. Monarchy will prevail, but it will be years acoming and it will not be this Charles who sits in his palace at Whitehall again.'

'The Roundheads will win?' It was as if a chill wind had stirred the air. 'What will happen to the King?'

Nona drew her shawl more closely around her. She looked suddenly weary enough to drop. 'A martyr's crown. This is his reward.'

Doom rolled in Cassey's ears like the thunder of drums. What could she mean? Would the King die in battle? But further enquiry was useless; the power had gone from Nona; she was already wrapping the cards in their cocoon of silk. She moved slowly, her years sitting heavily upon her.

'Sleep, my dear,' she said at last. 'Lie by your man and may your dreams be peaceful.'

'And you?' Cassey slipped off her shoes, climbing on to the bed.

Nona paused at the entrance flap of the wagon, looking back to say: 'I need little rest. The moon is full and I have herbs to cull which can only be done at this time.'

Cassey stretched out at Leon's side,

careful not to rouse him, unable to face the condemnation in his eyes. Her mind was too active to allow her deep sleep, one thought uppermost...the coming child. What was she to do? But presently peace began to wash over her. She cushioned her face against Leon's broad shoulder; in spite of all, this moment was good...just to know he was there...his presence making all things wonderful.

She lay dreaming, asleep, yet not asleep, aware, though her eyelids were closed, of the interior of the wagon, lit by a single rush. Something had awakened her, a sound, maybe, and she came to full consciousness with a start, knowing that someone had entered. She opened her eyes in astonishment. Morag was leaning over the bed, her attention fixed wholly on Leon, an expression of unendurable anguish on her features. She seemed unaware of Cassey's presence.

'Oh, Leon,' her voice broke on a whispered sob. 'My God, what have they done to you?'

Gone was her stubborn pride, her fierce hatred; now she was only a woman, broken by emotion and guilt. 'I did not mean them to hurt you.' She reached out and

312

gently stroked his face. 'Please wake and tell me that you understand and forgive me.'

In spite of the sleeping mixture, habit was strong, that soldier's training which alerted him so that his eyelids snapped back to stare at her without comprehension for an instant. Then a black scowl darkened his face.

'What do you here, Morag?'

'I had to see you.' She shrank back as if scorched. 'Oh, don't hate me, Leon. You left me for her. I hated her and wanted the Roundheads to take her so that you would love me again. Forgive me, please, Leon!'

He dragged himself into a sitting position. 'Get out, before I kill you!'

Emboldened by the fact that she was out of reach and his strength obviously sapped, Morag began to argue. Their voices rose, a brutal exchange which reverberated through the thin canvas walls, the commotion awakening the camp. In minutes Anthony Lalow was framed in the entrance, his mother close at his heels, and Will, with alarmed eyes, pushing in behind them.

'Morag! Do you dare to come back?'

313

The Duke's voice cut like a lash. 'Were you not forbidden to set foot here again? You have brought disgrace upon us. Living among the *gorgios,* dressed in breeches, like a man! Unnatural wench! You are *mochardi!* Unclean, wallowing in filth!'

'What do you know of it?' She spat at him viciously, as ferocious as a wild cat at bay. 'You speak of things of which you understand nothing! I couldn't wait to get away! My life has been rich and exciting! I've seen and done things of which you could not even dream, stuck out here in the forest, living like an animal!'

'And what of me?' Will seized her by the arm so that she swirled round to face him, her eyes sparkling dangerously. Cassey had never seen Will so angry...gone, the patient, obedient soul...here was a man goaded beyond endurance.

'You!' Morag's lip curled contemptuously. She raised an eyebrow and looked him up and down. 'Loutish clodhopper! Did'st really think that I could be forced into wedlock with you, to spend my days in toil and the rearing of brats as ignorant as yourself? I've been loved by a Lord! A real man, not a dirty, cheating horse-thief!'

She snatched her arm free, lunged past

the Duke and leaped the steps to the grass below. But Will moved as swiftly as she, yanking her round to face him, his knife flashing down to plunge between her ribs. She gave an astonished gasp, then slumped heavily into his arms. A stunned silence fell on the onlookers.

The day was not yet four hours old. Darkness was lifting slowly. Trees loomed through the dimness. The smell of leaves was in the air, and that of the damp, trodden earth to which Will gently lowered her.

'Come inside, my child.' Nona Lalow rested an arm about Cassey's shoulders as she stood, dumbfounded, at the top of the wagon steps. 'She flouted our laws, well knowing the price she would have to pay if she was caught returning here. Will did what he knew he must.'

Later that day, the Duke summoned Cassey to his presence. Wonderingly, she went out to find him. He was seated on a log by one of the fires smoking, and took the clay pipe from beneath his teeth, regarding her seriously for a moment before speaking.

'It is not often that I ask help from a *gorgio*,' he began. 'But you owe us a favour in return for the assistance we have given you.'

'Of course. What would you have me do?' Her voice sounded high and thin in her own ears, shaky with the terror with which his peculiar eyes filled her.

He leaned over to knock the ashes out of his pipe, then kick a log into place so that a tongue of flame shot through the sullen smoke. He threw a glance at her.

'Morag must be buried and it is not right that she should be wearing the breeches and doublet of a man. My people do not like touching the dead. Will you prepare her for burial?'

Revulsion swept her, but she was more afraid of refusing him, so nodded her consent. They took her to the clearing where Morag had been laid and Nona brought a bundle of garments, obviously very uneasy and leaving as soon as possible. Only Edward came to assist her.

It was with a sense of detachment and unreality that she stripped and washed the body, seeing the blood clotting darkly on the soiled white shirt, and the gaping lips of the wound through which Morag's life had slipped away so fast. Was this really the arrogant, vital woman whom she had hated with such intensity? This body had lain with Leon in the rutting heat of the bed; those long, slender legs had twined with his; that mouth, now locked in death, had softened under his lips, and those dark eyes, glinting dully through half-closed lids, had gazed into his with passion.

Cassey could not understand why she was without feeling. Not even relief permeated this numbness. Morag was now nothing more than a piece of meat, soon to rot, all that beauty turning to corruption, while within her own warm flesh new life already existed, and would soon be stirring. And she could not even experience triumph over the dead girl.

Edward and she worked in silence as the day grew increasingly warm. Once she paused to straighten her aching back, glancing through a gap in the briars, seeing beyond, a field rich with stooks of golden corn and the trees drowsy with thick summer. Rooks cawed in the elms above her head, and she went back to her work. Edward helped her to dress Morag in the traditional garb of a gypsy woman, sliding gold rings through her ear lobes, a chain belt about her waist, a scarf over her plaited hair, black shoes with fine silver

317

buckles on her feet.

They wrapped her in a blanket and laid her in the ditch at the roadside, covering her with earth and bracken, as the Duke had instructed them to do. As they returned to the camp, they saw a couple of men burning the discarded clothing. Drained, and weary beyond words, Cassey trailed back to Nona's wagon to renew her vigil over Leon. Later, she was thankful that they did not tell her that day that Will would scout for them no more. He had been found hanging from an oak in the depths of the wood.

Twelve

On the night of their arrival in camp, messengers had been sent winging to find the Queen's party with warning that they had been betrayed. Within hours the Duke's swift riders had returned with good news. They had been successful in intercepting her. Richard had scribbled a hasty message to Leon, informing him that a secret route, known only to one or two, would now take them to Pendennis Castle. Once within the walls of that fastness of Royalism, the Queen would be safe, until a ship could be found with a Master willing to risk a dash across the Channel, bearing her home to France. He added a rider to the effect that, as soon as she had departed, he would make for Kestle Mount and meet up with Leon there.

The gypsies were restless, eager to move on from a spot where two such tragic deaths had taken place. They feared ghosts more than almost anything, and spent the nights huddled together round the fires, conversing in whispers, glancing fearfully over their shoulders into the black mass of the woods which seemed to be peopled with rustling unnameable objects of terror.

Their fear was infectious; Cassey found herself reluctant to linger outside the camp even in the bright light of day, ashamed of this overpowering desire to scurry back to the comparative shelter of the circle. She forced her trembling limbs to obey her, adopting an exaggeratedly dignified gait, least someone should see and mock her. But at night even very firm talking to herself was of no avail. All the monsters, demons and hobgoblins of childhood tales came flooding back to haunt her. Then, she was only too thankful to creep into the back of the wagon, braving the strained silence which existed between Leon and herself these days.

Much of the time he was soundly asleep, sedated by one of Nona's brews, and Cassey would duck under the covers at his sleeping side, curling up against his back, pulling the blankets over her head, hardly daring to breathe as darkness thickened beyond the pale light thrown by the cake of wax floating in a silver basin.

Though never at ease with them, wholly

distrustful, she listened, intrigued as Nona and the Duke told her about the days before the war when Leon spent much time with them as a lad. Whenever he could escape his duties as heir to Kestle Mount, he would join their roaming band, learning their lore, adopting their skills, developing their native cunning. As lean and swart as they, it had amused him to pass as one of them, unrecognized as he bargained with some of his own tenants when he went horse-dealing in the villages, not at all adverse to employing the sharp practices taught him by the Duke.

The gypsy chief had taken to him, treating him almost as a son, but there had been an unfortunate repercussion. Morag, one of his nieces and high-born among them, had fallen in love with him, refusing to listen to reason or advice, defying the elders and their customs and following him off to war. And Will, who loved her and to whom she had been promised in marriage since birth, had gone with them, torn between loyalty to the man whom he admired so much, and jealousy and anguish because his woman behaved like a wayward slut. Tragedy had been inevitable.

Nona's treatment was proving most effective. Leon was much stronger now, able to get to his feet, though stiff and sore. He was taciturn and moody, bitingly sarcastic to Cassey, when he spoke to her at all, which was seldom. He seemed obsessed with the idea of returning to Kestle Mount, fearing reprisals from Grantley and his men. He avoided the Roundhead officers who had helped him to escape, shunning Edward's company and spending much time with the Duke, while Cassey suffered the torments of the damned, longing to be with him, wounded by the contempt in his voice, the coldness in his eyes whenever they were together. There was a wall between them which she could not penetrate.

His raw temper was inflamed by impatience of his own weakness, his frustration at being unable to ride full tilt for Kestle Mount, there to reorganize his garrison and strengthen the fortifications. Cassey suspected that he was also experiencing uneasy pangs of guilt concerning Morag's death. The gypsies attached no blame to him for this; in their eyes the woman had been responsible—she was well aware of their code, had deliberately broken it, and had been punished accordingly. The matter was closed, the score settled, paid in full—in blood.

The gypsies had packed up their belongings and were ready to move, letting the strangers know that here their help ended and they must part. Edward came seeking Cassey with plans for their future on his mind.

She was sitting dejectedly on a tree stump on the edge of the clearing, elbows on her knees, chin cupped in her hand, brooding about Leon and her own unhappy state, bewailing the day she had set eyes on him. Yet, she looked up expectantly on hearing the sound of footfalls on the turf, her heart skipping a beat, hoping against all hope that it might be Leon come to beg her forgiveness and understanding, that blank, withdrawn expression banished from his handsome face.

'All is ready for departure, Cassey.' Edward dropped on his heels at her side. Cassey did not object when he took both her hands in his. The last thing she wished was to hurt him, though his touch left her cold, and filled her with regret that it was not Leon kneeling at her feet. He was trying desperately to find the right words.

323

'It would be best if we left Treviscoe to find his own way back to Kestle Mount. No doubt, some of the bolder gypsy boys will accompany him. They seem to look upon him as some kind of blood-brother.' His voice had a cutting edge, betraying the storm beneath his calm exterior. Whenever he and Leon met and were forced to any interchange of conversation, they were always icily polite as became men of honour.

Now he glanced up at her hesitantly; the sunlight dappling through the trees gave his yellow hair a fiery tinge. 'Come back to Mawnan with me.' She was about to reply, but he held up a finger to silence her and hear him out. 'You are still my wife and I love you. I will be patient and, in time, you will forget him!'

'Never!' she said wildly, but he rose and drew her to her feet, imagining that he might still move her. He was suddenly alight with energy.

'Oh, Cassey, but consider. There is so much for you at home. A secure life, money, position, children. You'd see Beth again. Would that not please you? Mawnan would be yours. Yourself, the most respected lady in the district. Just

324

think of the good life we could have.'

Cassey wanted to sink her head into her hands and weep. What inscrutable workings of fate had thrown them all together, each to suffer so much? She saw herself with merciless clarity, knowing that she often tried to justify her actions, blaming the war—but this was not true and just a weak excuse for her own instability. There was that within her which, through her own impetuosity, always led her into trouble. Edward deserved a wife far better than she; yet she could fully understand and sympathize with his feelings. Was she not, too, hopelessly and eternally in love with someone not really worthy of such devotion?

She hated this power which gave her the awful responsibility of shattering for ever the hopes and dreams of this man whom she loved like a brother. Why could he not be satisfied with friendship? 'And would you be content with a pale platonic relationship with Leon?' asked that devilishly cool facet of her personality which always seemed to be sitting in judgement. Of course she would not! She could never look on Leon in any other light than that of a lover. She had made a valiant attempt to feel her old love for Edward when she had married him at Mawnan. She had failed miserably, and knew it to be a waste of time to try again.

For an instant, Cassey contemplated all he had to offer. Even the child would be accepted by him; she could lie her way round its date of conception, somehow. She would hate herself for this, but it would have to be done for her baby's protection. But within her, mixed with all the other feelings, was a growing indignation. It was not fair of Edward to burden her with his own longings. She had more than enough to contend with in regard to her own miserable state without being tortured by qualms of conscience because of him. There was one way to put a stop to his insistence, probably damning her future. The brutal truth.

'I am with child, and it is not yours.' She brought it out on a note of defiance.

She saw the light go out of his face and his mouth harden. He let go of her hands and went slowly to the path to stand with his back to her, while, between them, his dream dissolved. A dead stillness held Cassey.

He turned to her. The colour had drained from his face which had become suddenly grey and old, bereft of hope, empty of desire.

'Is it Treviscoe's?' The question seemed superfluous but had to be answered. She nodded and there was an uneasy silence; then he asked: 'Does he know?'

She shook her head forlornly and he read in that movement all of her fears, and his love for her welled up like a throbbing wound. 'Come home with me and I'll rear it as my own.'

He was so good, making her feel unworthy and all that she could do was regret that it was not Leon. She began to cry; the pent up emotion, the shock of the last few days washing over her, and Edward held her, patting her awkwardly till her sobs abated. She kept her face pressed against his shoulder, finding some comfort through her nose felt swollen with tears and her throat hurt.

She was absorbed in her anguish and he in his confusion, and they were not aware that someone else had entered the glade until a snapping twig made them look up. Leon was standing watching them with an inscrutable expression.

'Cassey!' he barked, black brows curving down alarmingly. 'What ails you?'

Edward released her and swung round to him. 'My Lord, there is something you should know.'

'The Queen! Has harm befallen her? By God, Ruthen, if aught has happened to her through you...!' Leon made a threatening gesture, but Edward broke in:

'As far as I know, she is safe. This concerns yourself and Cassey, and, indirectly, myself, though I am only her husband!' There was a cold, sarcastic bite to his voice which Cassey had never heard before. Both men were growing so angry that, although they had not moved, the air seemed to crackle between them.

Puzzled, Leon looked from one to the other. 'Well, what is this matter of such importance that we stand here discussing it instead of getting to horse?'

Edward's fingers bit into Cassey's arm. 'Tell him, Cassey,' he urged.

Slowly she lifted her eyes to that dark face that she loved so well, appalled by the distrust and suspicion which she read there. 'I am to have a child,' she faltered.

'Whose?' The intensity of his stare seemed to bore right through her. She could hardly believe her own ears; it had not occurred to her that he would doubt its parentage.

'Yours, of course!' she flung back at him.

He gave a harsh bark of laughter in which there was no mirth. 'Mine, forsooth! That I do not believe! He is your husband, after all.'

The lovely day was abruptly blighted, all that wild, beautiful burgeoning of nature seemed suddenly barren.

'It was conceived before I left Kestle Mount,' she protested weakly.

His mouth was stern and pitiless. 'D'you expect me to believe that? You have proved yourself to be a liar and a traitor. Between you, you foiled my design to help the Queen. How much did they pay you, Cassey, to give them directions to find her? Or did you do it for him, your husband and the father of your child?'

Cassey was stunned by the enormity of his accusations, unable to credit that it was really Leon speaking. But she saw with horror that the confused dream state of his delirium still clouded his mind, warping his normally clear thinking. He had suffered gruelling physical torture but, more than that, his pride and confidence had been severely shaken. He would trust no one now.

'I give you my word.' Edward was watching them, feeling the bitter tug of their love which eddied into black swirling anger, misunderstanding and desire. 'Would that it were otherwise, Treviscoe, but, alas, she loves you!'

'Love!' Leon spat the word out. 'Lust, more like, which any man could satisfy. You are like all the rest, Cassey, disloyal and completely false!'

'How can you say that, after all we have been through together?' Cassey's face was white and pinched, her distress adding to Edward's anger.

'Your actions have damned you.' Leon was unapproachable, locked in with this demon which he had allowed to possess him—someone had to take the blame for his failures—she saw this clearly and bitterly—knowing that it was useless to argue with him in his present frame of mind. Now he turned away, ignoring her.

'I intend to make all haste to Kestle Mount.' His eyes were hard as granite as they flicked over Edward's face. 'I presume that you will not try to prevent me, sir?'

'My position is difficult.' Edward was equally formal. 'I doubt not that Scarrier will be after my blood for aiding you. I had thought to return to Mawnan for a while. I think it unlikely that he will hunt me at present. He'll be hell-bent on chasing the Queen. I have asked Cassey to come with me but she refuses.'

'It is quite immaterial to me where she goes, or with whom.' Leon's lip curled unpleasantly, his manner making Edward's hackles rise.

'I want to come with you,' Cassey burst out.

'And I will play my part to escort you there,' Edward added.

'There is no need,' Leon said ungraciously. 'I can manage full well alone, and I must leave at once.'

' 'Tis not your safety which concerns me, I assure you.' A dark angry flush suffused Edward's cheeks. 'Cassey is the one who matters.'

Leon shrugged, gave Casssey one long, searching glance, and stalked out of the clearing, as if impatient for his body to follow his thoughts.

'You'll really come with us? What of your service with the Parliamentarians?'

In this black hour of despair, Edward's care for her was like balm, but Cassey was working with the top of her mind only, longing to snatch up her skirts and fly after Leon, to beg him to have faith in her again.

'If I'm caught, I shall be shot as a deserter, unless I can come up with a really plausible tale.' Edward's voice was weary and disillusioned; he had had time of late to consider seriously the actions of his party, no longer convinced that they were right. Now, it did not seem to matter so very much after all. 'You will need someone there to protect you. Treviscoe is still in no fit condition to defend either himself or you, if there is trouble on the way.'

There seemed to be no more to be said and Cassey went back with him to the wagons where his men were already saddling their mounts and waiting his word of command. Leon was taking farewell of the Duke, the old man standing with a hand on his shoulder, giving a final piece of advice. Then there was no call for further delay. Nona drew Cassey to her and planted a kiss on her forehead, almost like a blessing, and they swung into their saddles and turned their beasts' heads in the direction of Kestle Mount.

The going was hard. To add to the problems, it began to drizzle, a steady rain which looked as if it might go on for a long time. They rode mostly in silence, Edward, Cassey and Leon sunk in their own melancholy, hardly aware of the damp beauty about them. The hedges were still heavy with summer blossoms and they jogged past waving fields of coppery corn sprinkled with scarlet poppies, star-like columbines and bright blue cornflowers. The meadows gave way to rolling moorland, softened by purple heather, vivid green bracken, and dazzling yellow gorse.

They paused for a rest and to water their horses at a brown, peaty stream which broke round gleaming stones. Food was eaten in a gloomy silence, then they fell to discussing the best road to follow, deciding to make a detour of the small grey towns and pass speedily through the villages lest their sudden appearance drew too much attention.

They dared not delay long and rode hard all the afternoon, but by the time drab twilight had begun to gather, it was patiently obvious that Leon was in no condition to continue. His face was grey with exhaustion under his tan, and he, who usually rode as if born in the saddle, now drooped wearily, hardly able to control his beast.

Edward drew rein and they gathered about him, a dejected enough group hunched into their cloaks, hats pulled well down against the fine, persistent downpour.

'We are not far from Mawnan.' Edward swept a glance over them. 'I suggest that we shelter there tonight...'

'But what of Leon?' Cassey protested.

'I have thought of that,' he added quickly, stopping her before she could begin to argue. 'No one there will know what has taken place. News travels but slowly in these parts. I can say that you, my Lord, are my prisoner on parole. I can easily satisfy my mother's questions. It will give you a chance to rest before we press on.'

No fault could be found in this sensible plan. There was a slight risk that a troop of Grantley's soldiers might have been dispatched to seek Edward at his home, but he detailed one of his men to reconnoitre, and he returned to report that all was quiet at the manor. Soon they were riding through the dusk which followed about them, towards the walls and gatehouse. Dusk was everywhere. Dusk and then darkness. Their coming stirred the old house to life. Lights leaped to windows. Lanterns bobbled in the courtyard and twinkled above doors. Lady Amelia appeared at the top of the stone steps leading to the main entrance, hands outspread to welcome her son.

Then there were questions and explanations and a catching up on all the news, and frosty glances at Cassey, who moved wearily towards the fire in the Great Hall, drawing off her gauntlets, holding her stiff, chilled fingers to the blaze, glad to see that Leon still had his wits about him to join in the charade.

There was no disbelief expressed at Edward's tale of his capture of Leon. They even seemed to accept his highly improbable story of Cassey working as a spy for the Roundheads, which explained away her appearance in their midst clad in the soiled, tattered garb of a peasant woman. That night, Lady Amelia's joy at seeing her son swept away too much awkward probing, and she bustled about seeing that her unexpected guests were provided with hot water, a change of clothing and comfortable rooms.

Cassey was accompanied to the Master bedchamber by an astonished, round-eyed Beth. When they were at last alone, the two women flung their arms about each other, almost crying with delight. Then Cassey incoherently poured out her adventures, while Beth listened with alarm and horror crossing her pert, snubbed-nose features.

'Oh, ma'am...' she ventured, when at last Cassey paused for want of breath. ' 'Tis so good to see you again. My dear lady, you can have no notion of the gossip that has been mouthed abroad by your sudden disappearance.'

Cassey had a very shrewd idea of what they thought of her. Her mother-in-law detested her, she was sure of that now. And his sisters? Well, she had not liked the look in the eyes of Jessica, the youngest, when she first saw Leon.

During her absence that young woman had grown far too attractive. She could only hope that Leon was feeling too ill to respond. It was obvious that she was to be frustrated at any attempt to be alone with him...here she was Edward's wife...and she would be obliged to share the same room and bed to avoid any scandalized stares. And Leon would occupy a guest room, some distance from her.

This thought made her so agitated that she paced the room distractedly, in jerky disjointed sentences telling Beth of the new development in their stormy relationship.

'A baby, ma'am?' Beth rushed to her at that, then paused at her tortured expression whilst pride, love and despair warred in Cassey.

'What are you going to do, my lady?' Beth was looking at her with unquestioning devotion, wanting only to aid her. Cassey's spine stiffened with resolve.

'Do?' She sprang to her feet, making for the huge carved wardrobe which housed her clothing, abandoned so many weeks before. 'First of all, dear, help me out of these stinking rags. I'd not have him see me such a fright a moment longer. I'faith, I've quite forgot what it is like to don an elegant gown.'

This was Beth's happiest province, and they temporarily forgot the more unpleasant issues at stake whilst they rummaged through dresses and petticoats, and rifled drawers in search of stockings, fans and high-heeled pumps. Cassey washed away the stain of travel whilst Beth lit the candles in sconces on either side of the dressing-table mirror. Then Cassey was able to relax under her ministrations, seated on the low stool, watching their reflections, bending forward a little to touch rouge to her cheeks and lips, to add a trace of blue shadow to her lids, and apply a blackened brush to her thick sweeping lashes.

There was the crisp feel of stiff petticoats against the silk hose covering her legs, the half forgotten but instantly familiar sensation of the restriction of small satin shoes on her feet which had become accustomed to the hardness of leather boots, and the tightness of a boned busk crushing her ribs, this discomfort of no consequence compared with the knowledge that it took inches from her waist.

Her neckline was low, her breasts fuller than before, sure signs of early pregnancy, and she felt a sudden surge of confidence; she was still beautiful. Leon should not ignore her.

Between them, they had managed to wash her hair; Beth imperiously ordering the maid-servants to stagger up with buckets of rain water. Her heavy locks no longer twisted in greasy snarls about her face. There was no time to affect a fashionable coiffure, but, when it was dry, it hung in a soft, scented cloud on her bare shoulders. She felt well able to face Jessica when she entered a few moments later, with the excuse of clean towels over her arm. Really, she was eager to hear Cassey's adventures which had brought back colour into her drab existence.

'Cassandra! Oh, 'tis so good to see you again.' She almost danced across the room, laying her burden over the back of a chair. 'Mama says that supper is almost ready and will you come down?' Her eyes shone with genuine admiration and pleasure. 'Oh, how lovely you are! Would that I were like you, then perhaps he might notice me.' She blushed slightly, eyes bright. 'Oh, tell me, pray...who is this Lord Treviscoe? I vow and declare, I've never seen anyone half so handsome!'

It was like a smack in the face with cold water, rude and shocking, and it made Cassey angry because it frightened her so much. But why should it, she told herself, annoyed by her own abysmal lack of confidence. This girl could never mean anything to him, she was far too innocent and child-like...besides, she was a Roundhead! But the eager questions continued to tumble from Jessica's lips, her cheeks pink with excitement, her blue eyes shining like stars, making her really pretty.

'My dear child, he is a Cavalier.' Cassey found herself wanting to explode any myth of chivalry which Jessica might be building up in her mind. 'Your brother's prisoner, quotha! Would you so much admire your enemy?'

Her voice was tart and edgy and she caught Beth's warning stare. She stood abruptly, snatching up her fan, giving herself one final approving glance in the mirror, anxious to see Leon, to assure herself that he could not possibly find her rather gauche sister-in-law in any way attractive. In any case, she kept reminding herself, he is still too ill!

Jessica fetched a deep sigh. 'He is such a gentleman and seems so very sick. When I went to his room just now with clean clothing, he treated me like a queen, so kind and polite.'

'You went to his room?' Cassey's voice rose an octave and Beth gave her a sharp nudge in the ribs. She fought for control; if Jessica or anyone else guessed the truth, there would be trouble. His safety depended on her discretion.

'I think, my dear, such duties should be confined to the servants,' she said more reasonably, and the troubled cloud lifted from Jessica's features. She had failed to understand why Cassey, whom she so much admired, seemed to be cross with her.

Once they had been friends. When Cassey had lived there, motivated by sheer mischief and boredom, she had spent time encouraging both of Edward's sisters to take more interest in their appearances. It seemed that she had succeeded only too wel in the case of Jessica who had already changed for supper and was wearing a gown of dark blue satin, with the overskirt caught up in pink bows and roses pinned in the glossy brown curls bunched over each ear. As she moved closer to Cassey, the scent of orange-flower water floated about her, and she had obviously been using the lip-paste and orris-root powder which she had given her. Cassey was in a very bad mood as the younger girl slipped her arm through hers and they went down to supper together.

It was the most miserable meal which Cassey had ever eaten. Edward was glued to her side and his mother's eyes rarely left her. She felt herself to be under close, critical scrutiny. The four soldiers who had accompanied Edward were gentlemen known to Lady Amelia, locally born with plenty to discuss, eager to learn how matters were in the village, and if the war was taking its toll of their properties and business interests. And while the conversation dipped and soared, the plentiful plain food and decanters passed round, Cassey was only aware of Leon seated opposite her, with one of Lady Amelia's daughters on either side of him.

She strained her ears to hear what he was saying to them, but Edward was talking loudly to his mother, and one of his bluff lieutenants endeavouring to capture her attention on her other hand. After supper was no better, for then they drifted from the Hall to the with-drawing room. She still could not get near him, surrounded by other members of the household who wanted to hear of her exploits. And Cassey, whose eyes followed Leon wherever he went, even when she seemed preoccupied with something else, was furious when

Jessica managed to manipulate him into a corner alone with her. They sat on a settle, near the fireplace and began to talk.

Jessica was chattering animatedly to him and smiling widely, her eyes glowing with admiration. She was half consciously using on him all the pretty little tricks of the natural flirt. Leon, though still strained and tired, sat and watched her and occasionally made some remark which invoked her gay laughter. He was looking so remarkably handsome that Cassey's back and legs tingled, and she wanted to get her arms round him. They had found him clean linen, and the servants had been at work on his clothes, brushing away the mire. His short cloak was scarlet, showing, as it fell apart, a scarlet doublet, laced with silver, and he carried his black beaver hat, curled about with scarlet feathers. It was no wonder that Jessica was impressed, though he seemed only lazily amused by her, but Cassey was in a ferment of anguished jealousy.

He was deliberately ignoring her, even, cruelly, leaning a little too close to Jessica when he saw that she was watching them. Cassey bit her lower lip to stop it trembling, wanting to scream and cry, yet, at the same time, seething with rage against him and that impertinent jade, Jessica! She did not know what to do. As a prisoner on parole, Leon had perfect freedom of movement within the house and was treated as an honoured guest, all political questions laid aside.

'I'll speak to her mother!' Cassey thought furiously. 'Warn her of his reputation with women. That should stop her game!' But she could do nothing yet; the evening was wearing on, soon they would take candles and go to their rooms. Nothing had really happened; he had merely talked with Jessica, but Cassey was following her unerring feminine instinct which had warned her immediately, as soon as he and Jessica had exchanged a single glance.

There was one crumb of consolation; besides her mother's vigilance, Jessica had her own personal maid, a dragon of a lady called Mrs Jenkins. She tried to comfort herself with the thought of their mutual concern over Jessica's virtue, able to dip a goodnight curtsey in answer to Leon's bow and leave on Edward's arm, mounting the wide staircase with its shallow oaken treads, which led up to their bedchamber.

'When can we leave?' Cassey shot at him as soon as the door was closed, angrily backing up to Beth so that she might unlace her bodice.

He was loosening his collar band and unfastening the row of small jet buttons down the front of his doublet. His face was shadowed and she wondered what he would expect of her that night. A reinstatement of connubial rights, perhaps?

'Leave?' he repeated thoughtfully. 'But we've only just arrived. We should be safe here for several days, I think. It will do us all good.'

'No!' she snapped, flinging off the rest of her clothes impatiently, jerking her head towards the door to dismiss an anxious Beth. 'I want to get away at once!'

Wearing only her thin silk shift, she tossed back the bedclothes and climbed in. She pulled the bolster from beneath the pillows and laid it purposefully down the centre of the mattress. Forced to share his bed, she had no intention of lying close to him.

'There is no need for that,' Edward said, quietly. ' 'Tis true that you are the most desirable creature on God's sweet earth, but you have nothing to fear from me. It

345

is your love that I need, as well as your body.'

'You'll never have it!' Her tone was vicious; someone had to suffer for her pain, and all the time she was seeing how the candlelight had shimmered on Leon's dark head bent close to Jessica's, touching her hair with gold. Would he sleep alone tonight?

Edward laid back the covers on his side, then crossed the room, rummaged in a little chest on the table, and produced a pipe and tobacco. Sitting on the edge of the bed, he puffed for some time. They were silent, while outside the rain pattered, and the window shutter creaked in the wind, and somewhere in the depths of the house a door swung to and fro till it shut with a crash.

'I hate to see you torturing yourself, Cassey,' Edward rapped out, then thrust the pipe back into his mouth.

'You are aware, I suppose, that your sister fancies herself in love with Leon already?' Cassey tossed restlessly. 'For her sake alone, we should move on with all speed.'

'For her sake or yours?' He eyed her shrewdly. 'Sweeting, how can you ever imagine being happy with a man whom you trust so little? Don't you see that it will always be the same? You will never be able to let him out of your sight for an instant.'

What he said was perfectly true. She could not dispute it, but such bald facts were not to be faced. She lay stiffly in the bed, brooding gloomily on her misfortunes. Edward rose, laid aside his pipe and occupied the space reserved for him. He reached over and snuffed the candle. Silence followed and Cassey could not relax, very aware of his breathing. There was a draught down her back caused by the hump of the virtue-protecting bolster. Unhappily, she reflected that there would be little sleep for her that night.

An hour crawled by on feet of lead and her torment increased as images stalked behind her closed eyelids. Jessica and Leon. Supposing she was with him at this very moment? But no, surely Jessica's ladylike upbringing would prevent her from taking such precipitous action? Then she remembered how she had meddled in a spirit of malicious mischief, and had encouraged Jessica's rebellion against family traditions. She was now faced with the prospect of having her own advice turned against her. She herself had been reared to be a lady, but that had not prevented her from flinging herself at her drawing-master. And the stable-hands later? And then, Leon...

She could bear it no longer. Edward seemed to be sleeping, so she quietly slid from bed, fumbled for her dressing-robe and sped across the moonlit room, pushing her arms into the sleeves as she went. The door opened soundlessly and she was in the corridor. It had stopped raining, the clouds had cleared and bright shafts of moonlight pierced the small panes of the long narrow window.

His room was not difficult to find. There was no guard at the door; to have posted one would have been an insult. He was a gentleman and to be trusted.

'With his word, if not with women!' whispered that cold, cynical voice in her brain. The room was like a warm cave, smelling of beeswax and the dying fire. The heavy velvet curtains were not quite closed and the moon made a silver arrow-head almost to her feet. As her eyes grew more accustomed to the gloom, she made out the shape of the massive four-poster, a dark cavern mouth within a cave. There was only one shape within it...Leon, lying flat on his back, legs straight, arms at his sides, like an effigy on a family tomb.

Relief swept every other consideration from Cassey's head. Without any hesitation she mounted the wide wooden steps which surrounded the bed, lifted the quilt and snuggled beside him, her arms going about him, consumed with love and longing.

'Leon...oh, Leon...' she murmured against his face.

He came fully awake and his arms went round her automatically. Then he realized who it was he held and, though he did not move, she could sense his withdrawal. It was like the most gross of insults.

'Cassey! What are you doing here?'

She could dimly see his face, and could only guess at his expression, but his voice chilled her. But nothing he could say would stop her now; she had thrown away all vestige of reserve and pride. She clung to him, rabid for affection.

'Don't push me away, darling...' she begged, raised on one elbow, trying to see his face. The shadows played strange tricks, tilting his eyes at the corners, hooking his nose. His hair curled crisply under her fingers, the rims of his ears felt velvety. Her hands moved over his naked flesh; her mouth slid wetly over his cheek and found his mouth. She kissed him greedily, forcing him to respond to her, determined to break through his ill-temper and moods. She recalled the words of Nona Lalow—he was her man and no one else was going to get him.

She had learned many sensual tricks whilst living with Leon and now did not hesitate to use them, knowing well how to rouse him, at last feeling the returning thrust of his tongue against hers, his hands sliding across to fondle her breasts. Then she no longer had to seduce him; he became the aggressor, harsh and demanding. Cassey had never wanted him so much, whimpering with pleasure as his weight crushed her back against the soft mattress. It was not till afterwards that she realized that he treated her like a trollop, a thing to be used, and that he spoke no single word of tenderness to her.

When he had finished, he rolled away from her, violence and passion spent, and her heart sank with disappointment and frustration. Usually, when they had done making love, they would lie quietly, limbs entwined, enjoying the peace. Now he did not touch her, almost seeming to draw as far away from her as possible, in brutal dismissal.

She tried to tell herself that she was imagining this complete withdrawal, but could not deny that certainty which chilled her. She tried out one or two efforts at words, but these fell on dead air. It seemed that he slept, he was so quiet and still, and she lay on, trying to comfort herself by thinking of the life within her, imagining herself, large, maternal, swollen with milk, holding his child to her breast, feeling its mouth on her nipple. The thought was so sweet that it made her heart ache, so that she turned on her side towards him, pressing her hands to her chest with joy. She wanted desperately to share this emotion. And who else should be the recipient but the father of her baby?

'Leon...darling, don't turn away from me. Please say something.' There was a wealth of agony and longing in her voice, but he cut her short.

'Go back to your husband, woman!' he said in impatience and exasperation. 'He will be awaiting you!'

351

Thirteen

All afternoon Cassey had been forced to listen to Jessica prattling on about Leon. They were in the solar; Jessica attempting to concentrate on her sewing and failing, and Cassey putting up the pretence of absorption in a book. At first, Lady Amelia and the elder girl had been with them, then they had gone off on some errand to the still-room, and then Jessica had given full rein to her tongue.

To Cassey's intense annoyance, Jessica and Leon had spent much time walking in the garden together that morning. Jessica returned to dine with starry eyes and that silly, bemused expression on her face which made Cassey's palm itch to slap her. She had spied on them from an upper window, furious with herself but unable to stop, seeing them across the stretch of smooth, verdant lawn, Jessica's face upturned to him, like a flower to the sun, he looking down indulgently, an arm

353

laid lightly about her waist. Their shared laughter had floated across as if to mock Cassey.

Dinner had been a nightmare, listening to Jessica's inane, excited chatter, with Lady Amelia so polite and cordial to her enforced guest. They all seemed charmed by him, and Cassey felt a hot wave of hatred towards Edward for his stubborn refusal to leave. Apparently, he had pressing business concerning his estate which it was necessary to settle before departure.

'I cannot let Mawnan go to rack and ruin, even for you, my love,' he had expostulated at her urgent demand. She had started on him as soon as they awoke, sickened to find herself back in his bed when she yearned to be with Leon. 'Why in such an almighty sweat to be off, darling?' he had wanted to know. 'We are safe here, and surely, you can see the sense of allowing Treviscoe to recover?'

Oh, she could understand very well the real reason behind his desire to remain, guessing that he hoped she would grow to love the place as much as he and wish to stay. But her torment gave her no peace. Her jealousy was reaching obsessive proportions; she found herself day-dreaming of ways to kill Jessica. And last night had brought no relief; Leon had treated her like a whore, dismissing her crudely when he had finished with her. She had crept away to Edward's bed like a whipped puppy, any hope of touching his heart completely fled. Now he seemed to be deliberately encouraging Jessica, whether to pique Cassey or out of genuine interest it was impossible to tell.

'He is so wonderful!' Jessica was enraptured. 'I've never met anyone like him!'

'Nor like to!' Cassey retorted sharply, raising her eyes from the book where she had just read two whole pages without taking in a word. 'I tell you, he is not respectable. Why, he conducts his castle like a brigand's lair. I was a prisoner there...I know!'

Jessica sprang to her feet, almost scattering the contents of her embroidery basket. She winged to Cassey's side. 'Of course! I had not realized that it was he! Oh, Cassandra, tell me what it was like! If only it had been me!'

Cassey cursed herself for a fool, suddenly aware that to paint him in such a romantically villainous light would but add fuel to the fire of Jessica's inexperienced longings.

'You must forget him.' Something in her tone arrested Jessica, and for a moment their eyes met and they understood one another. The contrast between the two could not have been greater; one very plainly dressed in tobacco brown with only the relief of white at throat and wrists, the other much more flamboyant in her attire. Both were beautiful, but one was obviously innocent and naive, whilst the other was entirely the reverse. But it was more than that; there was an air about Cassey which suggested passion, recklessness and a lust for life which was stronger than was good for her.

'What is it to you?' Jessica asked slowly, and there was the dawning of realization in her eyes, of suspicions which she did not want to begin to believe. Cassey was her dear brother's wife. She admired him so much that it was almost inconceivable that a woman fortunate enough to be married to him should not remain entirely faithful in thought, word or deed, and be blissfully happy.

Cassey had a wild longing to tell her, to see the astonishment and outrage wiping the polite smile from those well-bred features. There was that wicked devil whispering in her ear again, urging her to kick aside convention, yell aloud that she was Leon's mistress and carried his child! To see the collapse of Jessica's girlish dreams would have given her a savage satisfaction. But she dared not; there was too much at stake.

'I do not wish to see you make a fool of yourself, Jessica,' she advised, though somewhat tartly. 'Remember, men do not admire forward chits. Be modest and quiet, as becomes your station. Above all, do not be deceived by fair words. Men are only too willing to take advantage of foolish young girls.'

'The silly jade is probably ignorant of the simple basic act of love!' she thought irritably, 'and hasn't the wit to see that she toys with a tiger!'

Edward came tramping in then, weary with poring over the accounts, ledgers and documents, wanting her to ride with him round the estate, assuring her that the fresh air would do her good.

'You are looking pale, my love.' He touched her cheek lightly, and she knew that this was true. It was partly due to sleeplessness, and partly because of the nausea which swept her often these days, particularly in the morning when she first lifted her head from the pillow.

Reluctantly, she trailed off to change into her riding habit, unable to refuse him because Lady Amelia had come in and was looking at her with questions in her eyes. To her chagrin, Jessica scampered off to the Long Gallery, in a rush of taffeta petticoats, to play chess with Leon.

The ride was as tedious as Cassey expected; she was even foiled in her desire to have a blazing row with Edward. He refused to be provoked into an argument about leaving. Cassey fumed, driving her sedate white cob hard, desperately worried. She was a married woman, whilst Jessica was free. But he'd never wed such a simpleton! she assured herself. To add to all, they fought on opposite sides, which would make such a match well nigh impossible! Then she remembered hearing that one of the King's Generals, Lord Wilmot, had married a Parliamentarian lady for her wealth; an action which had put him in bad odour with His Majesty.

The nagging worry gave her no peace. Jessica had a substantial dowry and Leon liked money. If he could compromise the girl, then Lady Amelia would have to consent. One part of her brain told her firmly that such conjectures were madness, but she could not wait to get back to the house, none the less. Leon was up to something, of that she was convinced. She knew him well enough to recognize the signs. Oh, why the devil could not Jessica be plain, like her sister!

They only really met at meal times, stilted affairs where conversation was kept strictly neutral, everyone pretending that civil war was not taking place, and that there was not the embarrassment of vastly different viewpoints among them. Yet Cassey was nervous and jumpy, hourly expecting some confrontation with Grantley, dreading the sight of armed men hacking into the courtyard, the hammering of Roundhead soldiers at the door. Edward tried hard to calm her. She knew that he had men posted on the outskirts of the village, and all this done without rousing Lady Amelia's suspicions.

Afterwards, she never knew how she got through that long day, but all things pass and at last she lay again in the vast nuptial bed, waiting tensely for Edward's breathing to become deep and regular, telling her that he slept and, as on the previous night, she crept away to Leon's room.

He was lying in bed, propped on one elbow, reading book held towards the single candle flame on the bedside table. He glanced across as she came in, and his expression was none too pleasant.

'What do you want, Cassey?'

She sped across the room, slender and pale in her flowing cambric nightgown and matching, lace-trimmed over-robe, hair spilling across shoulders and breasts, eyes wild and voice pleading:

'Leon... Oh, Leon...I had to see you. We must talk.'

'There is nothing to say.' He laid the book down on the coverlet, but kept his thumb between the pages as a marker as if his only concern was to get back to it as soon as possible, once he had got rid of this troublesome nuisance. The action was highly offensive and Cassey could feel hot anger rising in her.

'You are Ruthen's wife,' he continued calmly. 'Your place is here. After all, you are pregnant with his heir...'

'That's not true!' she blazed. 'How can you say such a wicked thing? 'Tis just an excuse to be rid of me!'

He shrugged, his naked shoulders very tanned against the white bed-linen, and Cassey's fingers tingled with the urge to strike him across that indifferent face, to smash through that cold reserve even if he killed her for it! Yet, at the same time, part of her wanted to scream out to him to take her in his arms, to kiss away this enmity between them.

'I have told you oft enough, that I do not wish to be bothered with you.' His words cut through her, knife-like in their cruelty.

'And what of Jessica?' She was trembling and could not keep her voice steady. 'She's mooning after you like a love-sick jackanapes. D'you wish to be troubled with her?'

'She is more tractable than you.' He sat up, hugging his knees humped up under the quilt. 'A nice little thing...pretty, too.'

He knew but too well how to rile her. Normally, she could resist rising to the bait, but now every vestige of self-control had vanished.

'Have you lain with her yet?' She was her own tormentor, but could not restrain herself from asking.

He shot her an impatient stare. 'That is none of your concern.'

It was true. She had no claim on him...the bald truth reared up to mock her. Yet, after all their adventures, the perils they had shared, the passionate hours of love, she refused to believe that she meant nothing to him.

'Have a care,' she warned him, her voice low and menacing. 'Do not forget that your life lies in my hands. The authorities would give a great deal to know where you are. I have but to say the word to Lady Amelia, to tell her the truth.'

His eyes narrowed and his mouth clamped into a hard line. He flung aside the covers and stood up, reaching for a brocade, fur-edged robe which lay across the foot of the bed. His naked body was superb, marred only by the half-healed scars on his back, and fire blazed in her loins at the sight of him, that familiar, hopeless, frustrated desire. But his face wore a look of angry contempt.

'You'd do it too, would you not? You jealous bitch!'

At once she was contrite, knowing that she had gone too far. She wanted to fling her arms about him, to kiss away that look of baffled anger.

'No. I'd never betray you, Leon,' she said in a soothing conciliatory tone, taking a step nearer. 'But you try me sorely. Can't you see that I love you? Oh, please stop being angry with me. Listen to me, Leon; let me come home with you...together we'll fight to keep Kestle Mount...all the others can go hang!'

She was so passionately convinced herself that she was almost sure that she could move him and thus get her way, but his answer was a painful disappointment.

'No!' There was such a look of dark rage on his features that she stopped in her tracks. 'Leave me in peace, slut! There is no more to be said!'

For an instant Cassey continued to stare at him, now as angry as he, every last attempt at reason failing her. 'Oh!' she yelled, almost hysterical with fury and pain. 'I hate you, Leon Treviscoe!' She swirled round and fled from the room, slamming the door after her to relieve her feelings. 'I hope I never set eyes on you again!' she sobbed to herself as she dashed headlong down the passage to her own apartment. 'This is the end! I've taken the last insult and humiliation from you!'

The next day she refused to leave her room at all, spending hours lying on the bed, sunk in misery, furiously going over in her mind all the hurt and despair of her affair with Leon. To make matters worse, she was queasy with early pregnancy. Beth crept in, bringing trays of food which she offered hesitantly, half expecting them to be flung at her. Cassey ignored them, leaving the lovingly prepared morsels to grow cold, the wine to stand untasted in the crystal goblets. Afternoon shadows lengthened into evening. Cassey crawled from the bed. Her head ached persistently, her eyes were red and sore with so much weeping, and the sight of herself still wearing her crumpled nightgown, hair tangled, face pale and haggard, made her even more miserable.

Edward had kept well out of her way and this hurt her. She had never felt more lonely and depressed. Beth came in carrying a branched candlestick, giving her a worried glance. In spite of herself, Cassey could not help asking:

'Have you seen Lord Treviscoe today?'

Beth nodded, and Cassey watched the flames spring one by one to light at the touch of the long taper. Beth's warm sympathy reached out to soothe her. 'Aye, that I have, ma'am, and mighty black were his looks. Come, my dear lady, let me brush your hair. You must try to put aside this mumpish humour. 'Twill do you or the baby no good at all. D'you want it to be born melancholy? Lady Amelia seems satisfied by your husband's tale of your having an attack of the ague, but you cannot stay up here forever.'

Cassey sagged before the mirror, taking a kind of morbid enjoyment in seeing how wasted she looked. Blaming the men in her life for her ruin, quite forgetting her own impetuous part in it. And the war of course, that disastrous conflict when brother fought brother, father against son, and the women were riven by conflicting loyalties. She stabbed about for excuses. If it had not been for the war and its disruptions, why, she might be married to an Earl by now, with her father's wealth behind her, not pregnant of a bastard child by a man who did not love her.

Her life stretched bleakly before her. Edward's wife forced into a provincial existence, under the shadow of her mother-in-law, never to see Leon again, for it seemed that having returned home, Edward grew ever more reluctant to leave. He had told her that, high in favour with Lord Essex, he could, no doubt, wheedle a pardon for his part in Leon's escape, if he were able to invent a story good enough to convince his Lordship. Here, in this peaceful oasis, one could almost forget strife, and Edward longed to revert to his role of country squire, but all that it meant for Cassey was an eternity of boredom.

It grew ever darker outside the ornately draped windows. The moon had not yet broken through the obscuring layer of cloud. From below, came the domesticated sounds of the orderly household, servants going about their duties, the rattle of china and clink of silver as the long oak table in the Hall was being set for supper. Then there came the flurry of footfalls in the corridor outside and Jessica burst in without knocking, very worried.

'Cassandra, have you seen Leon?' The agitated words tumbled from her lips.

Cassey gave her an annoyed glare; she was the last person she wanted to set eyes on in her present mood, astonished to see that she was dressed to go out. She was painted and perfumed, her hair was curled and she wore her new dark green woollen dresss which was usually reserved for special occasions. The bodice was low by Puritan standards; Lady Amelia's attention must have been diverted when the seamstress cut it out, and her small, round breasts rose and fell swiftly for she had been hurrying. Her hooded cloak was flung carelessly over her shoulders.

Cassey rose slowly, turning to face her. 'Leon?' she questioned, noticing that the formality of his title had disappeared from Jessica's vocabulary. 'Why no. I have not seen him since yesterday.'

'Oh, where is he?' Jessica began to pace up and down, brows drawn into a worried crease, wringing her hands together dementedly. 'I've searched the whole house and gardens. He is nowhere to be found.'

Growing suspicion made Cassey grip her suddenly, slewing her to a halt. She gave a savage shake. 'What has happened? Tell me, you little fool!'

Overwhelmed by events which she could only dimly understand and terrified by the violence of her sister-in-law, Jessica began to cry. 'He said he would take me with him.' She sobbed.

'Take you where?' Cassey's fingers dug

into her upper arms and she gave her another shake. 'What have you done, you stupid ninny?'

The sight of her scared eyes and the loud sound of her crying infuriated her. She had a sudden brutal longing to kill her.

'He said that if I helped him to escape, he'd take me too.' Jessica's words came with the shock of a thunderclap. Cassey stood stock-still for a moment, staring at her in astonishment. 'I was to meet him in the meadow. He said he'd manage to get two horses from the stable and I'd already given him the money...'

'Money!' Cassey shouted at her. 'What money?'

'That which was laid aside for my dowry. It was in the chest in Mama's room. I took it, and the contents of her jewel-case.' Jessica's face was white, her eyes enormous with fright.

'What!' Cassey's breath came out in a hiss, and she released the cowering girl. Her lips curled in contempt as she ran a scornful eye over her. 'Well, mistress, he deceived you well and truly, did he not? Did you really think he could love such as you?'

She felt suddenly very cold, calm and

triumphant. She had been right in her guess about him. He had been plotting this all along.

'But he wouldn't have run off like that, ma'am,' put in Beth, glad that Cassey had loosened her deadly hold on Jessica for she had been sure that she was about to do her an injury. 'He's a gentleman, he'd not break his parole.'

'He did not give his word not to attempt to escape.' Cassey was at the wardrobe door, searching for her riding habit. 'That was Edward's story. It never actually happened.' She was throwing off her robe and nightgown, getting into her clothes swiftly. 'Fetch Edward!' she ordered.

While Jessica continued to sob and tremble, Cassey dressed quickly, pulling on her high boots, sweeping a few necessities into a valise. By the time Beth returned with Edward, she was ready, clapping on her wide-brimmed hat. She had not felt so full of energy for days.

Without hesitation she explained to Edward what had taken place, and his face turned hard and angry. 'And that goose-brained idiot sister of yours has let him give us the slip!' she concluded viciously.

'Where are you going?' he demanded as she snatched up her crop from the floor.

'To Kestle Mount. That is where he will go!' She could hardly be bothered to answer him, single-minded in her determination to follow Leon without delay.

'You can't go alone!'

'Try and stop me!' She glared up into his face, hating anyone who would prevent her. Jessica, Mawnan Manor, Lady Amelia, none of them were of any importance any more. She stared at Jessica with eyes hard as agates, and wanted to laugh in her face. He had used her, and Cassey was glad.

'I'll come with you.' Edward was insistent, and she knew that she would be safer and more likely to reach her destination if he rode at her side.

'Do as you wish.' She was impatiently swishing at her long velvet skirt with her whip, eager to be off. She rounded on Jessica who shrank from this fierce-eyed shrew whose powerful presence seemed to dominate the room, afraid that she was going to hit her. 'And you, dolt, will have some explaining to do to your Mama!'

'And what of me, ma'am?' Beth was at her elbow, willing to go with her to the ends of the earth, if need be.

'Oh, Beth,' Cassey slipped an arm round her, hugging her warmly. 'My dear, I cannot leave you here to face whatever retribution might fall on you because of me. You'd best prepare and ride with us.'

Beth ran off to her own quarters to pack a bag, while Cassey and Edward took the back stairs to the stable. Leon had helped himself to one of the best horses...Edward's favourite. The old stone building was illuminated by a horned lantern hanging from an iron hook set in the wall, and they worked fast, saddling the horses. There was the smell of suppers being cooked from the kitchens close by and the grooms were away at their evening meal.

'Which is just as well, under the circumstances,' muttered Edward grimly, busy fastening girths. It was while they were thus engaged that Beth came running in to find them. She was sweating and breathless, followed closely by one of Edward's scouts.

' 'Tis soldiers, sir,' he panted urgently. 'I've run all the way from Dyke's Hill.'

'He was too late to warn you,' Beth gabbled at Edward. 'Colonel Scarrier is this minute at the front door. I caught a glimpse of him talking with Lady Amelia in the Hall.'

God! They were almost too late! Cassey came out in a cold sweat of fear, cursing Edward's pig-headed refusal to leave before this happened. She flung herself on to her mount, from the tail of her eye seeing Edward and Beth do the same. Then they clattered across the yard and out through the back way, knowing that pursuit was inevitable.

It was dark but they plunged on, riding furiously through the night, only Edward's considerable knowledge of the terrain keeping them from getting hopelessly lost. At last the first bird calls and a lightening of the sky heralded dawn and, above them, loomed Kestle Mount, that mouldering, ivy-hung castle with its red-roofed turrets which reminded Cassey of witches' hats.

Slowly they picked their way up the stony road which twisted through the woods to the castle entrance. The drawbridge was raised but Edward shouted across the rocky precipice which separated the castle from the road, and soon a guard appeared, sticking his head through one of the narrow windows of the gatehouse.

'Is Lord Treviscoe within?' Edward's voice echoed among the crags. 'We bring him warning. You must let us in.'

The man disappeared and there was a frustrating delay, with Edward keeping a keen eye on the road behind them, on the lookout for any sign of Roundhead troops. Then, at last, the drawbridge rattled down and they were able to ride across. Leon was at the gate to meet them. He looked dusty and travel-worn, and as if he had not got in much ahead of them.

'Well,' he demanded, pacing about impatiently, his men following his every move with watchful, anxious eyes, that high-mettled group of seasoned fighters who were his to command. 'What has happened that you come speeding after me as if the devil himself pursued you?'

'You are not so very far from the truth, my Lord,' Edward replied heavily. 'Colonel Scarrier is on our tail.'

'Is this some kind of trick?' Leon loomed over him, big and menacing. 'Why should you come to aid me, of all people?'

'Cassey would have ridden alone, else.' Edward was quiet and very dignified, facing that sombre, hawk-like man, whose awe-inspiring rage could make even the bravest cringe. 'But the way in which you cheated my poor sister was ill repayment for my hospitality.'

Leon's hand was at his sword-hilt, his eyes glittering. 'D'you wish to meet me to settle the score? I can call upon my seconds at any moment.'

'This is not the time nor the place for personal vendettas,' Richard intervened, and Cassey was very relieved to find him there. He had already greeted her with his rather lop-sided grin. She felt a little calmer, heartened by his presence, something of the cold terror abating.

Leon cooled down, once more in command of the situation. 'You are right. Let us deal with these rebel swine first.'

The castle burst into activity at his orders. It was already a well organized military encampment. Men were posted at every loophole facing the road. There was another entrance which led in from the cliffs and men were despatched to drive in the cattle grazing on the short springy grass, while every man, woman or child who resided within the ancient walls were collected or alerted before the gate was firmly closed and barred. Under

374

siege, they might manage to hold out until help arrived. Once defying a command to surrender, they all knew full well that the life of every person would be forfeit should they be taken.

Leon had not even acknowledged Cassey's existence by a single word or glance, but Richard was obviously delighted to see her, a broad smile lighting up his pleasant features. A peaked eyebrow shot up at Leon's clipped order that both she and Edward were to be kept under strict surveillance lest this should be a ruse for the Roundheads to gain entrance to the castle. Edward had looked furious enough to strike him dead at this, and the astute Richard very quickly guessed the real reason behind their hatred.

He gently teased Cassey about it when they stood together in the Hall, with armed men and messengers milling about them, and Leon far too busy fortifying his home to pay her any heed.

Cassey bit her lip with vexation; she found it difficult to hide anything from the shrewd Captain, and he had soon wheedled the whole story out of her. He shook his head and chided her:

'You should have thrown in your lot

with me, sweeting. I told you that long ago.'

'You'd not want me now, I'll warrant.' She could never resist flirting with him a little, even now under these desperate circumstances. She gave a toss of her curls and glanced up at him sideways, mouth smiling invitingly. 'I am to have a child.'

'And this but makes you all the more attractive,' he assured her, pausing in their conversation to grab a passing guard and give him a curt order.

'What of the Queen, Richard?' She was serious now, concerned about the safety of that tragic lady.

'She has escaped to France.' He pulled a rueful face, his eyes sorrowful. 'And not without much difficulty. Poor lady, she was the woefullest spectacle that I have ever had the misfortune to see. Doctor Wintour firmly believed that she would die this time. But she hung on...she is full of courage...and she was borne on a litter till we reached Pendennis Castle. In Falmouth bay lay a little fleet of friendly Dutch vessels and we managed to get her aboard at last. I left then, returning here, hoping to rejoin Leon. And then I find him pounding in alone but an hour since, in the foulest mood I have ever had to face! Lord knows what you have been doing to him, you little witch!'

'I have always been true to him,' she protested, as he helped her up the steep, rickety stairs to the battlements where he was posted to keep watch. 'But I could not bear to see him tortured. Richard, would you have not done the same, in my position?'

'God dammit, Cassey, don't ask me what I would do were I a female.' He leaned his back against the sun-warmed stones, lazily scanning the view. 'They are the most unpredictable of creatures!' Then seeing that she was really distressed, he grew serious. 'But he is my friend. I suppose that I admire him above all others, save King Charles; mayhap I should have found it impossible as you to hold my tongue. I do not blame you, Cassey.'

'He does,' she said mournfully.

'It is his damnable pride which has always been his bane.' He squeezed her waist comfortingly and she was glad to lean against him, joining him in looking down on the bay.

The cliffs rose up like sheer walls, capped with dark green furze, while below them sprawled weird black rocks which stretched far out into the deep sea beyond. Castles, spires and wings of jagged ironstone. Surely, this side of the building was impregnable; no one could scale it but:

'We cannot be too careful,' Richard cautioned.

There was a sweeping mile-long bay beneath this drop from the walls, ridged with blown sand, bright with golden trefoil and crimson lady's-fingers. A small river flowed into it, its banks grey with polished pebbles. The cove was paved with coloured rocks, streaked with a pink line of shells stretching out to the West, and laced with white foam, its strata set up on edge or tilted at strange angles.

They paced round to face the landward side which was all richness, softness and deceptive peace; out to sea a calm for the moment, which could turn to a bowling waste of rock and roller, should the weather turn. And it seemed indeed that peace was over. As Cassey and Richard stood looked towards the road, they saw the glint of steel and Roundhead troopers approaching the castle, a large body of men on foot behind them, and the unmistakable figure of Grantley riding at their head.

Soon his trumpeter was sounding at the gates and Leon went to stand on the battlement above it, hearing Grantley's summon to surrender. The decision he had to face was a hard one. His garrison was thin; a large number of his men were out on a foraging expedition and had not yet returned. When they did, they would assuredly be intercepted by Grantley. Stocks of food were low and there were many dependent mouths to feed, helpless women and children at risk. But...Kestle Mount...the home of the proud Treviscoes...he had sworn to keep it for the King. Yet more and more men were joining Grantley, till the forest and road opposite the castle were thick with them; a formidable army.

There was a long pause during which Leon stood deep in thought. Then Grantley broke from the throng of officers wheeling their mounts around him, sitting his roan a little apart from them, his mocking voice rising to harangue him.

'Ho, there, Treviscoe! Will you think to fight us? We are too strong for you. Save your followers, or all shall meet the fate of this soldier captured but lately.'

There was a commotion beneath the

trees. Cassey, straining her eyes, saw a young man, bound on his horse, a noose about his neck, the other end fastened to the spreading branch of an oak. She recognized him as Farriday, the lad whom she had prevented Leon from shooting in what seemed a life-time ago. Grantley raised his arm and the lad's horse was whipped from under him. An angry roar went up from Leon's watching men.

Grantley was shouting again, face up-turned to them, his voice holding a note of savage triumph. 'I'll hang you too, Treviscoe, and that Jezebel, Cassandra Ruthen, when I get my hands on her!'

He sounded mad. Cassey had long felt him to be unbalanced and now she was sure of it. Leon's eyes had narrowed to slits as he gazed down on his enemy.

'We'll fight!' he snarled at Richard who was standing at his side. 'Let us take a few of the bastards with us before we die!'

Richard's lips lifted in a wolfish grin. 'I'm with you, sir, every inch of the way. He's out for blood and vengeance, and like to kill us anyway, even if we surrender.'

Fourteen

Leon gave Grantley his answer, and very high-handed it was, as if he was the attacker not the attacked and the garrison settled down to wait Grantley's next move.

Nerves taut as bow-strings, Cassey wandered the castle, eventually going to join the women where they had been gathered in the Great Hall. This was situated within the inner Keep and one of the safest places. The meagre rations were distributed, the largest share going to the soldiers, and the gruelling watch continued all day, any change in the Parliamentary forces immediately reported back to the Commanders. It was like no fight Cassey had been in before, for in defence there is no fierce exultation and stirring of the blood as there is in attack.

Darkness thickened, shrouding all. From the walls could be seen pin-points of light betraying the whereabouts of Roundhead pickets. A gloomy silence pervaded the castle; there was something in the tense

381

air which compelled them to reduce their voices almost to whispers. It was as if every sense was strained to listen for the first suspicion of attack from outside. Even the children were unnaturally quiet, and those of the garrison not on duty, slept fully armoured, weapons in hand.

Cassey could not rest, huddled into her hooded cloak, trailing uneasily up to the battlements in search of Richard. She found him at last, on guard, and kept him company through the long, bleak hours till dawn. She knew that Leon had been persuaded to rest at last. He had not gone to bed, and Cassey had come across him rolled in his cavalry cloak, stretched out on the hearth in the Hall with his dogs beside him. She had wanted to lean tenderly over him, to ease a cushion under his sleeping head, but they had growled and stared at her with fierce yellow eyes. Now she recognized the breed; his hounds were very much the same as those she had seen tied to wagons in the encampment, his close companions with whom he seemed more at home than with humans. She did not venture to touch him again.

The watch had been puzzled by fires and activity on the South side of the castle, and with first light the mystery was revealed. Grantley had done the unexpected. Under cover of darkness he had brought artillery up, draught horses hauling the heavy pieces along the cliff path to face the less well defended South gate, and, as daylight grew stronger, they began to bombard the wall.

The castle cannons had been prepared, and they soon gave answer with case and round shot, but the Roundheads began to come on, advancing with order and resolve, helping themselves with faggots and scaling ladders against the ditch and wall. And among the defenders there was little of song or battle-cry...they fought in grim silence, save for the shouts of command, the hard breathing of laboured men, and the shriek of steel and shot.

Grantley was an experienced soldier and knew that it was pointless to waste troops attacking the almost impregnable main entrance with its crevasse and raised drawbridge. He concentrated his forces on the weaker gate, driving them mercilessly to scale the rocky way leading to the cliffs, and soon cries from below the Great Hall, told that the enemy had entered, pouring over the wide breach blasted by his cannons in the stout wall. They were thronging in by port and parapet. The deadly struggle of hand to hand fighting rent the air. It was only a matter of time before the advance party of Roundheads overpowered the guard at the portcullis. Once the drawbridge was down, cavalry would come pounding in and all would be over, save the slaughter.

Now all who could among the defenders were fighting their way to the Hall in its safer position within the Keep. Men were struggling to gain entrance, wounded, bleeding and desperate. Their women ran to cling to them, their terror infectious, knowing that they would be put to the sword by the vengeful enemy, and their children too.

Panic was spreading and Cassey's eyes raked the crowd, seeking Leon, and at last he came in, battered and bloody, sword in hand. The door was barricaded behind him. From without came the screams of those who had not been quick enough and were now being cut down.

'Quickly,' he ordered, his voice rising above the cries of alarm and terror. They were accustomed to taking their cue from him and now his calm quietened them. 'To the cellars, everyone. There is a way out by an underground passage. Follow me.'

Mothers snatched up their frightened young, older women struggled with bundles of possessions, while what remained of the fighting men reformed into some kind of order, allowing them to precede them down the narrow, twisting stairs to the vast cellars beneath.

Cassey hung back, the last to go, though Beth was frantically urging speed, but she wanted to remain close to Leon, and he let everyone else go first. Then Richard and Edward swept her away with them, brooking no further delay.

Following the light from smoking torches carried by those ahead, they ran through the echoing, arched chambers, storage places for the Castle kitchens, and past the wine vaults with their vats, barrels and presses, coming at last to the furthest cellar, low-ceilinged and gloomy. The men heaved at a trapdoor, which lifted to reveal a dark aperture winding down even deeper, carved from the solid rock.

'Find your way to the caves,' Leon was instructing them, seeing that everyone dropped through safely. 'There are boats waiting. Row to the next cove and make your escape inland.'

A chill, muttering wind swept past them, and Cassey stumbled blindly down an almost unending stair hewn from the rocks. The steps were slimy and treacherous. Someone had ignited the flares which hung at intervals against the slippery walls, or else it would have been very possible to miss one's footing and plunge down that unrailed drop.

At last her feet touched the floor at the end of which was the sandy bottom of a large cave, where water lapped ceaselessly and Leon's men were already hustling their dependants into rowing boats and moving off to where a dim glow betrayed the cave entrance opening into the sea.

Beth, who had been struggling along in Cassey's wake, was terrified of heights and, never very agile, she suddenly slipped on a patch of damp lichen, a cry of pain escaping her as her ankle twisted beneath her. Cassey stopped and, without a thought to the consequences, ran back for her. It was while they were struggling along with Beth leaning heavily against her, unable to put her right foot to the ground, that Cassey became aware of a commotion behind them. A quick glance round showed her the hated pot helmets and uniforms of Roundheads close behind.

Cassey stood there for an instant with a throat dry as ashes and her brain all wild confusion and terror, then she gave a strangled cry as she recognized Grantley leading them.

'You!' His face was aglow with triumph and revenge. 'At last I've caught you! You'll not get away this time!'

He made a grab at her and she screamed, struggling in his iron grip. Leon, busy directing those embarking heard her and spun round.

'Let her go, Scarrier!' he commanded, and advanced across the cave floor. 'Turn and face me, coward!'

With an oath, Grantley released her, bearing down on Leon, sword raised. They circled warily, blades at arm's length. Around them, fighting had broken out between Leon's followers and his, but all of Cassey's attention was focused on them. With the sudden, seering clang of steel, their blades met and engaged.

Both of them were quick and fierce, expert swordsmen, fighting with reckless fury. And Cassey pressed back against the chill, wet rocks, watching them, her eyes going from one to the other. Beth crouched at her side, still moaning with pain, sure that their last hour had come. Edward and Richard were duelling savagely with a couple of Grantley's men, while the others had already fallen in the reek of flash and shot from a couple of Leon's musketeers.

With growing horror, Cassey realized that Leon was still weak from the flogging, and that he had already been fighting for hours. He was panting with exertion, and when Grantley's sword pierced his shoulder and dark blood spread over his doublet, she gave a scream and started forward. Richard, who had dispatched his adversary, threw an arm about her waist and pulled her roughly back.

'Distract him now, darling, and he's done for,' he growled.

The sound of swords ringing and clashing echoed through the cavern, their shadows flung grotesquely on the shining wet walls by the flickering torches. Both men were fighting desperately for their lives. They moved quickly back and forth, slashing and hacking, but unable to get through each other's defences and draw blood again. Then, suddenly, Leon lost his footing on the slippery sand. He crashed down to one knee and Grantley was upon him, knocking up his guard. He paused for an instant, his face a hideous grinning mask of satisfaction, weapon raised to come down in one final thrust into Leon's chest. But, swift as lightning, Edward moved, his own rapier intercepting the blow.

With an enraged howl, Grantley turned on him and, before he could regain his balance, he had driven his sword into his ribs with such force that the tip appeared through his doublet at the back. In the same instant, Leon leaped to his feet and lunged at Grantley, his blade plunging into his side. Grantley's sword clattered to the ground, he buckled to his knees, bloody foam bubbling from between his lips. He tried to speak but choked in his own blood, as he slowly crumped and fell to the ground.

Cassey rushed forward to where Edward lay, dropping on her knees at his side. For a moment horror and shock rendered her speechless, then she took his head on to her lap, cradling him against her breasts, a frightened, dismal sob breaking from her and tears falling on to his upturned face.

'Oh, Edward...dear Edward...' She knew that he had done it for her sake, not through any liking for Leon, and her hands moved gently over his forehead, his temples, his eyelids.

Behind her, Leon was pushing Richard's kerchief beneath his shirt to staunch the blood. There he stood, hands on his hips, feet spread, looking down on Edward, his face grim and bitter. His chest was heaving with effort, sweat running down from his hair, great arcs of it staining his doublet, under the armpits and across his back.

Edward stirred restlessly, as if trying to escape the pain. He coughed slightly, and blood trickled from his lips and Cassey continued to sob. He raised his heavy eyelids and looked at her, attempting to smile.

'Don't cry, Cassey...it is better thus. Now you will be free. You said that you could never love me, and I could not settle for less.' A spasm of agony twisted his features, and sweat broke out on his face, then he relaxed again, turning his head a little and fixing Leon with his eyes. 'And you, Treviscoe, I swear to you that Cassey has always been yours. Surely you will take the word of a dying man? I'd not condemn myself to Purgatory by lying now.'

Leon had bent and was wiping his sword on a corner of Grantley's cloak, before slipping it back into its scabbard at his left hip. He did not answer and Cassey laid Edward back on the sand, rising swiftly and going across to hang on Leon's arm. 'What he says is true, darling. You must believe me.'

He was looking at her with a strange expression of bewilderment and sadness, shaking his head as if thoroughly confused. 'Go to him, Cassey. He's dying...he needs you.'

Yet still she insisted...maybe her whole future hung in the balance. 'But what of us, Leon?'

Just then Edward gave a strange choking cough, bringing up a great clot of blood, and she ran back to kneel beside him, but she saw that his still-open eyes stared blankly. They were looking directly at her, as if he had been straining to look at her, even at the last.

Richard came over to raise her, and his eyes were on his leader.

'That was a brave man, my Lord. I'll stake my oath that what he said was true. Come, let us to the boats and away before yon rebel rinse-pitchers raise the alarm and send more men after us.'

Leon paused, giving her a long, searching stare, then he swung her up easily, laying her across his shoulder, carrying her effortlessly, wading into the shallow water to put her in the leading boat. Richard was behind them, bearing a protesting Beth, then the two men climbed in themselves, the oarsmen leaned to their work and the boat glided out through the cave mouth to the open sea.

Cassey and Leon stood on the poop deck near the prow of this neat little sloop which had been anchored in the next bay. During their journey in the rowing boat he had told her that it was used to smuggle exiles abroad, and to bring men and money back, too, to aid the King. It was evening and the red ball of the sun was just sinking as they made their way sea-ward between portals of sloping turf, lighting up the golden sand and crimsoning the intense blue of the ocean.

Cassey was very conscious of the new sensation of the lift and swell of the ship beneath her feet. She rested her hands on the rail, the wind lifting her hair, blinded by the scarlet light which seemed to be gouging a path for them across the water. Soon the sun would disappear entirely, leaving a peacock glow across the dark clouds of night which were rushing in. She felt that they were alone in an emptied world.

Now Leon was pointing to the cliffs which they were just passing. 'Look, there's Kestle Mount.'

The old castle seemed to dominate the headland, squat and menacing, yet, somehow lonely, clinging stubbornly to its rock, vanquished now...its long fight for the King over.

'We'll come back when the war ends, and whichever way it goes,' Leon said softly.

'And I?' Now the barriers were down. She could talk to him again.

He was smiling down at her. 'You, my dear, will obey me and stay in France till peace comes.'

Panic seized her; she gripped his arm fiercely. 'You'll be coming back to fight alone?'

'I cannot stay out of the war.' He was impatient again, pulling away from her, and she knew that she could never hold him. He would stultify in safety whilst there was still conflict raging in England. Her place would be to wait for him and rear his heir, knowing that he would return to her, if and when he could. With this she would have to be satisfied.

But for a few days he would be hers, then it would all start again, the daring, the danger, the crippling anxiety, and it was life's breath to him. Richard had warned her, laughing, that it was not only the King which called him to the roving life of a mercenary. For all his noble ancestry which went right back to the Normans, he was an incorrigible rogue.

She watched the fading light; soon only the boat's lanterns would pierce the dark wall of night, and she thought of Edward...darkness had closed over him for ever. She shuddered as she saw in her mind's eye, the dead face of Grantley. What black pit of hell did his soul inhabit?

Leon, feeling her tremble, thought that she was cold and drew a fold of his cloak over them both, a simple friendly action which gave her a sense of pleasure and deep contentment. She was in his charge, belonging to him, dependent on him and, for the first time ever, he seemed to be accepting the role.

Cassey felt a rising surge of confidence, facing the wind, breathing in the fresh evening air. She laughed aloud and, clasping him round the neck, drew his head down to her kiss.

The publishers hope that this book has given you enjoyable reading. .... Print ...... are especially designed to be easy to see and hold. .... people ...... a complete list of ...... titles ...... write ...... full local library or ...... directly to:

Dales Large Print Books Long Preston, North Yorkshire, BD23 4ND, England.

This Large Print Book for the Partially sighted, who cannot read normal print, is published under the auspices of

THE ULVERSCROFT FOUNDATION